John Baillie

Life-Studies or how to Live

Illustrated in the Biographies of Bunyan, Tersteegen, Montgomery, Perthes, and

Mrs. Winslow

John Baillie

Life-Studies or how to Live
*Illustrated in the Biographies of Bunyan, Tersteegen, Montgomery, Perthes, and Mrs.
Winslow*

ISBN/EAN: 9783337016111

Printed in Europe, USA, Canada, Australia, Japan

Cover: Foto ©Raphael Reischuk / pixelio.de

More available books at **www.hansebooks.com**

"—and its sign of **the Rising Sun.**"

OR,

How to Live.

ILLUSTRATED **IN** THE BIOGRAPHIES **OF**

BUNYAN, TERSTEEGEN, MONTGOMERY,
PERTHES, **AND MRS. WINSLOW.**

BY **THE**
REV. JOHN BAILLIE,
AUTHOR OF "MEMOIRS OF **HEWITSON**," "ADELAIDE NEWTON," ETC.

" **He** hungereth to feed on facts."

NEW YORK:
ROBERT CARTER & BROTHERS,
No. 530 BROADWAY.

1860.

PREFACE.

How to live—how to dispose worthily of **that** *one life* which is all wherewith each of us has to face Eternity—is confessedly the **gravest** problem which a sane man **can be called to solve.**

A lump of salt **is** dissolved in a basin of water; the salt is gone, but its savor has reached the remotest **atom** in the basin. Our one life is like that lump of salt : gradually it is melting away, and in a brief season it will be **gone; but its savor** will reach the remotest hour in the Eternity to come.

How is this one life to be lived? Where **is** the power which shall carry me victoriously through its struggle? **It will not do to take me to** the monk's pillar, or to **the** hermit's cell—you **must** show me how to go up to life's battle, and to **go** through it, erect and unharmed.

It was **a** fable of the ancients, that the god who presided over each river had his residence in a cavern at its source. Is not the fable **an** intense reality in each man's course ? Is not the presiding power of each man's life *at its source ?* It is of no use **to deliver** homilies about the beauty of virtue or **of self-sacrifice, or** about the vanity of this passing scene; **men** go from such homilies, complacently as before, to their worldliness or **to** their sins. There is one power, and only one, which can energize the heart. And it is the purpose of this book to call **up** certain scenes where that power put forth its strength.

"**I want,**" said a young corporal one day to Hedley Vicars, "to **have** more of Jesus *in this life.*" CHRIST CRUCIFIED is **not** a mere fund in reserve—a kind of "extreme unction"—to teach men how **to** die; **it is** the lever which is to move **the life.**

The savage, in certain regions, is said to have a belief that the spirit of every enemy he slays passes into his own bosom—giving to his heart new courage, and to **his** arm new power; and therefore his one watchword is—"Slay, slay, slay !" Is it not true that each new victory we gain over sin, is a new accession of moral power ? To retire from life's conflicts, is only **to keep the** passion in abeyance; to meet the temptation and to overcome, is that by which alone we "live."

The Christian athletes here sketched are marked

by varying idiosyncrasies; but they all fought **man-fully** the good fight, **and** they all **have** gotten the victory. **God's grace** " is manifold **;" and it may comfort** and stimulate **the** wrestlers **in** the various places of the field to know **that** others occupied the post before them, and " stood in the evil day."

For the facts in the following Biographies, **we** are indebted chiefly to existing Memoirs. And we shall feel thankful **if the** sketches here given lead to **a** more earnest study **of** the models themselves.

Contents.

I.

The Good Soldier:

JOHN BUNYAN.

"Faith may rise into miracles of might."

"**All** my springs are in THEE."—*Ps.* lxxxvii. 7.

> "Be this, then, a lesson to thy soul, that thou reckon
> nothing worthless,
> Because thou heedest not its use, nor knowest the
> virtues thereof."

BUNYAN is his own Pilgrim embodied into life. "God," says he, in the preface to his Autobiography, "did not play in tempting of me; neither did I play when I sank as into the bottomless pit—when the pangs of hell caught hold upon me: wherefore," he adds, "I may not play in relating of them, but be plain and simple, and lay down the thing as it was." His "fears, and doubts, and sad months," were "as the head of Goliath in his hand;" and the very sight and remembrance of them, like Goliath's sword to David, "did preach forth God's deliverance to him."

There may fall upon these pages the eye of some fainting "soldier of Jesus Christ," whose heart will take new courage as he communes with this stalwart warrior.

CHAPTER I.

The wayside village—The young tinker—Book of Sports—Visions—
Apprehensions—Hair-breadth escapes—A parallel—The adder—The
militiaman—Marriage.

In one of our **wayside English** villages, **with** its rustic cross, **and its** Maypole, and its sign **of** the "Rising Sun," there might be seen, some two **centuries** ago, of an evening on the village green, a **band** of roystering lads, intent on certain rude sport. **The** soul **of** the frolic is **a** broad-shouldered, brawny youth, with **piercing eye and** massive forehead—born a tinker, but evidently **shaped** by Nature **as a** future "king of **men."** The village is Elstow, in Bedfordshire, and the young tinker is John Bunyan.

The times are loose—it is the age of James and of his "Book of Sports;" and the villagers, young and old, "singing and saying very devoutly" once or even twice a day at church on Sunday, "retain" most contentedly "their wicked life." Our youthful hero falls in with the prevailing way—oaths on the green, and a devout "**Amen**" in the Sunday-pew. "It was my delight," he tells us, "to be led captive by the devil at his will. I had few **equals, both** for cursing, swearing, **lying, and** blaspheming the holy name of God." And **these** are **no** mere momentary ebullitions. "So settled **and** rooted **was I** in these things," **says** he, " that they became a kind of second nature to me."

But **it is** not all sunshine. Even in his ninth or **tenth year** he is scared with fearful dreams and visions. Often, after " spending this and the other day **in sin," he is "** greatly afflicted, while asleep, with the apprehensions of devils and wicked spirits, coming to draw him away with them." And his waking hours are haunted with " the thoughts of **the** fearful torments of hell-fire." "Oh, that I were a devil!" he will whisper to himself, " for it were better to be a tormentor, than to be tormented myself!"

Awakened suddenly one night in his hammock by a violent sea which has broken over the crazy ship, a sailor-lad, hastening up the " companion," is met half-way by the captain, shouting "Bring a knife with you—the ship is going down!" Returning for the knife, he is succeeded on the ladder by another, who, the moment he reaches the deck, is washed overboard. There is no time to lament him; and all hands labor at the pump, expecting every moment to be the **last. As the** day brightens, and the sea calms down a litttle, the lad endeavors, with an ill-**disguised** uneasiness, **to cheer** one of the sailors with the prospect that in a few days this distress will serve them **" to talk** of over a glass of wine." " No," replies the other, with tears in his eyes; " it is too late now." But, after other four-and-twenty hours of pumping, the peril passes by, and another of his "deaths oft" is over. The lad is the future John Newton, of Olney.

Bunyan also, in these days of his ungodliness, has many hair's-breadth escapes. Once, "falling into a creek of the sea," he "hardly escapes drowning." Another time he is precipitated from a boat into the Ouse; but "mercy preserves him alive." On a third occasion, being in the field with one of his companions, an adder chances to pass over the highway; and, "having a stick in his hand," he "strikes her over the back;" the animal is "stunned," and he "forces open her mouth with his stick, and plucks her sting out with his fingers." And still another escape he mentions. Now, in his seventeenth year, and having enlisted as a soldier during the civil war, he is "drawn out to go to the siege of Leicester," and is just on the eve of starting, when one of the company desires to go in his room. "He took my place," says he; "and coming to the siege, as he stood sentinel, he was shot in the head with a musket-bullet, and died."

. But these "judgments mixed with mercy" do not "awaken his soul to righteousness." He "sins still, and grows more and more rebellious against God, and careless of his own salvation."

A few years pass over; and he leaves the army, and gets married. "Though we came together," he tells us, "as poor as poor might be, not having so much household stuff **as a dish or** spoon betwixt us **both,** yet this she had for her part—'The Plain Man's Pathway to Heaven,' and ' The Practice of Piety,' which her father had left her when he died." These two volumes are read, and re-read; and another book is read—the " living epistle" of her godly father's life. The result **is, "a** desire to reform his **vicious life, and to** fall in very eagerly with the re**ligion of the** times."

CHAPTER II.

Superstition—New awakening—" Game at cat"—The voice from heaven—"Too late"—The reproof—Legal workings—Self-complacency—The church-bells—Stri**vings—The three poor** saints—Living epistles —" Dwelt alone"—Evangelist.

"**Man**," it has **been** said, "with sinuous ease, escapes from lie to lie." Earnest hitherto in worldliness, the tinker is now scarcely less earnest in " credulities of weakness."   At church " with the foremost," he **is** " overrun with a spirit of superstition," adoring with great devotion "**the high-place, priest,** clerk, vestment, service, **and** what else ;" counting all things **holy** that are therein contained, and especially **the** priest and clerk **most happy,** and, without doubt, greatly blessed, because they are servants, and are principal, in the holy temple, to do His work therein."

Cowper has written—

" **For** though the Pope has lost his interest **here,**
And pardons are not sold as once they were,
No papist's more desirous to compound
Than some **grave** sinners upon English ground."

Bunyan's whole **soul is** now **intent on** this **work.** So strong in **a** little while does the feeling grow **upon** him, that, does **he** but "see a priest though **never** so **sordid** and debauched in his life," he will "find **his spirit** fall **under** him, reverence him, and knit **unto him**; yea, for the love he bears unto them, supposing **them** the ministers of God, he feels **as if he could lie** down at their feet, and be trampled on **by** them; their name, their garb, and work, do so intoxicate and bewitch him."

Once more, however, he is awakened to a crushing sense of sin. All this while, he has "kept from considering, that, **what** religion soever he follows, sin will damn him **unless he be** 'found in Christ.'" But one **day** a sermon **on** Sabbath-breaking startles him; he "falls **in** his conscience under it," and goes **home** "with a great burden upon his spirit."

The "trouble" threatens to "benumb the sinews **of** his best delights;" but, before he was well dined, **it** begins to wear off, and that evening he is at his old sport on the village green, "solacing himself therewith." **The** arrow, however, is not gone. He **is** "**in the** midst of **a** game of Cat," and is just about to "strike **it a** second blow from the hole," when suddenly a voice darts **from** heaven into his soul **say-ing,** "Wilt thou *leave* thy **sins** and go to heaven, or *have* thy sins and go to hell?" **At** this he is "put to an exceeding maze," the Lord **Jesus** seeming **to** "look **down** upon **him from** heaven **in** hot displeas-**ure.**" **His** heart **sinks within** him. **It is** now "too late for him to look after heaven." Christ will never forgive him ; **and, concluding** he may " as well be damned **for many sins as for** few," he " rushes **desperately to his** sport again," fearing lest he should die before he gets his " fill of sin."

One of our poets has described "sin's **round,"** thus :—

> " My words take fire from my inflamed thoughts,
> Which spit it forth like the Sicilian hell."

Standing one afternoon **at a** neighbor's shop-window, he begins to **" curse and** swear **and** play the madman" after such **a fashion, that** the woman of the house, **overhearing him, comes** out, and, though herself **" a very loose** and ungodly wretch," protests **that it** " makes her tremble to hear **him."** " You're enough," she adds, " to spoil all the youth of the town, if they come but in your company." At this reproof he is " silenced ;" and he hangs down his head, " wishing with all his heart he were **a little** child again, that his father might teach him to **speak** without swearing."

The swearing is now abandoned, so that **" it is a** wonder to **himself to observe it."** And the **conversation** of **" one** poor man," **who** " did talk pleasantly of the Scriptures," **leads him** to " his Bible," which he " begins to take great pleasure **in** reading, especially the historical part thereof ;"—though, " as for Paul's Epistles and such-like Scriptures," he " cannot away with them—being **as** yet ignorant, either

of the corruptions of his nature, or of the want and worth of Jesus Christ to save him."

A new enterprise now engages him. "I fell," says he, " to some outward reformation, both in my **words** and **in** my life, and did set the commandments before me for my way **to** heaven ; which command-**ments I** also did strive **to** keep, and, as **I** thought, **did keep** them pretty well sometimes, and then I would have comfort ; yet now and then should break one, and so afflict **my** conscience : but then I would repent, and say I was sorry for it, and would promise God to do better next time, and there get help again ; for then I thought I pleased God as well as any man in England."

This process continues for about a year, all which time his neighbors " take him to be a very godly man—a new and religious man, marvelling much to see such great and famous alteration in his life and manners." And great is his self-complacency as he hears the people's comments on him. " Now," says he, " they began to praise, to commend, and to speak well **of** me, both **to** my face and behind my back. Now I was, as they said, become godly ; now I **was** become a right honest man. But oh ! when I **un-**derstood those were their words and opinions of me, **it** pleased me mighty well. For, though **as** yet I was nothing but a poor painted hypocrite, yet I loved to be talked of as one that was truly godly. I was proud of my godliness."

But the conscience is not at rest. He has " taken

much delight in ringing the church bells;" but now he "begins to think, How if one of them should fall?" For safety, he first "chooses to stand under a main beam which lay athwart the steeple;" but "then," says he, "I thought again should the bell fall with a swing, it might first hit the wall, and then, rebounding upon me, might kill me, for all this beam." He next "stands in the steeple-door," thinking now he is safe enough; for, if the bell should fall, he can "slip out behind those thick walls." But standing there one day, "it comes into his head, How if the steeple itself should fall?" And "this thought continually so shakes his mind, that he dares not stand at the steeple-door any longer, but is forced to flee."

These are real, not imaginary fears. " Poor wretch that I was," he says, "I was all this while going about to establish my own righteousness; and I had perished therein, had not God in mercy showed me more of my state by nature. If I had died thus, my state had been most fearful."

A better day, however, is now to dawn. Sauntering, one morning, along a street in Bedford, in pursuit of his calling as a tinker, he stumbles upon "three or four poor women sitting at a door, in the sun, talking of the things of God." John stands still, and listens. "Their talk is about a new birth, the work of God in their hearts, as also how they were convinced of their miserable state by nature; they tell how God has visited their souls with His love in the Lord **Jesus**; moreover, they reason of the suggestions and temptations of Satan, and tell to each other by what means **they** have been afflicted, and how they **were** borne up under **his** assaults. **They** also discourse of their **own** wretchedness of heart, and **of their** unbelief, contemning, slighting, and **abhorring** their own righteousness, as filthy and insufficient **cient** to do them **any** good."

This **is a** new region **to** him. "**I** heard," says he, "but understood not; for they were far above, out of **my** reach." And yet there is something about these humble Christians which bespeaks an intense reality. "Methought," says Bunyan, "they spake as if joy did make them speak; they spake with such pleasantness **of Scripture** language, and with such appearance of **grace in** all they said, that they were to me as if they **had** found **a new** world—as if they **were** 'people that dwelt alone.'"

The result is, a harrowing **of** soul such **as** he has not **yet** known. His heart "begins **to** shake;" for he **sees that, in all** his thoughts "about religion **and** salvation," the new birth has never entered into his mind. He goes **to** his employment, but his heart "tarries with them;" and often he "makes it his business to be going again and again into their company," being greatly affected with their words, both because he has been convinced **by** them that he "wants the tokens **of a truly** godly man," **and** also because they have taught him "the happy and blessed condition **of him** that **is** such **an** one."

These three **poor** saints are **his** "Evangelist," at once deepening his convictions of sin, and pointing him hopefully to the wicket-gate and to the cross. "**A** very great softness and tenderness **of** heart," **he says,** "now came upon me, so that it lay like a horse-leech at the vein, **still** crying **out, 'Give,** give!' **I** was so fixed on eternity, that neither pleasures, nor profits, nor persuasions, nor threats, could loose me or make **me** let **go my hold."**

CHAPTER III.

HERBERT, in one of his Odes, has written—

> "Of what an easy, quick access,
> My blessed Lord, art thou! how suddenly
> May our requests thine ear invade!
> If I but lift mine eyes, my suit **is** made:
> Thou canst no more not hear, than thou canst die."

And Bunyan **is,** one day, to comprehend this truth, and **to** delineate **it** with a matchless pathos in the scene at **the Cross.** But, as yet, it is only the grey dawn **of day.**

The dawn, however, is gradually brightening; and from **the** Word **the** cheering beams shine. "Now, methought," he says, "**I** looked into the Bible with new eyes, and read **as I** never read before; and especially the epistles **of Paul were** sweet and pleasant to me." He is "never out of **the** Bible, either by reading **or** by meditation—still crying **out to**

God, that he may **know the truth, and the way to** heaven and **glory."**

Like many earnest souls at this stage, he **is driven** upon the rocks of inward frames. This always **"is** running in his mind, 'But how if I want faith ? **how** can I tell I have faith ?'" Travelling one afternoon from Elstow to Bedford, "the temptation is hot" upon him to say to "the puddles in the horsepads, 'Be dry ;' and to the dry places, 'Be you puddles !'" If he can work the miracle, it will **prove he** "has faith indeed." But, just as he is about to speak, the thought comes into his mind,—" **But** go **under** yon- der hedge **and pray first, that God** would make **you** able." **And another thought** "comes hot" upon **him** —" What **if I** pray, and try to do it, and yet **do** nothing, notwithstanding ? then to be sure I have **no** faith, **but** am a castaway, and am lost."

Grotesque as this appears, is it not **in** substance the method adopted by "fearful" souls to ascertain their standing before God ? They **do** not command the "puddles" to become dry ground, or wait for the "troubling" of the Bethesda **pool** ;—but do not **they look** into **the** "waters" **of** their own inward frames, and, according as these waters are "troubled" **or** stagnant, are not they joyous or joyless ?

A kind of waking vision opens to him **a** glimpse of the way **of life.** The poor saints of Bedford he sees one **day as** if on the sunny side of some high mountain, refreshing themselves **with** the pleasant beams **of the** sun ; while he himself **is** shivering and shrinking in the cold, afflicted with frost, snow, and dark clouds. "Methought, also," he says, "betwixt me and them I saw a wall, which did compass about this mountain. Now, through this wall, my soul did greatly desire to pass—concluding that, if I could, I would even go into the midst of them, and there also comfort myself with the heat of their sun." But is there a way through the wall? After a long search, at last he discovers "a narrow gap, like a little door-way, very straight, and narrow." He labors to get in, but in vain—even until he is "well-nigh quite beat out." **At** length, with great striving, he at first gets in his head, and then, "by a sideling striving," his "shoulders, and **his** whole body." Exceeding glad, he goes and sits down in the midst of them, and **so is** "comforted with the light and heat of their sun."

The vision is thus "**made** out" to him: The mountain is the living Church; the sun which shone upon it, "the comfortable shining **of** God's merciful face on them that are therein;" the wall is that which "does make separation betwixt the Christians and the world;" and the gap in the wall is "Jesus Christ, the way to God the Father—'I am the way, and the truth, and the life; no man cometh to the Father **but** by **me.'**" And, "forasmuch as the passage was wonderful narrow," it shows him that none can enter life but those who are in downright earnest, and **un-less** also they leave that wicked world behind them; for here is only room for body and **soul, but** not for body, and soul, and sin.

Still he does not personally "sit in the sunshine." One temptation besets him, and then another, and another. "Am I elected?" at times so "offends and discourages" him, that, though he is "in a flame **to** find the way to heaven and glory, and though nothing can beat him off," he is "as if the very strength of his body also were taken away by the force and power thereof."

"You had as good leave off," whispers Satan to him one **day,** "and strive no further; for if, indeed, you should not be elected and chosen of God, there is no hope **of** your being **saved; 'for it is not of him** that willeth, **nor of him that** runneth, **but of God** that showeth **mercy.'"**

Driven **to his** wits' end, he is "ready to sink where he is, with faintness of mind." But one night, as he **is** now "quite giving up the ghost of all his hopes **of** ever attaining life," the thought occurs to him— "Begin at the beginning of Genesis, **and** read to **the** end **of** the Revelation, **and see** if you can find **that** there **were ever any that** trusted **in** the Lord and **were** confounded." That thought **"doth** still ofttimes,"** he says, "shine before my face."

Another temptation tries him—"How if the **day** of grace should now be past **and** gone? How **if** you have overstood the time **of** mercy?" He goes up and down, bemoaning his sad condition, counting himself "far **worse** than a thousand fools for standing off thus long, and spending so many years in **sin."** "Oh!" he cries, "that I **had** turned sooner! **Oh,** that I turned seven years ago!" For many days he is "vexed with this fear," until he is "scarce able to take one step more." At length, however, these words break in upon his mind—"Compel them to come in, that my house may be filled;" and "yet there is room." There must still be place enough in heaven **for** him; for did not the Lord Jesus, in speaking **these** words, think individually of him? This he "verily believes." And the comfort is the greater, that the Lord should have thought of him so long ago, and should have spoken those words on purpose **for** his sake.

And another temptation besets him—to "return again to his **old ways.**" But one thought at such moments always outweighs every other—"that *sound* sense of death, and of the day of judgment, which abides, as it were, continually **in his** view."

Is it not the want of this "sound sense of a com-**ing** judgment" which encumbers the Church with so many loiterers, and so many lookers-back?

> "I sum up half mankind,
> And add two-thirds to the remaining half,
> And find the total of their hopes and fears
> Dreams, empty dreams."

The Church in Sodom consisted of four members: of these how many were **true** souls?

The goodly tents of Israel grow gradually more attractive in his eyes. How "lovely" now is "every **one** that **he** thinks **to be** converted, whether man or

woman ! They shine ; they walk like a people who
carry the broad seal of heaven about them." Christ
" called unto Him **whom He** would." **Never** does
he read of any whom Christ called but he presently
wishes—" Would I had been in their clothes ! would
I had been born Peter ! **would** I **had been** born
John ! **or,** would I had been by and had heard Him,
when He called them ! how would **I have** cried, ' **O
Lord, call me also !' "**

CHAPTER IV.

"Hast thou watched the dawn of sunlight brighten into perfect day?
Seen the rippled waves of ocean lashed to surf, and foam, and spray?"

The Bedford centurion—The escape—The gaming-table—"Great
peace"—The pastor—Interviews—Two wonders—Inward pollution
—The cross—"My love"—Rest.

THERE lived at that time in Bedford a minister of
God's Word, who had passed through a strange bap-
tism. Originally a major in the army, and a devoted
royalist, he had been apprehended with eleven others,
and been sentenced to death. It is the eve of the
fatal day, and his sister comes in to bid him a last
farewell. The guard is asleep, and his companions
are intoxicated. "Why not," she whispers, as she
enters the cell, "escape instantly for your life?"
Cautiously stealing his way out, he lies concealed for
three days in the bottom of a great ditch, and then
flies in disguise to London.

After a while, returning to Bedford, he bethinks
him of venturing upon the practice of physic. One
night, at the gaming-table, having lost a considerable
sum, he is plunged into the most horrible profane-
ness, raging at the providence of God, and threatening to put an end to his life. He gains his own

chamber; **and,** as he sits solitary **and in despair,** a sentence **catches his eye, in a** book lying **open on** the **table.** Conscience is smitten, and for a month **he** has no rest. **But** at length the way **of** forgiveness through **the** atoning blood of Christ comes home **to** him so sweetly and so forcefully, that his whole soul is filled with joy and peace; so that, for " five years together, he never loses for one hour the comfortable light of God's countenance."

Like Saul of Tarsus, he " assays to join himself **to** the disciples ;" **but so** notorious has been his **enmity to** serious godliness, **and** also **so exceedingly vile his life,** that only **a warm attachment and a** naturally **bold spirit secured for** him **a** place **in their** fellow- ship. Beginning, however, bye and bye to speak **the W**ord of God—at first in private, and afterwards more publicly—John Gifford is attended **with so re-** markable a blessing, that the people with one consent choose him as their pastor; and he **gives** himself **up** to serve them **in the Gospel of His Son.**

Among the humble flock of this true minister **are the " three poor women." Breaking his** mind one **day to** these saints, Bunyan **is named by** them to Mr. **Gifford. After a** private interview **with** him, he in-**vites him** repeatedly to his house, to hear him " con-**fer with** others about **the** dealings of God with their souls." The result is, **a** deeper conviction of " the vanity and inward wretchedness of his wicked heart" —his **inward** exercises being only " as **a clog** on the leg **of a bird, to** hinder **it from** flying."

Yet the case is not so desperate as to himself it seems.

> "Fractures well cured, make us more strong."

He who has been "breaking" these "bones" is preparing for the troubled man a firm and lasting joy. But Satan does not willingly let go such a prey. The tinker is like the child brought to Christ, who, "while he was yet coming to Him, was thrown down by the devil, and also so rent and torn by him that he lay and wallowed, foaming." Drawing nearer into God's own light, he sees things now more in their true proportions. Two things especially often make him wonder. The one is, when he finds " old people hunting after the things of this life, as if they should live here always;" the other is, when he sees " professors much distressed and cast down when they meet with outward losses." "Lord, thought I, what ado is here about such little things as these! What seeking after carnal things by some, and what grief in others for the loss of them!"

And another reality which grows more vivid to him is his " original and inward pollution." He " sees it at a dreadful rate;" it is always "putting itself forth within him," and he " has the guilt of it to amazement." He feels as if none but the devil himself could " equalize him for inward wickedness and pollution of mind;" sin and corruption as naturally bubble out of his heart as water out of a fountain

He is " more loathesome in his own eyes than a toad ;" **and** he " thinks he is so in God's eyes, too."   **And** yet " this sight and sense of terror of his own wickedness **ho is** afraid to let go quite off his mind ;" for **he** finds that, " unless guilt of conscience be taken off in the right way, that is, by the blood of Christ," a **man** " grows rather worse for the loss of his trouble of mind."

But God's " comforting time" is now come.

> " Sweeten **at** length this bitter bowl,
>   Which thou hast poured **into** my **soul:**
> Thy wormwood **turn to health ; winds to fair** weather."

Now in sight **of** the **Cross, he begins to** lift up hopefully and expectingly this prayer.

One day, **in** the humble meeting, a preacher is discoursing most tenderly of Christ's grace to sinners. Bunyan is there ; and two simple words* fix themselves in his mind, and reach his bleeding **heart.** " What !" he thinks, " *I* loved by Him when loveless ! loved **without a** cause ! **loved,** though despised **by** the world ! **loved,** when tempted and self-destroyed !" And **as he saunters homewards, the** words " twenty times **together kindle in** his spirit," until, " waxing stronger **and warmer," they** " begin to make him look up."

Days pass on, **and the** " Word **over and over again makes** this joyful noise within **his** soul— ' Thou art my love ; thou art my **love ; and** nothing

* " My love."—Song of Sol., iv. 1.

shall separate **thee** from my love.'" **His heart is now** " filled full of comfort and **hope ;" now** he " can believe that his sins will be forgiven him." And so **taken is** he with the love and mercy of God, that he **feels as if** he " could speak **of it to the** very crows **which sit upon** the ploughed land by the wayside, were they capable to understand him."

It is the "pilgrim" gazing at the Crucified, until **his** burden sinks into the open grave, and until the **tear** of lowly thankfulness glistens **in** his beaming eye. And now he can sing with his own Pilgrim—

> "**Thus far** did I come **laden** with my sin;
> Nor could aught ease the burden I was in
> Till I came hither: what a place is this!
> Must **here be** the beginning of my bliss?
> Must here the burden fall from off my back?
> Must here the strings that bound it to me crack?
> Blest cross! blest sepulchre! blest rather be
> The MAN that there was put to shame for me!"

CHAPTER V.

The house Beautiful and the conflict—Apollyon—"A very great storm"—"A thousand pounds for a tear"—"Alone, alone!" —"I will cool you"—The sword—"A good word"—"A sweet glance"—A wayside musing—Fireside message—Right mind— Faithful—Mr. Gifford—"Former and latter rain."

"The Church militant," it has been said, "inherits the condition of Jesus Christ." It endures His conflict; otherwise it is not the Church.

And each member of the body has the same conflict; so that, if suddenly the Church were reduced to one living person, "nothing would be changed but the number"—that one individual would "fill up that which is behind of his afflictions." The same conflict, therefore, awaits Christ's good soldier. In Christ's afflictions, what feature more marked than His conflict with the tempter!

Before the Pilgrim met Apollyon, he had been "harnessed from head to foot" with armor. Bunyan himself is less fully girded.

A presentiment, indeed, of coming peril is not wanting. "About a week or a fortnight after this," he tells us, "I was much followed by that Scripture,

'Simon, Simon, behold, Satan hath desired **to have you ;'** and sometimes **it** would sound as loud within **me,** yea, and **as it were call so** strongly after me, that **once,** above all **the** rest, I turned **my** head over my shoulder, thinking verily that some one behind **had** called **me. It came, as I have** thought since, to stir me up to prayer and watchfulness—to **ac-**quaint me that a cloud **and a** storm **were coming down** upon me."

But he " understands it not." **And** so, ere **long,** **" a very great** storm" does come down. Deep calls to deep; darkness seizes upon him ; blasphemous suggestions " **do so** overweigh his heart, both with their number, continuance, and fiery force, that he feels as if God **has** given him up to them, to be car-**ried away** by them as **by** a mighty whirlwind."

The temptation lasts **" about a** year." Fearing **at** times that he may have **committed the sin** against the Holy Ghost, he " envies **the condition of the dog** and of the toad ;" counting " the **estate of everything that** God has made far better than this dreadful state **of mind."** His heart, too, is so " exceeding hard, **that, if he should give a** thousand pounds for a tear, **he** cannot shed one ; no, nor sometimes scarce desire to shed one." Some he sees, who can mourn and lament their sin ; **others who** can rejoice **aud** bless **God for** Christ ; **and others again,** who can quietly talk of and gladly remember the **Word** of God : but he himself is only in the " storm **and** tempest," and there, as he thinks, **aloue—**

> "**Alone,** alone—in the world alone;
> Pacing the **desert wild.**"

And yet not **alone!** The devil will be "continually at him in **time of** prayer, **to** have **done—to** break off." "**Make haste,**" he will whisper to him; "you **have** prayed enough; and stay **no** longer."

At other times, "when laboring to compose his wandering thoughts and to fix them upon God," he **will** "with great force distract and confound **him,** by presenting to his fancy the most silly **and trifling** objects."

And again, **when he "has some** strong and heart-affecting apprehensions **of God," his** heart "putting **itself forth with** inexpressible groanings," Satan will **come** to him, saying—"You are very hot for mercy; **but** I will cool you—this frame shall not last al**ways.** Many have been as hot as you for a spirt; but **I have** quenched their zeal."

At that he **will** remember some who have "fallen off," **and will begin to tremble** lest he should "do so **too.**"

"But I am so glad **that this has come into my** mind: **I** will watch, and take what care **I can.**"

"Ah! though you do," Satan whispers, "I shall be too hard for you; I will cool you insensibly, by degrees, by little and little. What care I, though I **be** seven years **in** chilling your heart, if I can do it **at** last? Continual rocking will lull a crying child asleep: I will **ply it** close but I will have my end accomplished. Though **you be** burning hot at present,

I **can** pull you from this fire; I shall have you cold before it be long."

Grasping his sword, the brave warrior exclaims :— "I am persuaded that neither death, nor life, nor angels, nor principalities, nor powers, nor things present, nor things to come, nor height, nor depth, nor any other creature, shall be able to separate us from the love of God which is in Christ Jesus our Lord." "And now," he says, "I hoped that long **life** would not destroy me, nor make me miss **of** heaven."

The "fiery darts" still fly thick around him. One day, sitting in a neighbor's house, he "says in his mind—'What ground have I to think that I, who have been so vile and abominable, shall ever inherit eternal life?' But suddenly that word comes upon **him**, 'What shall **we** say to these things? if God be for **us**, who can be against **us**?'" Another day "a sweet glance" surprises him, from **the** text, "He hath made Him to be sin for us, who knew no sin, that we might **be** made the righteousness of God in Him." And, again, a "fragrant breeze" freshens his drooping spirit, **in** the words, "Because I live, ye shall live also." Still these words are but "hints, touches, short visits; though very sweet when present;" only, they "last **not**, but, like Peter's sheet, **of** a sudden are caught **up** from him to heaven again."

The "visits," however, grow **at once** more frequent and less transient.

One day, as he is travelling into the country, and is musing on the enmity which is in his heart to God, that Scripture comes into his mind—" He hath made peace by the blood of His cross." "I was made to see," he says, " both again and again, that God and my soul were friends by His blood ; yea, I saw that the justice of God, and my sinful soul, could embrace and kiss each other, through His blood. This was a good day to me ; I hope I shall never forget it."

Another day, he is sitting by the fire in his house, oppressed with a sense of his natural wretchedness ; and " the Lord brings to him that Scripture—' Forasmuch, then, as the children are partakers of flesh and blood, He also Himself likewise took part of the same, that through death He might destroy him that had the power of death, that is, the devil, and deliver them who through fear of death were all their lifetime subject to bondage.' " And " the glory of the words is so weighty" on him, that he is " both once and twice ready to swoon ;" yet " not with grief and trouble, but with solid joy and peace."

Thus, for the time, does the Lord " more fully and graciously discover Himself" to him, and, indeed, " quite deliver him, not only from the guilt which by these temptations has been laid upon his conscience, but also from the filth thereof ;" for " the temptation is removed, and he is put into his right mind again."

In the earnest pastor of the humble flock at Bedford, Bunyan now finds at his side another " Faithful." " At this time," he tells us, " I sat under the ministry of holy Mr. Gifford, whose teaching by God's grace was much for my stability." It is precisely such teaching as he at this season needs. "That man made it much his business," he says, " to deliver the people of God from all those hard and unsound tests, which by nature we are prone to. He would bid us take special heed that we took not any truth upon trust, as from this, or that, or any other man or men, but cry mightily unto God that He would convince us of the reality thereof, and would set us down therein by His own Spirit in the holy Word; 'for,' said he, 'if you do otherwise, when temptations come strongly upon you,—you, not having received them with evidence from heaven, will find you want that help and strength now to resist, which once you thought you had.'" This is "as seasonable to his soul as the former and latter rain in their season :" wherefore he prays, that, in "nothing which pertains to God's glory and to his own eternal happiness, will He suffer him to be without the confirmation thereof from heaven ;" for now he "sees clearly, there is an exceeding difference betwixt the notion of the flesh and blood, and the revelation of God in heaven—also a great difference betwixt that faith which is feigned and according to man's wisdom, and that which comes from a man's being born thereto of God."

CHAPTER VI.

Cowper—The balm—" Led from truth to truth"—Nothing at **second-hand**—The only Teacher—Assurance—A scene at Erfurth—Luther and Bunyan—Fears within—A pattern—Temptation.

THE poet Cowper **was not uttering an unfelt** joy, when **he** wrote—

"Scripture is the only cure of woe.
That field of promise, how it flings abroad
Its odor o'er the Christian's thorny road!
The soul, reposing on assured relief,
Feels herself happy amidst all her grief."

Bunyan now, **with a kindred** joy, ponders, **day by** day, the sacred page. **" Oh !** how my soul," he **says,** " was led from truth to **truth !** There was not anything which I then cried to **God to** make known to **me but** He was pleased to do **it** for me—I mean, not **one part of** the Gospel of the Lord Jesus **but** I was orderly led **into it."**

And he adds—" Methought I was **as** if I had seen Him born—as if I had seen Him grow up—as **if I** had seen Him walk through this world from the cradle to **the** cross, to which also when He came, I saw how gently **He gave** Himself to **be** nailed on it **for** my sins and wicked doing. I have seen also as if He had leaped **out of the** grave's mouth, for joy that He **was** risen again **and had** got the conquest **over** our dreadful foes, saying, '**I** ascend **unto** my **Father** and your Father, **and to** my God **and** your **God.'** I have likewise in the spirit seen Him a Man **on** the right hand of God the Father for me, **and** have seen the manner of His coming from heaven **to** judge the world with glory."

Bunyan takes nothing at second-hand. If ever a man's faith was " established, not in the wisdom of men, but in the power of God," it is his. "Truly in those days," he writes, "**let** men say what they would, unless **I** had **it with** evidence from heaven, **all** was nothing **to me—I** counted myself not set **down in** any truth of **God.** **It** would be too long to tell **in** particular how God did set **me** down in all the things of Christ, and how He did, that He might do **so,** lead me into His words; yea, and also how He did open them unto me, and make them shine before me, and **cause** them dwell with me, talk with **me,** and comfort me over and over. Oh, friends, cry to God to reveal Jesus Christ unto you; there is none teacheth like **Him."**

Herbert once wrote :—

> "Why do I languish thus, drooping and dull,
>   As if I were all of earth ?
> Oh ! give me quickness, that I may with mirth
>   Praise thee brim-full."

The seer of Bedford, also, growing in heavenliness, feels how imperfect and **"in part"** is all here. Often does he "long **and** desire **that** the last day **were come,** that he may be for **ever** inflamed with the sight and joy and communion with **Him** whose head was crowned with thorns, whose face was spit upon, and body broken, and soul made an offering, for our sins." For, "whereas before," he says, "I lay continually trembling at the mouth of hell—now, methought, **I** was got so far therefrom that, **when I** looked back, I could scarce discern **it. And, oh!** thought **I,** that **I were fourscore years old now, that** I might **die quickly, that my soul might be** gone to rest !"

In the town of Erfurth, a century previous, there might **have** been seen, in the library of its Augustinian monastery, a grave earnest man, poring for days and weeks together over **a** Bible chained **to a** reading-desk, and hitherto **a** sealed **book. It is** Martin Luther, inquiring **of** God, "What shall I **do** to be saved ?" Deep and mysterious **are the** struggles **in that** strong **heart.** But light **arises ;** and masses, austerities, bead-rolls, penances, strivings, **frames,** "weighed and found **wanting," give** place **to the** righteousness **of Jesus,** bestowed as **a** free gift, and received by **faith** alone. Taught his theology thus at the **feet of** Christ, the monk goes **forth** among **his fellows,** uttering in tones of thunder the great secret **of his own joyous** hope.

Bunyan **is "** greatly **longing** to **see some** ancient

godly man's experience," when "God casts into his
hand one day a **book so old** that it is ready to fall
piece from piece if he but turn **it** over." The book
is "Luther **on** the Galatians." "Perusing **it** but a
little way," he "finds his own condition **so** largely
and so profoundly handled, that the book might have
been written out of his heart." "Besides," says he,
"it doth most gravely debate of the rise **of** these
temptations, namely, blasphemy, desperation, and the
like; showing that the law of Moses—as well as
the devil, death, and hell—hath a very great hand
therein." "The which at first is very strange" to
him; but, "considering and watching," he "finds **it**
so indeed."

Bunyan and Luther were cast in moulds not un-
like; and the period when they met—not in personal, indeed, **but** in mutual and spiritual converse—
may be regarded as the era which gave to Bunyan's
practical theology its type of broad common-sense,
and **of** plain-spoken dealing with the human conscience **and** the human heart. "Of particulars
here," **he** says, expressing his own sense of his
deep sympathy with the great Reformer, "I intend
nothing; only this, methinks, I must let fall before
all men—I do prefer this book **of** Martin Luther
upon the Galatians (excepting **the** Holy Bible) before
all the books which ever I have seen, as most fit for
a wounded conscience."

CHAPTER VII.

> " And now, methinks, I am where I began
> Seven years ago; one vogue and vein,
> One air of thought usurps my brain.
> I did toward Canaan draw; but now I am
> Brought back to the Red Sea, the sea of shame."

> " I gave to Hope a watch of mine; but he
> An anchor gave to me."

Luther—His conflicts and triumphs—Face **to face** with Satan—Bunyan—"Sell Him"—Wrestlings—A stroke—Gleam of light—New struggles—Not content—**The** "flesh" and the "spirit"—The unpardonable sin—"False opinions"—Satan's aim—Sunny gleams—"Flying fits"—The voice—" No use praying"—" Ancient Christian"—The settle—An echo—A mill-post at his back—Self-dedication.

LUTHER oftentimes—so vivid were his heart **experiences**—seems to stand before **us** in actual **face-to-face** conflict with **Satan. At one moment, he** puts him **to flight with a joyous hymn of praise; whilst,** at another, **he** dares **him** to write, **at the** bottom **of a catalogue of his sins,** the Scripture—" The **blood of** Jesus **Christ cleanseth** from all sin"—and the tempter disappears. **Not less** vivid are Bunyan's wrestlings with the arch-fiend.

Scarcely has the Lord "set him down so sweetly, **in the faith** of His holy Gospel," and he has felt his " affections cleaving to Christ," and his **love to Him** "as hot as fire"—when "the tempter comes upon him" with a temptation "more grievous and dreadful" than he has yet known. The temptation is, "to sell and part with this most blessed Christ—to exchange Him for the things of this life, for any thing."

For the space of a year, the suggestion follows him continually, so that he is not rid of it one day in a month, and at times not one hour in many days together, except when he is asleep. "Sell Christ for this," whispers the tempter, as he is "eating his food, stooping for a pin, chopping a stick, or casting his eye to look upon any object;" "sell Christ for that; sell Him, sell Him !" Sometimes it will run in his thoughts, "not so little as a hundred times together, 'Sell Him, sell Him, sell Him !' " whilst "for whole hours together, he is forced to stand as continually leaning and forcing his spirit, lest haply, before he is aware, there arise in his heart some wicked thought which may consent thereto." And, notwithstanding, "the tempter at times succeeds in persuading him he has consented ;" whereupon he is "as one tortured upon a rack for whole days together."

After a while he recovers the shock; but again the temptation to consent " puts him into such fear," that, by " the very force of his mind in laboring to gainsay and resist this wickedness, his body is put into action or motion by ways of pushing or thrusting with his hands or elbows"—the " destroyer" still saying, "Sell Him!" and the tried man still answering, until he scarce well knows where he is or how to be composed again—"I will not, I will not, I **will** not! no, not for thousands, thousands, thousands of worlds!" The "reckoning" is, to make sure that, in the midst of these assaults, he does not set too low a value on Him.

On other occasions, the tempter appears as an angel of light "dragging **him into** bondage." At these seasons, **he** will **"not** let him eat his food at quiet;" but, "forsooth, when he is set **at** the table at his meat, he must go hence to **pray—he must leave** his food, now, and **just now—so** counterfeit **holy,** also, would **this devil be."**

"Now I am at meat," he will "say in himself," at such moments, "let me make an end."

"No, you must do it now, or you will displease God and despise Christ."

And then he will feel "as **guilty,** because **he** has not obeyed **a temptation of the devil, as if he had** broken the law of God indeed."

The **reader** will remember Christian's "dreadful fall," when Apollyon, "gathering up close" to him, "had almost pressed him to death." One morning, Bunyan is lying awake, harassed by "the wicked suggestion still running in his mind, as fast as a man could speak, 'Sell Him, sell Him, sell Him, sell Him!'" and "**in** his mind he is answering, **at least** twenty times together—'No, **no, not for thousands,** thousands, thousands!'" when, at last, "after much striving, even until he is almost out of breath," he feels this thought pass through his heart, " Let Him go if He will ;" and he thinks also that he " feels his heart freely consent thereto." The battle seems lost; and " down he falls, as a bird shot from the top of a tree, into great guilt and fearful despair." Hastening out of **bed,** he " goes moping **into the** field"—where, for the space of two hours, he is "like a man bereft of life—past all recovery, and bound over to eternal punishment."

And **yet he** " concludes, with great indignation both against his **heart** and against all assaults, how he would rather be torn in pieces than be found a consenter thereto." **In** spite of his self-condemnatory reasonings his heart is true and loyal.

The " new man" is **of** God, and cannot act against God ; the "old man" is of **the devil, and** cannot act for God. It is Jacob and Esau struggling together in the same womb. The " flesh" is essentialy hellish and devilish ; the " spirit" is as essentially heavenly and divine. **Hence the** struggle and the victory : what is **of God** must encounter Satan's enmity, and **must** also overcome. **"I** write **unto you, young** men," says **John, "**because ye have overcome **the** wicked one." The tempter was not finally beaten back ; but each new conflict ended in a new triumph. Such **a** triumph is awaiting Bunyan ; but, this time, it is not till after a protracted fight.

The fear " tears and rends" him—" Have I committed **the** unpardonable sin ?" And this though presents itself—"How loathsome shall I be to **the saints at the day of judgment!**" Scarcely can **he** see a good man, whom he believes to have a good conscience, but, "he feels his heart tremble at him while he is in his presence." And then this—"Oh, what a glory in walking with God! and what a mercy to have a good conscience before Him!"

Again; he is tempted to "content himself by receiving some false opinions;" as, **that there** is no such thing as a day of judgment, or **a** resurrection;—the tempter suggesting that, "even though these things should **be true, it would** be a present relief not to believe **them.**" **But, as** he listens to this lie, he "sees judgment and the judge" at the very door, "as if they were come already." And the lesson he learns is, that "Satan will use any means to keep the soul from Christ;" an "awakened frame of spirit" being that which he hates; and "security, blindness, darkness, and error" being his "very kingdom and habitation."

Yet gleams of sunshine flit across these dark **scenes.** This Scripture "rushes" upon him—"He **hath** received gifts for **men,** even for the rebellious." "Am not I **a** rebel?" he asks himself; "and then why not for **me?**" And such cases as David, Peter, **Solomon,** Manasseh, comfort him; for, "though all the sins of these saints, and of other great offenders **were** put **together in one,** and though his own sins were bigger than all, cannot the blood which had virtue enough in it to wash away their sins, wash away his also?"

On another occasion, he is "fleeing from God as from the face of a dreadful judge." But, "in these flying fits," this Scripture calls after him—"I have blotted out, as a thick cloud, thy transgressions, and as a cloud thy sins; return unto me, for I have redeemed thee." It cries aloud with a very great voice, **so that** he "makes a little stop, and, as it were, looks over his shoulder behind him to see if he cannot discern **that** the God of grace follows him with a pardon in his hand."

One day, as he **is** "walking to and fro in a good man's shop," again bowed down by the fear of having committed **the** unpardonable sin, and praying in his heart that, if his **sin do** differ from that against the Holy Ghost, the **Lord will** show it to him—"suddenly there is, as if there rushed in at the window, the noise of wind upon him, but very pleasant; **and** as if he heard a voice speaking, 'Didst thou ever refuse **to be** justified by the blood of Christ?'" In an instant, **his** "whole life of profession" **is opened to** him; and **he** sees that designedly he **has not,** and his "heart answers groaningly, No." Light **comes,** and a calm silence—stilling the tumult of "those thoughts which, like masterless hell-hounds, have roared and bellowed, and made so hideous a noise within him."

Another temptation, however, tries him. Can he **have the face** once more to go to the feet of that

Saviour against whom he has so vilely sinned? Oh the shame which now attends him, when he thinks of going to God by prayer! "It is no use your prayers," whispers Satan; "for God is weary of you and of your unbelief, in not going up to possess the land." The man is stunned. "Oh! who knows," says he, "how hard a thing I found it to come to God in prayer!" But, whilst "pinched very sore," he thinks he can but die; and, so, pray he will and must—even though it should once be written, "Such an one died at the foot of Christ in prayer."

At this crisis, harassed and perplexed by every passing wind, he breaks his mind to "an ancient Christian," telling him he is afraid he has sinned the sin against the Holy Ghost. "I think so, too," is the reply. This is "cold comfort;" but he is relieved on finding that, though a gracious man, he is "a stranger to much combat with the devil." So he hies him back once more to God again, beseeching mercy there.

But a strange cloud still shrouds God's face. He thinks of Jesus—of His "grace, goodness, love, kindness, gentleness, meekness, death, blood, promises, and blessed exhortations, comforts, and consolations;" but all this "goes to his soul like a sword," for the thought comes, "Ay, this is the Jesus, the loving Saviour, whom I have parted with; and oh, what I have lost!"

One day, in this troubled mood, he is pacing the streets of a neighboring town—when, ready to sink, he sits down upon a "settle," and "falls into a very deep pause" about his sin. "Methinks," says he, as he lifts up his head after a long musing, "that sun grudges to give me light; and those stones in the street, and tiles on the houses, band themselves against me." And, heaving a heavy sigh, **he** adds, "How can God comfort such a wretch?"

A sunbeam, however, once more penetrates his **soul.** "This sin of thine," an echo seems to answer, "is not unto death." It is as if he "had suddenly **been** raised out of the grave," and he exclaims— "Lord, how couldst thou find out such **a word** as this?" For he is "filled with admiration at the fitness and the unexpectedness of the sentence, and at the rightness of the timing of it, and at the power, and sweetness, and light, and glory, which has come with **it.**" His sin, he now thinks, is pardonable ; and great **is the** "easement" to his mind—it **is** a release " from his former bonds, and a shelter from his former storms."

For two days that sentence "**stands like a** mill-post **at his** back." But by and by **it** begins **to** leave him, and **to** "withdraw its supportation" from **him ;** and so, again he finds himself on his knees under **his** "old fears," and crying—"O Lord, I beseech **thee,** show me that thou hast loved me with everlasting love." Scarcely has the cry gone forth, when, like an echo, there returns upon him—"I have loved thee with an everlasting love." He goes **to** bed in quiet; also, when he awakes next morning, it **is** fresh upon **nis** soul, and he "believes it."

Leaving once more the ashes and the " pots" among which he has been lying, he soars aloft into the soul's proper rest and home—

"On steady wings sails through the immense abyss,
Plucks amaranthine joys from bowers of bliss."

And the " love and affection" which now again **"burn** within him toward his Lord and Saviour," **work** " such a strong and hot desire of revengement upon himself for the abuse which he has done to Him, that, had he a thousand gallons of blood within his veins, he feels he could freely spill **it all** at His **command,** and at His feet." **And** such a passage **as this** stimulates him—" **There is** forgiveness with thee, **that thou mayest be** feared **;" for it** is " thus made **out"** to him—that **the** great God doth set so high an esteem **on the** love of His poor creatures, that, rather than go without their love, He will pardon their transgressions. And then **another** word is " fulfilled **on** him"—" They shall **be ashamed** and confounded, **and** never **open their** mouths **any** more, because of **their** shame **; when I am** pacified **toward them** for all **that they have** done, saith the Lord **God."** And thus **his** soul at this time—and, as he then thinks, **for ever** —is " set at liberty from being afflicted with **his** for**mer** guilt **and** amazement."

CHAPTER VIII.

Heart-ache—Deep gulf—"Yet I will pray"—"Clapping on the back"—
"Able"—"For thee"—"A grace-giver"—Napoleon—"Has left Him"
—A calm—Christ in heaven—Brainerd—Love.

"Security," it has been said, "is the greatest of our dangers." To this peril, certainly, Bunyan is **not** exposed. His Christian life hitherto has been one continuous conflict; **nor** is the battle yet over.

Many weeks **have not** passed when again his "**heart** begins to ache," **lest he** "meet with disappointment at last." And **he sets** himself most diligently **to** examine his former comfort, fearing that one **who has** sinned so grievously against light may be shut **out from** all right to peace **and** joy. "Rejoice not, O Israel, for joy, as other people"—startles him; for, though there is cause of rejoicing **for** those who "hold **to** Jesus," has not he cut himself off by his transgressions, **and left** himself "neither foot-hold **nor** hand-hold **among all** the stays **and** props in the **precious Word of life**?" And so again he "sinks **into** a gulf, **as a** house whose foundation is destroyed," **the** darkness brooding **over** him for many months.

One day, the thought occurs to him—" Men ought always to pray and **not to** faint." But **no** sooner has he set himself with new earnestness to this exercise than the tempter " lays at him very sore," saying —" Neither the mercy of God, nor yet the blood of Christ, **does** at all concern you, nor **can help you for** your sin ; therefore it is vain to pray."

" **Yet,** I will pray," he secretly says to **himself.**

" **But** your sin is unpardonable."

" Well, I will pray."

" It is to no boot."

" But I *will* pray."

And, going upon his knees, he says—" Lord, Satan tells me that neither thy mercy nor Christ's blood is sufficient to save my soul : Lord, shall I honor thee most by believing thou wilt and canst? or him, **by** believing thou neither wilt nor canst? Lord, **I** would fain honor thee by believing thou wilt and canst." Scarcely has he spoken, when it seems **as** if " some one was clapping him on the back," saying —" O man, great is thy faith."

Another day, after continuing from **the** morning **till** about seven or eight at night, " again **much un-der** this question, ' Whether the blood of Christ is sufficient to save his soul,' "—suddenly, **as** he is quite worn out with fear, these words " sound within his heart, ' He is able.' " " Methought," says he, " this word ' able' was spoke loud to me ; it showed a great word ; it seemed to be writ in great letters, **and** gave such **a jostle to my fear** and doubt as I

never had from that time, all my life, either before or
after."

Yet, even this bright gleam is of short duration.
A fortnight after, his sky is again overcast, and he is
crying—

" Whither away, delight ?
Thou cam'st but now; wilt thou so soon depart
And give me up to-night ?"

But now the sun returns more speedily. One morn-
ing, as he is on his knees, that word " darts in" upon
him—" **My grace is** sufficient." A short time before,
the same **word** " could not come near his soul with
comfort," **so that** he had " thrown down his book in
a pet ;" but now **it is** " not large enough" for him—
it is as if **it** " had **arms of** grace so wide" that it
could " enclose, **not him** only, but many more be-
sides." A few weeks elapse, **and the** thought occurs
—" But is this grace for *me ?*" He has left out " for
thee ;" and, once more, he is in the fearful pit. One
evening however, as he is in a meeting of **God's** peo-
ple, full of sadness and terror, suddenly there " break
in" upon him, with great power, and three times together, the words—" My grace is sufficient for thee ;
my grace **is** sufficient for thee ; my grace is sufficient
for thee." And, **" oh !** methought," says he, " that
every word was a mighty word unto me ; as ' my,'
and ' grace,' and ' sufficient,' **and** ' for thee ;' they
were then, and sometimes **are** still, far bigger than
others be."

With touching pathos a poet has written, concerning the soul's inner struggles—

"I struck the board, and cried, 'No more!
I will abroad.
What! shall I ever sigh and pine?
My lines and life are free; free as the road,
Loose as the wind, as large as store.
Shall I still be in suit?
Have I no harvest, but a thorn
To let me blood; and not restore
What I have lost, with cordial fruit?
Sure, **there was** wine,
Before my sighs did **dry** it; there was corn,
Before my tears did **drown it.**
Is the year only lost to *me?*
Have **I no** bays **to** crown it?
No flow'rs, no garlands gay? all blasted?
All wasted?
Not so, my heart! but there is fruit;
And thou hast hands.
Away, take heed!
I will abroad.
Call in thy death's head there.   Tie up thy fears.' "

The time is **now** at hand **when** this great soul is to
go forth in giant-might, **" the** joy of the **Lord"** his
" strength."   And, led by a way which he knows
not, he is struggling onwards to his sure rest.   " **I**
was," says he, **on** the occasion last named, " as
though I had seen the Lord Jesus look **down** from
heaven through the tiles upon me ;" and it sends him
home mourning, his heart broken and " filled **full** of
joy."

"Christ," said Martin Luther, "is not a new law-giver, but only a grace-giver." Bunyan now grasps more and more firmly this truth. One day, in a troubled agitation of his spirit about "Esau's birth-right," and about his own likeness to him in surrendering it, he appeals to God to bring the conflict to an issue by confronting with it His own grace. Instantly the "two Scriptures bolt" upon him, and they work and struggle strongly in him for a while, until at last "that about Esau's birthright begins to wax weak, and withdraw, and vanish, and this about the sufficiency of grace prevails with peace and joy." As he is "in a muse" about this, that Scripture "comes in upon him," "Mercy rejoiceth over judgment." This is "a wonderment" to him; yet he does not doubt it is of God, for "the word of the law and of wrath must give place to the word of life and of grace."

One day, at St. Helena, Napoleon was contrasting the force of Christianity with all other forces known among men. "Alexander," said he, "Cæsar, Charlemagne, and myself, founded empires; but on what foundation did we rest the creations of our genius? Upon force. Jesus Christ founded an empire upon love; and, at this hour, millions of men would die for Him." And, turning to Bertrand, he added, still resting upon this fact—"If you do not perceive that Jesus Christ is God, I did wrong to appoint you general." It is this divine characteristic of the Saviour which Bunyan, in spite of all Satan's wiles and even by means of them, is now day by day realizing more vividly.

One evening, that Scripture "most sweetly visits" his soul—"Him that cometh unto me, I will in no wise cast out." "Oh! the comfort," says he, "which had from that word, 'In no wise!' As if He had said, 'By no means, for nothing whatsoever which you may have done.'"

"But," whispers Satan **to** him, "greatly laboring to pull" it from him, "Christ did not mean *you*, or such as you."

"Nay, but here is in these words no such exception; 'him that comes'—'him'—any 'him;' 'Him that cometh unto **me, I** will in no wise cast out.'"

"And **so,**" he writes, "**if** ever Satan and **I did** strive for any word of God in all my life, **it was** for this good word of Christ; he at one end, **and I at** the other. Oh, what **work** we made! It was **for** this in John, I say, that we did so tug and **strive;** he pulled **and I** pulled; but, God be praised, **I overcame** him; **I** got sweetness from it."

Another **day,** "notwithstanding **all** these helps," he is still perplexed with the thought—"But have you not, like Esau, sold Him?"

"Well, suppose I have; does not that mean, 'I have freely left the Lord Jesus Christ to his choice, whether He will be my Saviour or no?' **for** the wicked suggestion is, 'Let Him go, if He will.' But **He** tells me, '*I* will never leave thee, nor **forsake** thee.'"

" Yes, but thou has left Him."

" But *I* will not leave *thee*."

He thanks God, and takes courage. Those Scriptures which once he wished out of the Bible, now
look " not so grimly" at him as he thought they did.
Election and sovereignty now shine as the **very glory
of grace.**

After these storms, **a sweet** calm settles down upon
his soul, and he sings :

> " King of Glory, King **of Peace,**
>   I will love thee.
> And, that love may never cease,
>   I will move thee.
>
> Thou hast granted my request ;
>   Thou **hast** heard me.
> **Thou didst note my** working breast :
>   **Thou hast** spared me.
>
> Though my sins **against me cried,**
>   Thou didst clear **me** ;
> And, alone, when they replied,
>   Thou didst hear me."

True, " some drops" **now and** then fall upon him ;
but it is **only " the** hinder part of the tempest"—the
thunder is gone **beyond him.**

One morning, as he is " passing into the field, and
that, too, with some dashes on his conscience, fearing
lest all be not right"—this Scripture comes upon his
heart, " Thy righteousness is in heaven."

" There," he exclaims, **looking** upward, " with the

eye of his soul," and beholding Jesus Christ at God's right hand, "*there* is my righteousness! Wherever I am, and whatever I am doing, God can never say, He does not see my righteousness; for it is just before Him, and that continually."

Thus he sees that it is not his own good frame of heart which makes his righteousness better, nor his bad frame that makes it worse; for his righteousness is Jesus Christ Himself—"the same yesterday, to-day, and for ever." And although, on going **home** and searching the Scriptures, he does not find these exact words, "Thy righteousness is in heaven," yet that other word comes before him—"He is made **of** God unto us wisdom, righteousness, sanctification, and redemption;" by which word he "sees the other sentence true."

Now do his "chains fall off his legs indeed." Brainerd describes his enlargement as **a fixed** and steadfast contemplation of God in Christ—the thought of his own peace or comfort, **or** even existence, scarcely entering his mind. Such also is Bunyan's experience at this season. "**Oh!** methought," he says, "Christ! Christ! there was nothing but Christ that was before my eyes. I was now for looking upon this and the other benefits **of** Christ apart, as of His blood, burial, **or** resurrection, but considering Him as a whole Christ! as Him in whom all these, and **all** other His virtues, relations, offices, and operations, **met** together, and that He sat on the **right hand** of God in heaven."

Love is **life.** God is love; and to dwell in God is to dwell in **love.** Love is the very atmosphere which God breathes; and the moment the Divine nature is communicated to a man in the new birth, the same atmosphere **is** breathed. Hence it comes **to** pass that the "new man," by a necessity of his nature, **loves.** "**It** is when we love," says Vinet, "that our salvation **is** realized. Love lends to the light of our **lamp its** liveliest and brightest **beams.** Faith and hope **are** of value, only because **they** conduct to love; and the soul would dispense with believing and hoping, if, without hoping and believing, it were possible **to** love." **Bunyan** now has reached this heavenly landing-place, **from** which Satan by his wiles has so long sought **to** intercept him. "The Lord," says he, "did lead me into the mystery of union with the Son of God—that **I** was joined to Him—that I was flesh **of His** flesh, and bone of His bone." **And** then he sees **that,** if Christ and he are one, Christ's righteous**ness is** his, Christ's merits his, Christ's victory also his. "Now," says he, "could I see myself in heaven and **on** earth at once; in heaven by my Christ, by my Head, **by my** righteousness and life; though on earth by my **body or** person." He is risen with Christ, and he **knows** it; he is a partaker of His resurrection-life; and the result is, his affections are **set upon** things **above, and upon Him** who is above.

CHAPTER IX.

The house Beautiful—The salutation—Aspirations—Foretastes—Church at Bedford—The Supper—Shadow of death—"Sickness doubled"—"Greatly pinched"—"A turn"—"Got on high"—Alleyne.

"Who can tell how joyful this man was when he had gotten his roll again? for this roll was the assurance of his life and of acceptance at the desired haven." So wrote Bunyan, many years afterwards, describing in his Allegory this stage in his own "progress." **And now,** nimbly mounting the **rest** of the hill, **and** passing unharmed the chained though roaring lions, **he is** entertained **in the** "house Beautiful" by its grave and comely inmates.

It was **a** touching salutation **with** which the wayfarer **was** welcomed—"She smiled, but the water stood in her eyes." The pilgrim was there victorious, but he bore the scars of conflict.

And how yearningly did he long for holier and **closer** fellowship than this place of tears and of shadows gives! "What is it," said Prudence, "which makes you so desirous to go to Mount Zion?" "Why, there," he replied, "I hope to see Him alive that did hang dead on the cross; and there I hope to be rid of all those things which, to this day, are an annoyance to me: there, they say, there is no death; and there I shall dwell with such company as I like best. For, to tell you the truth, I love Him because I was by him eased of my burden; and I am weary of my inward sickness. I would fain be where I shall die no more, and with the company who shall continually cry, 'Holy, holy, holy!'"

But until that bright land should be reached, pleasant foretastes were vouchsafed.

"Do you not find sometimes," asked one of the inmates of the palace, "as if those things were vanquished, which at other times are your perplexity?"

"Yes," said Christian; "and they are to me golden hours, in which such things happen to me."

"Can you remember by what means you find your annoyances, at times, as if they were vanquished?"

"Yes, when I think of what I saw at the Cross, that will do it; and when I look at my broidered coat, that will do it; also when I look into the roll, that I carry in my bosom, that will do it; and when my thoughts wax warm about whither I am going, that will do it."

Bunyan's "house Beautiful" is the humble church at Bedford. "After I had propounded to them," says he, "my desire to walk in the order and ordinances of Christ with them, and was also admitted by them; while I thought of that blessed ordinance of Christ, which was his last supper with His disciples before his death—that Scripture, 'Do this in remembrance of me,' was made a very precious word to me; for by it the Lord did come down upon my conscience with the discovery of His death **for my sins,** and, as I then felt, did as if He plunged me in the virtue of the same."

Scarcely has he joined the Church, when he **is** " suddenly and violently seized" with " something inclining to **a** consumption;" insomuch that he " thin**ks he cannot live.**"

Taken thus into the " valley of the shadow of death," he is brought face to face with " the innumerable company of his sins and transgressions," his " deadness, dulness, and coldness in his holy duties; his wanderings **of** heart, his wearisomeness in all good things, his want of love to God, to His way, and to His people: and " with this at the end **of** all—'Are these **the** fruits of Christianity ? are these the tokens of **a** blessed man ?'"

His "sickness is doubled" upon **him;** for now he is "sick in his inward man"—his soul is clogged with guilt. And, to add to his distress, his " former experience of God's goodness is taken quite out of his mind, and hid as if it **had** never been nor seen." " It seemed once more," says he, " as if all was over with **me,** my soul being greatly pinched betwixt these two considerations—'Live I must not, die I dare not.' Now I sunk in my spirits, and was giving up all for lost."

One day, however, as he is walking up and down in his house, " as a man in a most woeful state," this Scripture takes hold of his heart—" Ye are justified freely by His grace, through the redemption which **is in** Christ Jesus." And, " O ! what a *turn*" it makes **upon** him ! It is as if a voice had said to him—

> " Poor man ! where art thou now ? thy day is night.
> Good man, be not cast down, thou yet art right;
> Thy way **to** Heaven lies by the gates of Hell;
> Cheer **up,** hold out, with thee it shall go well."

Not more **joyful** was the pilgrim that morning, as he emerged **from** the dismal valley, than is Bunyan at this new glimpse of **his** heavenly standing and rest. He is " as one awaked out of some troublesome sleep and dream."

" Behold, my Son is by me," God seems to say to him through that Scripture; " and upon Him I **look, and** not on thee, and shall deal with thee according **as I am** pleased with Him." Now he " is got on high," **and** he sees himself " within the **arms** of grace and mercy ;" and, though he was " before afraid to think of a dying hour," yet now he " cries, ' Let me die !' "

Alleyne once wrote—" **Oh !** what a shame that **ever** we should live as if GOD were not enough for **us,** without anything else !" Bunyan now is to enter on a course which shall " declare plainly" what God is to him. " At this time," says he, " I saw more in these words, ' heirs of God,' than ever I shall be able to express while I live in this world. ' Heirs of God !' God Himself is the portion of the saints. This I saw and wondered at, but cannot tell what I saw." But his life is to tell—his earnest labors, and his calm patience, and his heroic self-denial.*

* Following Bunyan's own order, we have somewhat ante-dated the latter part of these temptations. His first two years of preaching preceded his full establishment in the joy and peace of the Gospel.

CHAPTER X.

God's vessels—"Thrust forth"—First preaching—His "orders"—The
honey and the lion—Bowels of pity—Divine signature—Scene in
churchyard—The student—Yearnings—Self-love and its refuges
—"Not many fathers"—Fruits—"Our joy"—"The net"—Homely
Saxon—Genial soul—"Pleading with men."

A HOLY man of God once uttered this aspiration :— ·

> " Wherefore **I dare not, I, put** forth my hand
> To hold the ark ; **although it** seems to shake,
> Through the old sins and **new** doctrines of our land,
> Only—since God doth **often** vessels make,
> Of lowly matter, for high uses **meet**—
> I throw me at His feet.
> **There** will I lie ; until my Maker seek
> **For some mean** stuff, whereon to show His skill :
> **Then is my time."**

Like **all true laborers** in God's harvest, **Bunyan is**
" thrust forth" by **the Divine hand.**

The intimation comes through the little company
of saints at Bedford. It is after **he** " has been five
or six years awakened," and, **has** " seen both the
want and the worth of Jesus Christ, **and has** been

enabled to venture his soul upon Him," that " some of the most able among them for judgment and holiness of life," " perceiving that God had counted him worthy to understand something of His will in His holy and blessed Word," and had given him utterance in some measure to express to others for edification the things which he had seen, " desire **him, with much** earnestness, to take in hand, in one of the meetings, to speak a word of exhortation to them." The proposal " does much dash and abash his spirit ;" though **at** length **he** consents, " in two several assemblies (but in private) twice to discover his gift amongst them."

The tinker **has no** " orders," **such** as colleges and ecclesiastics confer ; **but** He who has called him to His feet, and has forgiven him all his sins, gives him *His* commission—" Go and preach to every creature." And the mouth which He has opened, who may dare to shut ? " The people," says Bunyan, referring to the two occasions **just named, "** not only seemed **to** be, but did frequently protest, **as** in **the** sight of the great God, that they were both affected and comforted ; **and they gave** thanks to the Father of mercies for **the grace bestowed on me."**

He next " accompanies these men when they go forth into the neighboring villages"—where, though as yet he does not venture to " make use of his gift in an open way," he yet " sometimes speaks **a** word of admonition," to the great joy and edification of **souls.** And no wonder souls **are** gladdened. His lips distil the "honey which he has taken out of the carcass of a lion." "I have eaten thereof," he says, alluding to the manner in which God has educated him by his peculiar inward trials and temptations, "and have been much refreshed thereby. Temptations, when we meet them at first, are as the lion that roared upon Samson ; but, if we overcome them, we shall find a nest of honey within them." He has overcome ; and, more than conqueror, he brings from the spoiler fatness.

Now, in his twenty-eighth year, he is set apart by **the Church,** with fasting and prayer, to "the more ordinary **and public** preaching of the Word." Feeling in his **mind** "evidently" a "secret pricking forward thereto," **though** "with great fear and trembling at the sight **of his own** weakness," he "does set to the work." And **He who** "openeth and none shutteth," gives him for a season **a** door of utterance, "wide and effectual" to his heart's content. The **people** flock into Bedford by hundreds and by thousands, **to** hear the tinker and his burning message.

Trained for his mission in God's own school, his hands **have been** taught to war, and his fingers to fight. **"I** thank **God,"** says he, "He gives unto me some measure **of bowels** and pity for the people's souls, which also **does put** me forward **to** labor with great diligence and earnestness, to find out such a word as may, if God **will** bless it, **lay** hold of and awaken the conscience." And how piteously he pleads with **the** awakened !

"Arise, sad heart! if thou dost not withstand,
    Christ's resurrection thine may be.
  Do not, by hanging down, break from the hand,
    Which, as it riseth, raiseth thee.
                Arise, arise!
  And with His burial-linen dry thine eyes,
    Christ left His grave-clothes, that we might, when grief
    Draws tears or blood, not want a handkerchief."

And not unblest are his gracious words. "The good Lord," says he, "had respect to the desire of His servant; for I had not preached long **before** some began to be touched and be greatly afflicted **in** their minds at the apprehension of **the** greatness of their **sin,** and of their **need of** Jesus **Christ.** At first, he cannot believe that God should speak by him to **the** heart of any man, "still counting himself **un-**worthy." The divine signature to the work, however, is too real to be mistaken ; and though he still "puts it from him that they should be awakened by him, he begins to conclude that it may be so, that **God** has owned such a foolish one." He now, therefore, has joy ; the very tears of the awakened **both** solacing and encouraging **him. And** these things **are** another argument to him, that God has called him to this work, **and** stands by him in it.

One summer evening, in a rustic parish in Cambridgeshire, a thoughtless under-graduate is riding along the highway, when his attention is arrested **by a** gathering of people assembled in **a** church-**yard.** On **a** gravestone **stands a** plain working-man, addressing the vast crowd. Every eye is fixed intently on **the** speaker; and a strange solemnity—still as the **grave** over which he stands—pervades the motley group.

"What is this?" whispers the student, scarcely able to catch the ear, for a moment, of **a** lad who hangs on the outskirts of the crowd.

"**It's** the Bedford **tinker,**" replies **the** lad, **in a** tone of impatience, as if marvelling at such a question.

The student dismounts, and listens for a few moments, a sneer curling on his lip. But, as **the** preacher proceeds, the lip begins to quiver, and the tear **to** tremble **in** his eye;—it is the "deer hit of the **archer.**" A year or two later, and the mocking gownsman **is a bold** preacher of Christ.

Richard Baxter, **in his** "Reformed Pastor," puts this question—"Is it **not the great** and lamentable sin of the ministers of the Gospel, that they are *not fully devoted to God,* and give not up themselves **and all** that they have to the carrying **on** of **the** blessed **work** which they have undertaken?" If ever a preacher avoided this sin, it was Bunyan. "When I have been preaching," he says, "I thank God my heart hath often, all the time of this **and** of the other exercise, **with** great earnestness cried to God that He would make the Word effectual to the salvation of the soul—still being grieved lest the enemy should take the Word away from the conscience, and so it should become unfruitful." And he adds :—"When I have done the exercise, it hath gone to my heart to think the Word should now fall as rain on stony places—still wishing from my heart, 'Oh! that they who have heard me speak this day did but see, as I do, what sin, death, hell, and the curse of God is; and also what the grace, and love, and mercy of God is, through Christ, to men in such a case as they are, who are yet estranged from Him!' And, indeed, I did often say in my heart before the Lord, 'That if to be hanged up presently before their eyes would be a means to awaken them, and to confirm them in the truth, I gladly should be contented.'"

And he is "unto God **a** sweet savour of Christ." "I have been," says he, "**in** my preaching, especially when I have **been** engaged in the doctrine of life by Christ without works, as if an angel of God had stood by at my back to encourage me."   And, again :—"It pleased me nothing to see people drink in opinions, if they seemed ignorant of Jesus Christ and of the worth **of** their own salvation—of sound conviction for sin, especially for unbelief—of a **heart set on** fire **to** be saved by Christ, with strong breathings **after a** sanctified soul.   That it was which delighted me; those were the souls I counted blessed."

"Self-love," writes Isaac Taylor, "finds much aliment in the argument which is to end in showing that another—a former guide—has been the cause **of** whatever is blameworthy in the disciple." Bunyan is too intent on his great errand **to** give to the conscience any such shelter.   His one enemy is sin;

and, in taking the field against that enemy, he finds in every conscience a judge ready to pronounce a sentence of immediate self-condemnation. " I never care," he says, " **to** meddle with things which are controverted, especially things **of** the lowest nature'; I let them alone, because I see that they engender **strife,** and because neither in the doing of them, nor **in the** leaving them undone, do they commend **us to God to be** His. I see my work before me does **run into** another channel, even to carry **an** awakening **word; to** that, therefore, I do stick and adhere." **And he** adds—" It pleases me much to contend with great earnestness for the word of faith and the remission **of sins by the** sufferings and death of Jesus."

It was Paul's **complaint of** the Church at Corinth, that, though not **without** abundance of " instructors in Christ," they had " **not** many fathers." Bunyan **" never** can be satisfied, unless some fruits do appear **in his** work." " If I be fruitless," sa**ys** he, " **it matters** not **who** commends me ; but if I be fruitful, **I** care not **who condemns."** And again : " I have counted it as **if I had** goodly buildings and lordships **in** those places w**here my** children were born ; my heart hath been so **wrapped up** in the glory of this excellent work, that I count myself more blessed and honored of God by this **than if He** had made me the emperor of the Christian world, or the lord of all the glory **of** the earth, without **it.** Oh ! these words, ' He that converteth **a** soul from the error of his way doth save

a soul from death :' ' He that winneth souls is wise ;'
' For, what is our hope, our joy, our crown of rejoic-
ing ? Are not even ye in the presence of our Lord
Jesus Christ at His coming ?' "

It is at His word that he " lets down the net." " I
have observed," says he, " that where I have had a
work to do for God, I have had first, as it were, the
going **of God** upon my spirit to desire I might preach
there : I have also observed, that such and **such** souls
in particular have been strongly set upon my heart,
and I stirred up to wish for their salvation ; and that
these very souls **have, after** this, **been** given **me as**
the fruits of my ministry." **And he** adds : " I have
observed **that a** word, cast in by the bye, hath done
more execution **in a** sermon, than all that was spoken
besides. Sometimes also, when I have thought
I did no good, then I did the most of all ; and at
other times, when I thought I should catch them, I
have fished for nothing."

It is thus **that " for about** the **space of** five years"
this **true minister labors,** night and day for **souls.**
" How **much** learning," said Leighton one day **to**
some of his clergy, **" is** required to make these things
plain !" The " tinker has no learning from human
schools ; but he **has** sat at Christ's feet, **and** has
learned of Him." And this, with his homely Saxon
and his genial soul, opened a way for him into the
hearts and understandings at once of **the** rude country bumpkin, and of the **refined and** accomplished
graduate. Like **his** own picture in the house of the

Interpreter, his eye is lifted up to heaven, the best of books is in his hand, the law of truth is written upon his lips, the world is behind his back, a crown of gold hangs over his head, and he stands pleading with men—

" As meek as the man Moses, and withal
As in Agrippa's presence Paul."

CHAPTER XI.

The ancient prison—Howard—Bunyan's ring—A scene at Samsell—
The warrant—The "close"—The "Forlorn hope"—The prayer—The
constable—The parting—The Justice-room—"What arms?"—The
bond—The "mittimus"—The Judas-kiss—To prison.

In the town of Bedford, on one of the central piers of the rude bridge across the Ouse, there stood, in those days, an ancient prison. A century later, it was visited by Howard, who found the felons, men and women, associated together in a **court** not wider than fourteen feet, and **at night huddled** into two dungeons sunk within the piers—only **one** court **for** debtors and for felons, **and no** apartment for **the** jailor. The visit of Howard was its death-warrant; for, in a few more years, it was razed to the ground. In removing **the** floor of **one** of the dungeons, the workmen discovered Bunyan's ring.

How came he there? Had the tinker lapsed into his old ways, and merited a felon's brand?

It is a winter evening; and we are in the kitchen of a farm-steading, adjoining the village of Harlington, in Bedfordshire. After the labors of the day, the rustics are gathering, grand-dames and children, old men and maidens—each countenance lighted with an unwonted gladness, as if a joy **not** often tasted were in store. It is Bunyan who is coming **to** preach the Word, and to speak a word in season **to the** weary.

And yet **a** strange restlessness pervades the little gathering; for some mysterious whisperings are abroad that **a " warrant"** is out, to silence the preacher and to hurry him **off** to jail. As the darkness comes on, certain suspicious **visitors** have been seen prowling stealthily about, **as if** watching for some expected prey. And now **that the** place is filling, the farmer, grown somewhat **timorous, is** conferring with his wife **and** with one **of the shrewder** neighbors, whether **they** had not better separate and warn their friend **not to** come out to-night.

But there he is! All rise **to** welcome him, and his manly face has a radiant smile for **all.**

" Oh ! Mr. Bunyan," whispers the master, hurrying up **to him** with an agitated, anxious air, " there's **a** warrant **out against** you ; the officers are about; and we must separate **at** once, **or** you will be seized and imprisoned."

" What ?" says Bunyan, with the bold, decisive tone of a man who **has** counted **the** cost; " I will **not** stir, neither will **I** have the meeting dismissed

for this. Come, be of good cheer; let us not be
daunted ; our cause is good, we need not be ashamed
of it : to preach God's Word is so good a work that
we shall be well rewarded if we suffer for that."

Before beginning, however, he " walks into the
close," to lay the matter calmly before his God. " I
have showed myself," is his quiet soliloquy, as he
confers with his brave spirit, " hearty and courageous
in my preaching, and have, blessed be grace, made
it my business to encourage others ; therefore, if I
should now run and make an escape, it will be of a
very ill savor in the country. **For, what** will my
weak and newly-converted brethren think of it ? but
that I was not as strong in deed **as I** was **in** word.
Also, if I should run now that there is a warrant out
for me, may not I make them afraid to stand when
only great words are spoken to them ? Besides,
since God of His mercy would have me go upon
the *forlorn hope*, might not **my** flight be a discouragement to the whole body that may follow
after ? And further, might not the world take occasion, at my cowardliness, to blaspheme the Gospel, and have **some** ground to suspect worse of me
and of my profession than I deserve ?" His mind
made up and stayed on his God, he returns into the
house, " with a full resolution to keep the meeting,"
and to " see the utmost of what they can say or do
unto him. For, blessed be the Lord," he adds, " I
know of no evil which I have said **or** done."

The preacher enters. **All** fall upon their knees.

And, oh! how each heart pours itself out before the Lord!—

> "Of what supreme, almighty power,
> Is thy great arm—which spans the East and West,
> And tacks the centre to the sphere!
> By it, do all things live their measur'd hour;
> We cannot ask the thing which is not there."

And will He not restrain this wrath of man, and shield His servant?

Scarcely have they risen from their knees, and opened their Bibles and the text been announced, **"Dost thou** believe on the Son of God?" (so fitting a preparative for those stern trials which are at **hand; for the** words were the balm applied by the Master to **the** torn heart of that despised castaway),* —when "the constable and the justice's man" come in, and, presenting **the warrant,** demand that he shall follow them.

"But stay," says Bunyan, turning again to the startled company, "one parting word." The officers **are** silent, and he proceeds—"We are prevented, you see, of our opportunity to speak and to **hear** the Word **of** God, and are like to suffer for the same. But be not discouraged, my dear brethren; it is a mercy to suffer upon so good account. We might have been apprehended as thieves **or** murderers, or for other wickedness; **but,** blessed be God, it is **not** so—we suffer as Christians for well-doing, and we had better be the persecuted than the persecutors."

* John, ix. 34.

" We must away," shouts the constable, interrupting him. And the humble gathering rise, following their beloved teacher with their **tears.**

The scene changes; and **we are in the Justice-**room at Bedford. It is the time **of** the Restoration; and England's noblest sons are paying the penalty of patriotism and of Christian steadfastness, at the beck of a dissolute court and of a sycophant magistracy. A fitting tool is found at Bedford, **in** the person of Justice Wingate.

" What has he done ?" **is his** interrogatory, **as the** constable conducts **his** prisoner **into court: " where** were they met? **what had they** with them ?" meaning, what arms ?

" I found him at Samsell; there were no arms, but *they had Bibles;* and the prisoner was just beginning to preach."

" Well, prisoner," rejoins the Justice, gruffly, turning to Bunyan, " what say you? **why don't** you keep to your calling? **Y**ou are breaking **the** law."

" I go to these places," says **he,** respectfully but firmly, **"to** instruct the people, and to counsel them to forsake their sins and close in with Christ, lest they miserably perish; and **I** find I can **without** confusion both follow **my** calling **and** preach the Word."

" What !" exclaims the justice in a chafe, and losing his self-possession; " but I'll break the neck of your meetings. That I will."

" It may be so," says Bunyan, **calmly.**

" Produce your sureties, or you must go to jail."

Two friends stand forward, and give bail for his appearance at the sessions—the justice adding—" And remember, you are bound to keep him from preaching ; if he preaches your bonds are forfeited."

" Then I shall break them," interposes Bunyan ; " for I shall not leave speaking the Word of God— to counsel, comfort, exhort, and teach the people among whom I come. And I thought this to be a work that had no hurt in it, but was worthy rather of commendation than of blame."

" I tell you, if they will not be so bound, your mittimus must be made, and you shall go to prison."

At last the order is made out, and the constable leads him off. A crowd has gathered, as the news has got abroad; and we join it as it convoys him along.

" Stay !" whisper two " brethren," who have just come up in breathless haste, and are addressing the constable with an air of authority, " we must go back to the Justice." And, as Bunyan and the officers slowly return, the two friends joined by a third, hasten forward to the Justice's house.

" If you will just say a few words," whispers one of them to Bunyan, running out from the house to meet him, " it will be all right, and you shall be released."

" If the words are such," he replies, " as may be said with a good conscience, I shall; otherwise, I cannot." And as he enters, he " lifts up his heart to God for light and strength, to be kept, that he may not do anything which shall either dishoner Him, or wrong his own soul, or be a grief or discouragement to any inclining after the Lord Jesus Christ."

It is the old policy, tried sixteen centuries before with the fisherman—"Speak no more in this name." Affecting great kindness, a new personage appears on the scene, and accosts "Bunyan with such seeming affection as if he would have leaped on his neck and kissed him."

"**If** you will but promise," says this **new** meddler, fawningly, "to call the people no more together, **you** shall have your liberty **to go** home; **for my brother is** very **loath to send you to prison, if you will but be ruled."**

"Sir," said Bunyan, "pray what do you mean by calling the people together? My business is not anything among them, when they are come together, but to exhort them to look after the salvation of their souls, that they may be saved."

"There are none but a company **of** poor, simple, ignorant people come to hear you. Will you promise **that you will not** call them together any more?"

"**The** foolish and **the** ignorant have most need of teaching. I durst not leave off the work which God has called me to."

The Justice and his friend, after conferring **in an** adjoining room, once more repeat the demand; but Bunyan is not to be moved. "Then he must go to prison," says Mr. Foster, addressing the Justice; "and the sooner the others **follow** him, **the better."**

"**Thus** we parted," writes Bunyan. " And verily, as I was going forth of the door, I had much ado to forbear saying to them that I carried the peace of God along **with** me; but I held my peace, and, blessed be the **Lord,** went away to prison with God's comfort in my poor soul."

It is on November 12, 1660, and in his thirty-second year.

CHAPTER XII.

> " Ay! call it holy ground,
>   The spot where first they trod!
> They left unstained what they had found,
>   Freedom **to worship God.**"

The "**Den**"—**Gate** of heaven—Home-affections—Bitterest pang—"My poor blind one"—"Must do it"—Indictment—Felon's dock—The Justices—Examination—"Canting"—Sentence—"Home to prison" Prison-Rhymes—"Much content."

HE is now in the "Den;" but it is the gate of heaven to him. "I never in my life," says he, "had so great an inlet into **the** Word as **now.** Those Scriptures which I saw nothing in before, **are made in** this place and **state to** *shine* upon me. Jesus Christ also was never more real or apparent than now: here I have seen and felt Him indeed."

Bunyan has a heart for home-affections. One of our poets has written of the domestic hearth—

> "O happy lot, and hallowed even as the joy of angels,
>   Where the golden chain of godliness is entwined with the
>   roses of love!"

Such **a** home has Bunyan; and the bitterest pang of

this hour is the rude disruption of its lowly joys. "The parting with **my wife** and poor children," he says, "hath often been to me, in this place, as the pulling the flesh from my bones, and that not only because I am somewhat too fond of these great mercies, but also because I should often have brought to mind the many hardships, miseries, and wants that my poor family was like to meet with, should **I be** taken from them, especially my poor blind **child**, who lay nearer my heart than all **be-**side. **Oh!** the thoughts of the hardship I thought my poor blind **one** might go under, would break my heart in pieces."

Often, often **does** this thought rend his sensitively tender heart. "**Poor** child!" he whispers to himself, in the solitude **of that** dismal dungeon, "what sorrow art thou like to have for thy portion in this world! Thou must be beaten, must beg, must suffer hunger, cold, nakedness, and a thousand calamities, though I cannot now endure the wind should blow upon thee."

But, "recalling himself," he "ventures them all with **his** God;" "though it goeth to the quick," he adds, "to leave them." This is his infirmity—though a noble one, and not displeasing to the Lord. "Oh! I saw in this condition," says he, "I was as a man who was pulling down his house upon the head of his wife and children : yet, thought I, I must do it—I must do it; and now I thought on those two milch-kine which were to carry the ark of God into another country, and to leave their calves behind them."

After seven weeks' confinement, he is indicted before the quarter-sessions. Let us take our place at the felon's side—it is good to be in such companionship.

It is a cold winter morning in January :* but the people are up betimes; for many warm hearts are there, each man wishing that he himself might have "that preferment," and whispering like his own Pilgrim when Faithful was in the dock at Vanity Fair—

> "Now, brother, play the man, speak for thy God,
> Fear not the wicked's malice, nor the rod:
> Speak boldly, man! the truth is on thy side;
> Die for it, and to life in triumph ride."

The "Hate-goods," too, are there, in the shape of some half-dozen justices, "in order to his condemnation." As they take their seats, a strange terror seems to seize them, as if themselves consciously the culprits before another tribunal, whose decisions are already foreshadowed in the heart's dark chambers. And that felon, they feel involuntarily, is, in truth, beyond their jurisdiction. No heavenly halo is there, to proclaim his real citizenship; but the calm, sublime repose with which he abides his doom—the poor ministers of Satan quail before it and tremble.

The indictment is read. "My Lord," said the

* 1661.

accuser, at the trial of Faithful, " this man, notwith-standing his plausible name, is one of the vilest men in our country. He neither regardeth princes nor people, law nor custom, but doth all that he can to possess all men with certain of his disloyal notions, which **he** in the general calls principles of faith and holiness. And, in particular, I heard him once my-**self** affirm that Christianity and the customs of our **town** of Vanity were diametrically opposite, and **could** not be reconciled. By which saying, my lord, he doth at once not only condemn all our laudable doings, but us in the doing of them." This other Faithful is charged as follows :—" That John Bunyan, of the town of Bedford, laborer, hath devilishly and perniciously abstained from coming to church to **hear** divine service, and is a common upholder of several unlawful meetings and conventi-cles, to the great disturbance and distraction of the good subjects of this kingdom, contrary to the laws of our sovereign lord the king." And, having read the charge, the clerk asks, " What say you to this ?"

"**As** to the first part of it," answers Bunyan, " I am a common frequenter of the Church of God, and also, by grace, a member with the people over whom Christ is the Head."

" But do you come to church ?" interposes the presiding justice; " you know what I mean ; to the parish church, to hear divine service ?"

" **No, I do not.**"

" Why ?"

" Because I **do not** find it commanded **in the** Word of God."

" We are commanded to pray."

" **But** not by **the** Common Prayer-book."

" How then ?"

" With **the** Spirit. As **the** Apostle saith, ' I will pray **with** the Spirit, and with the understanding.' "

" But we may pray with the Spirit, and with understanding, and with the Common Prayer-book also."

" Sir, the Scripture **saith, that** ' **it is the** Spirit **that** helpeth **our** infirmities **; for we know not what** we should pray for as we ought **;** but the Spirit itself maketh intercession for us.' Mark, **it** doth not say **the** Common Prayer-book teacheth us how to pray, **but** the Spirit. And it is the Spirit that ' helpeth **our** infirmities,' saith the Apostle ; he doth not **say** it is the Common Prayer-book."

" At this," he says, " they were set." And he added : " But yet, notwithstanding, they that have **a mind to use it, they have** liberty ; that **is, I** would **not keep** them **from it—but,** for our parts, **we can** pray to God without **it.** Blessed be His name !"

" Who is your God ? Beelzebub ?" exclaims **a** Mr. No-good, sneeringly. " **You** are possessed with a devil."

" Blessed be the Lord for it," replies Bunyan, taking no notice of the taunt, and secretly asking the Lord to forgive it ; " **we** are encouraged **to** meet together, and **to pray,** and **to** exhort one another; for we have had the comfortable presence of God among us, for ever blessed **be His** holy name !"

" This **is** pedlar's French : you must leave off your canting."

" It is lawful for me, and such as I am, to preach **the** Word of God."

" Prove it."

" By this Scripture—' As every man hath received **the gift,** even so let him minister the same unto another, **as** good stewards of the manifold grace of God. If any man speak, let him speak as the oracles of God.' "

" I **am not so** well versed in Scripture as to dispute ; but **we** cannot wait upon you any longer. You confess the indictment, do you not ?"

" This I confess—we have had many meetings together, both to pray to God, and to exhort one another ; and we have had the sweet, comforting pres**ence** of the Lord among us for our encouragement, **blessed** be His name : therefore I confess myself **guilty, and** no otherwise."

" Then **hear** your judgment : ' **You** must be had back **again to prison,** and there lie for three months following : and, **at** three months' end, if you do not submit to go to **church to** hear divine service, and leave your preaching, you must **be** banished the realm : And if, after such a day as shall be appointed you to be gone, you shall be found in this realm, or be found to come over again without special license from the king, you must stretch by the neck for it, I tell you plainly.' Jailor, have him away!"

"As to this matter," says Bunyan, boldly, as he rises to leave the dock, "I am at a point with you; for, if I were out of prison·to-day, I would preach the gospel again to-morrow, by the help of God."

And all honor to thee, thou good confessor! This shall be remembered one day, when the Lord is distributing His crowns.

We rise, and follow him to the "den." And he enters it with a calm mien; for ANOTHER is there, whose approving smile is more to him than all human frowns. "I can truly say," he writes, "and I bless the Lord Jesus Christ for it, that my heart was sweetly refreshed in the time of my examination, and also afterwards at my returning to the prison; so that I found Christ's words more than bare trifles, where He saith, 'He will give you a mouth and wisdom, which all your adversaries shall not be able to gainsay nor resist,' and, that 'His peace no man taketh from us.'"

And there he kneels in his "prison-home," his spirit not bound, but enlarged into a new heavenliness by Him who knows how to vouchsafe to His tried confessors, even here, divinely-solacing compensations. "Verily, at my return," he says, "I did meet my God sweetly in the prison again, comforting of me, and satisfying of me that it was His mind and will that I should be there." And, in some of his rude rhymes, he writes:

> " For though men keep my outward man
>   Within their locks and bars,
> Yet, by the faith of Christ, I can
>   Mount higher than the stars.
>
> 'Tis not the baseness of this state
>   Doth hide us from God's face;
> He frequently, both soon and late,
>   Doth visit us with grace.
>
> We change our drossy dust for gold,
>   From **death to** life **we** fly;
> We let go shadows, and take hold
>   Of immortality.
>
> These be the men that God doth count
>   **Of** high and noble mind;
> These **be** the men that do surmount
>   What you in nature find.
>
> They conquer, when they thus do fall;
>   They kill when they do die;
> They overcome then most of all,
>   And get the victory."

In those " prison-rhymes" the martyr learns to sing **praises unto** God—" continuing, through grace, with **much content.**" " I have had sweet sights," says he, " of the forgiveness of my sins in this place, and of my being **with Jesus** in another world. Oh, the ' Mount Zion, **the** heavenly Jerusalem, the innumerable company of **angels, and God the** Judge of all, and the spirits of just men made perfect, and Jesus, have been sweet unto me in this place. I have seen that here, which I am persuaded I shall never, while **in** this world, be able to express."

CHAPTER XIII.

The palace and the prison—The **cell—The** lamp—The "Pilgrim"—The prison court—The preacher—The "three Jews"—Christ **a fellow-prisoner—The** "tagged laces"—The visitor—The **scaled eyeballs—The Clerk of the** Peace—The conference.

"**WHILE** the body is in a palace," says Foster, **alluding to** Peter's enchainment in the dungeon, and to the angel's visit, "the soul may be in prison; whereas, while *his* body was in a prison, **his soul was as in a** palace. And, even externally, he was soon to **have such** attendance there, as the dwellers **in royal and** imperial mansions **have not."** Angelic ministry is suspended **now; but he who is** with us as the Comforter **has a thousand** methods of making **the** wrath of man to praise Him.

Look into that cell! That Bible on the rude table, **and** that Concordance, **and** that book of Martyrs; and that feeble sunbeam, struggling through the grated window; and that dim lamp, after the sunbeam, has gone; and that undimmed orb shining so **brilliantly in** the confessor's happy **soul!** by these

the felon is to speak to all time. "In the prison," **is** the testimony of Charles Doe, who visited him, "he wrote, not only 'Grace Abounding,' 'The Holy City,' and other precious treatises, **but** also 'the Pilgrim's Progress, First Part.' This I had from his own mouth. What," he adds, "hath the devil **or** his agents got by putting our great gospel-minister in prison?"

Quitting for a moment the little cell, **we go** with him into the prison-court. "Imagination," wrote Howard, visiting the place **in** after-years, "can hardly realize the miseries of fifty or sixty pious men and women, taken from a place of worship, and incarcerated in such dungeons with felons—as was the case while Bunyan was a prisoner. How justly did the **poor** pilgrim call it a 'certain den!'" But what scene is this which meets us, as we enter the court? "When **I** visited him in prison," says the eye-witness already quoted, Charles Doe, "there were about sixty Dissenters besides himself, and two eminent Dissenting ministers, by which means the prison was very much crowded; yet, in the midst of all that hurry which so many new-comers occasioned, **I** have heard Mr. Bunyan both preach and pray **with that** mighty spirit of faith and plerophory of **Divine** assistance which has made me stand and wonder."

Describing the three confessors in the furnace at Babylon, Foster has written:—"They were seen act**ually** associated with a Being that belonged not to **the earth.** That space of fire was as a tract of another world. They could have no wish to come forth. It was **the** sublimest, most delightful region they had ever dwelt in **yet.** In their state of feeling, that burning floor was preferable to the marble pavement of the monarch's superbest palace." And is not the "den" of Bedford transformed, by the same Divine alchemy, into the very pavilion of God? "I never knew," says Bunyan, "what it was for God to stand by me at all turns, and at every offer of Satan to afflict me, as I have found since **I** came in hither; insomuch that **I have** often said, ' Were it lawful, **I could pray for greater trouble, for the greater comfort's** sake.' " And again:—" **I have been able to '** laugh **at destruction,' and to fear** neither the horse **nor** his rider."

> " Oh, happy he who doth possess
> Christ for a fellow-prisoner, who doth glad
> With heavenly sunbeams gaols that are most sad !"

But we return with him **into the** cell. It **is near** sunset **; and, with** the fading light, **how** earnestly **he** labors **at those " tagged** laces," to **finish the "** gross" for the **day! A** gentle **knock at the door** announces the expected visitor. It **is his little** blind daughter, come for **the** day's work, **from w**hich the desolate family are to obtain their precarious pittance.* And,

---

* " In prison," says **Mr.** Wilson, the Baptist minister, who **was his** fellow-prisoner, **"I** have been witness that his own hands ministered to his, and to his family's necessities, making **many** hundred gross of long-tagged **laces,** to fill up **the** vacancies of **his time."**

oh, how pleasant to him are the moments which this dear child is suffered to pass in the cell! Clasping her **to** his bosom, the manly confessor, whom no menances can browbeat, and from whom no sufferings can extort a sigh, is dissolved in a flood of tenderness as he gazes nightly on **this** child! And how yearningly he prays, as they kneel side by side upon the stone floor! These eye-balls are sealed; but the heart's eye—let the light shine there!

The three months have now elapsed, and a visitor of another kind is announced. It is the "Clerk of the Peace," sent from the justices to demand his "submittance."

"I am come," says he, "to tell you, that it is desired you submit yourself to the laws of the land; **or** else at the next sessions it will go worse with **you, even to** be sent away **out** of the nation, or else **worse than** that."

Not discomposed by the significant intimation, **the** confessor replies :—"I desire **to** demean myself in the **world as** becometh both **a** man and **a** Christian."

"But you must submit to the law **of the** land, **and** leave off those meetings which you were wont to have ; for the statute-law is directly against it, and **I am sent** to **you by the justices to** tell you that they do intend to **prosecute the** law against you, if you submit not."

"**Sir, I** conceive that **the law** by **which I** am in **prison at this time was made** against those who, designing to do evil in their meetings, made the exercise of religion a pretext to cover their wickedness. It doth not forbid the private meetings of those who plainly **and simply** make it their only end to worship the Lord, and to exhort one another **to** edification."

" Well, **I** don't profess to be a man that can dispute ; but, neighbor Bunyan, I would have you submit yourself. You may exhort your neighbor in private discourse, so be you do not call together an assembly of people. It is your private **meetings** that the law is against."

" Sir, if **I** may **do good to** one **by** my discourse, **why not to two ? And if** to two, why not **to** four ? And **if** to four, why not to eight ? And **so on."**

" But you may only do harm, by seducing people : you are, therefore, denied your meeting so many together, lest you should do harm."

" And yet you say the law tolerates **me** to discourse with my neighbor ! Surely there is no **law** tolerates me to seduce any **one :** therefore, if I may by **the** law discourse with one, surely it is to **do him** good ; and **if I,** by discoursing, may **do** good to **one,** surely by the same law I may do good to many."

" The law doth expressly forbid your private **meet-**ings, therefore they are not to be tolerated."

" But when I see that the Lord, through grace, **hath** in some measure blessed my labor, **I** dare not **but** exercise for the good of the people that gift which God hath given me."

" What if you should forbear a while, and sit still till you see further how things will go ?"

" Sir, Wickliffe saith that he which leaveth **off** preaching and hearing **of** the Word of God for fear of excommunication of men, **he** is already excommunicated **of God, and shall in** the last day be counted a **traitor to** Christ."

" Well, neighbor Bunyan, but indeed I would wish **you** seriously to consider **of** these things between this **and the** quarter-sessions, and **to** submit yourself. **You may** do much good if you continue still in the **land;** but, alas ! what benefit will it be to your friends, or **what** good can you do to them, if you should be sent **away** beyond the seas into Spain, or Constantinople, **or some** other remote part of the world ? Pray, **be ruled."**

" Indeed, sir," **interposes the** jailor, **"I** hope he **will be ruled."**

"I shall desire," says Bunyan, **"in** all godliness and honesty, **to** behave myself in the nation whilst I **am** in it. And, if I must be so dealt withal as you say, **I hope** God will help me to bear what they shall **lay** upon **me."**

The visitor **seems** awe-stricken, and he rises **to** leave, Bunyan thanking him for his " civil and meek discoursing" with him. The felon is left alone ; and, **as the** door closes, he lifts this aspiration—" Oh ! that **we** might meet in **heaven !"**

CHAPTER XIV.

Coronation-festival—Amnesty—"Suing out a pardon"—Christiana—
    The cell—The Swan-chamber—Sir Matthew Hale—The petitioner—
    "Clapped him up"—"It is recorded"—"Four small children"—"A
    tinker"—"God hath owned him"—The tears—Roman Catacombs—
    Prison joys—Dark clouds and bright.

IT is the Coronation-festival of the Second Charles.
The nation's heart is stunned; the fevered era of the
Commonwealth has given place to a collapse; and
the rollicking Court, mad with joy, has few thoughts
for the good confessors whom it has consigned to
the dungeons.

But coronations must have amnesties; and therefore the semblance of a pardon is vouchsafed. Bunyan and his fellows are allowed a year for "suing"
the royal clemency; so that for twelve months the
sentence of "banishment or of hanging" is held in
suspense.

In his homely rhymes, Bunyan describes Christiana and her boys thus:

"Tell them that they have left their house and home;
    Are turned pilgrims—seek a world to come;

> That they have met with hardships in the way,
> That they do meet with troubles night and day;
> And how they still
> Refuse this world, **to do** their Father's will."

The words touch the tenderest chord in the **holy** seer's heart. For, **let us** enter the cell again, and who is this **at** his **side** one morning, bending **so intently** over a paper which Bunyan is writing on the little deal table ?

It is the Midsummer assizes **;** and his devoted wife, just returned from a fruitless journey on foot to London, is concerting the plea with which she shall appear before the judges, and is committing it with him **to the** Lord.

The judges have arrived, and are seated one after-**noon in the** "Swan Chamber," with "many justices and gentry." Beneath the ermine of one of them there beats a heart **not** unresponsive to the sighs of God's saints. Early arrested in a career of sin, Sir Matthew Hale has been drawn to Christ's feet, and knows no higher joy than to wash them with his **tears.** "With abashed face and a trembling heart," **the** noble woman "ventures into their presence," to **"try** what she can do with them for her husband's **liberty** before they **go** forth of the town."

"My lord," she says, addressing Hale, whose mild **and** gentle **mien seems to** intimate that he is not an enemy, **"I make** bold **to come to your** lordship, to know what **may be done with** my husband."

"I would **do," replies the** judge, "both you and

him the best good I can : but they have taken that for a conviction which thy husband spoke at the sessions ; and, unless there be something done to undo that, I fear I can do thee no good."

"My lord, he is kept unlawfully in prison; they clapped him up before there was any proclamation against the meetings ; the indictment also is false : besides, they never asked him whether he was guilty or no ; neither did he confess the indictment."

" My lord," interposes one of the justices, " he was lawfully convicted."

" Nay," says the bold woman ; "for, when they said to him, Do you confess the indictment ? he said only this, that he had been at several meetings where they had preaching the Word and prayer, and that they had God's presence among them."

" What !" exclaims the other judge, very angrily, as if his conscience was not at ease, " you think we can do what we list ! Your husband is a breaker of the peace, and is convicted by the law."

" Bring me the statute-book," whispers Hale, aside, to one of the officers.

" My lord," shouts another of the justices, as if afraid that Hale would thwart their malice, " he was lawfully convicted ; it is recorded—it is recorded." " As if," adds Bunyan, narrating the scene as he had it from his wife, " it must of necessity be true, because it was recorded. With which words he often endeavored to stop her mouth, having no other argument to convince her but—' it is recorded—it is recorded.' "

" If it be," she replies, " it is false."

" Will your husband leave preaching ?" asks Judge Twisdon. " If he will do so, then send for him."

" My lord, **he** dares not leave preaching as long as he can speak."

" See here," says Twisdon ; " what should we talk any **more** about such a fellow ?. Must he do what he lists ? **He** is a breaker of the peace."

" **My** lord, he desires to live peaceably, and **to** follow his calling, that his family may be maintained : and, moreover, I have four small children that cannot help themselves, one of which is blind, and **we have** nothing to live upon but the charity of good people."

" Alas, poor woman !" says Hale, in a tone of deep sympathy, turning **round** to his brother-judge.

" You make poverty your cloak," rejoins Twisdon : " moreover, I understand he is maintained better by running up and down a-preaching, than by following his **calling.**"

" **What is his** calling ?" asks Hale again, **very** mildly.

" **A tinker, my lord,**" shout some half-dozen voices, eagerly ; " **a tinker !**"

" Yes," she **replies;** " and because he **is a tinker,** and a poor man, therefore he is despised, and cannot have justice."

" Since they have taken," says Hale, gravely, but somewhat sadly, " what thy husband spake for a conviction, thou must either **apply** thyself to the king, or sue **out his pardon, or** get a writ of error."

"My lord," exclaims Justice Chester, alarmed at Hale's counsel, "he will **preach, and** do what he lists."

"He preacheth nothing but the World **of** God," she says.

"He preach the Word of God!" says Judge Twis-**don,** rising in great rage **as if he** would have **struck** her; "he runneth up and down, and doeth harm."

"**No,** my lord, it is not **so;** God hath **owned him,** and done much good **by** him."

"God! **His** doctrine is **the** doctrine **of the** devil."

"**My lord, when the** righteous Judge shall appear it will **be** known that his doctrine is not the doctrine of the devil."

"Do not mind her," says Twisdon, hastily, turning to Hale, "but send her away."

"I am sorry," rejoins Hale, addressing her **very** kindly, "that I can do thee **no** good: **thou** must **do** one of those **three** things aforesaid—namely, **either apply** thyself **to the** king, **or** sue out his **pardon, or get a writ of error; but** a writ of error **will be cheapest.**"

Bursting into tears—not so much for their hard-heartedness against her and her husband as for "**the** sad account which such poor creatures **will** have to give at the coming of the Lord"—she quits the chamber and hastens back **to the** prison to report **her** ill success. "They will not call for you," she says, " and they will not remit the sentence." And, with that, they calmly kneel, appealing to a higher tribunal, and patiently waiting God's time.

Like the early confessors of the Roman Catacombs, **scarcely a** word **escapes** from Bunyan's lips **or** pen to intimate **his** prison-privations; only the bright hope **is seen.** " What gladness" **we** have him writing, for example, amidst the gloominess **of** that dismal cell—

> " What gladness shall possess our heart,
>   When we shall see these things !
> What light and life in every part,
>   Rise like eternal springs !
> O blessed face ! O holy grace !
>   When shall we see this day ?
> **Lord,** fetch **us to** this goodly place,
>   **We humbly to thee** pray.
>
> Thus, when in heavenly harmony
>   These blessed saints appear,
> Adorned with grace and majesty,
>   What gladness will be there !
> Thus shall we see, thus shall we be,
>   Oh, would the day were come !
> **Lord** Jesus, take us up to Thee,
>   To this desired home."

Before his imprisonment, " for not so little as **a** year together," he " could seldom go **to** prayer but this sentence or sweet petition, to be ' strengthened with all might, according **to** his glorious power, unto all patience and long-suffering with joyfulness,' would, **as it** were, thrust **itself into** his mind, **and** persuade him that if ever he should go through long-suffering he must have patience, especially if he would endure it joyfully." And the prayer is not unanswered now. "When God makes the bed," he writes one day from his cell, with its straw couch, "he must needs be easy that is cast thereon; a blessed pillow hath that man for his head, though to all beholders it is hard as a stone." And, another day, sending to his brethren of the Church at Bedford his "Grace Abounding"—"a drop of that honey which he has taken from the carcass of the lion," he says :—"I have eaten thereof myself, and am much refreshed thereby. The Philistines understand me not." And a while later :—"Now is my heart full of comfort. I would not have been without this trial for much; I am comforted every time I think of it, and I hope I shall bless God for ever for the teachings I have had by it." And, still later, he sums up all in one weighty line—

"Dark clouds bring water, when the bright bring none."

CHAPTER XV.

Ten long years **have now** passed in the dismal "den." " The school **of the cross,**" says he, " is the school of light, and lets us see **more** of God's mind." **Let us** enter **the cell once** more, and listen to his heavenly converse.

"**It** is not every suffering," he says to a visitor, one day, "**that** makes a man **a** martyr, but suffering **for** the Word of God after **a** right manner; to wit, in that holy, humble, meek **manner** which **the Word** of God requireth."

"**I have often** thought," rejoins the other, "**that** the best **of** Christians **are** found in **the** worst times."

"**Yes;** and I have thought **again,**" says Bunyan, "**that one** reason **why we are** not better is, because **God purges us no more.** Noah and **Lot,** who so holy as they in the time of their afflictions? and yet, who so idle **as** they in the time of their prosperity?"

" What is it," enquires the visitor, " which makes people so troubled about their afflictions?"

" They are too much addicted to the pleasures of this life; and so they cannot endure that which makes a separation between them. The Lord useth the flail of tribulation to separate the chaff from the wheat."

Another day we **join** him, and find him pleading with a visitor, thus :—" To be truly sensible of sin, is, **to** sorrow for displeasing of God—to be afflicted that **He is** displeased **by us, more** than that He is displeased with us."

" But how may I get this penitence? for my heart is so hard."

" The death of Christ gives us the best discovery of ourselves—in what condition we were, that nothing could help us but that; and also the most clear discovery of the dreadful nature of our sins. For, if sin be such a dreadful thing as to wring the heart **of** the Son **of** God, how shall a poor wretched sinner be able **to bear it?"**

It is the **Lord's** day, and we are with him in the cell once more. " Have a special care," he is saying, with a smile of holy joy caught from the holy day, " to sanctify this blessed festival. **Make** it the market for thy soul; let the whole day be spent in prayer or meditation; lay aside the affairs of the other parts

of the week; let the sermon thou hast heard be con
verted into prayer."

And, not in individual parleys only, but in wider colloquies, he finds, in these years, a door of utterance opened. For, He who gave Joseph favor in the sight of his Egyptian gaoler, has touched the heart of the Bedford turnkey, so that his prisoner enjoys stolen hours of fellowship with the brethren at their place of meeting, " exhorting them to be steadfast in their faith of Jesus Christ." It is recorded of the imprisoned confessors of Madeira, that their keeper would give them leave of absence for many hours, on no other security than their parole. The Bedford prisoner is even allowed on one occasion to " go to see the Christians of London." The visit, however, is scarcely over, when the rumor gets wind among the bishops that the gaoler is inexcusably lax; and an officer is dispatched from London to visit the prison.

That night Bunyan is out on leave. It is late; for the hours have slipped quickly past, as he enjoys a stolen hour of his children's prattle and of his wife's devoted affection. " I must away," he suddenly exclaims, interrupting the joyous moment; " I got leave to stay out to-night, but I think I had better return." Rising that instant, he hastens back; the gaoler remarking, as he opens the prison-door, that rather than come so late, he had better have waited till the morning.

A quarter of an hour elapses; and the iron knocker rattles, till the old rickety building reels again. It is the detective from London, arrived on his ungracious errand.

"Are all the prisoners safe?" he **asks,** in a tone of authority, as the gaoler cautiously opens the gate.

"Yes," replies the turnkey, with a peculiar emphasis, like one who feels he can safely make a clean breast of it.

"Is John Bunyan safe?"

"Yes."

"Let **me** see **him.**"

Bunyan is summoned, and **is** eyed **from head to** foot. The officer is crest-fallen, and leaves chagrined **and chafed.**

"**Well," says the gaoler to** him, as he conducts **him** back **to the** cell, with a strange awe upon **his** spirit—" you may go out again just when you think proper ; for you know when to return better than I can tell you."

And there he is! That hard bed ; and those gloomy walls ; and that earthen jug ; and those coarse garments ; and that calm, joyous soul. It is here the "Dreamer,"

> "Writing of **the way**
> **And** race of saints,
> Falls suddenly into an allegory
> About their journey, and the way to glory."

And such an allegory!

> "This book, it chalketh out before thine eyes
> The man that seeks the everlasting prize;

> It shows you whence he comes, whither he goes:
> What he leaves undone, and what he does;
> It also shows you how he runs and runs,
> Till he unto the gate of glory comes."

And who **shall** tell how many **souls,** now redeemed, owe to the voice which issued from that cell their everlasting **all?** "This **book,**" writes its author again in his **"Apology," as if** possessing a presentiment of its mission,

> "This book will make a traveller **of thee,**
> If by its counsel thou wilt ruled **be**:
> It will direct thee to the Holy Land,
> If thou wilt its directions understand;
> Yea, **it will** make the slothful active be,
> The blind also delightful things to see.
> Then read my **fancies** : they will stick like burs,
> And may be, **to the helpless,** comforters."

And how divinely **the mission has** been fulfilled, a coming " day" alone shall reveal.

It is the eleventh year of the imprisonment ; **and** we meet him one evening in the twilight **on** the bridge leading **to** the town. Into the rooms of a **humble dwelling,** situate in a back street, **are** crowded **a company of** grave, holy men, waiting for **the ex-**pected **visitor** and for his heavenly message. Bunyan comes in ; and a greeting welcomes him, such as only suffering saints **can** give. "I now once again," says **he,** after they **have** lifted their hearts to Him who **nears the** sigh of the prisoner, "that **you** may see my **soul hath** fatherly **care and desire** after your spiritual and everlasting welfare, **as** before from **the** top of Shenir **and Hermon, so now** from the **lions'** den, and from **the** mountain of the leopards,* **do** look yet after you all, greatly desiring to see your safe **arrival into the** desired haven.**"** And, as he **proceeds** with the heavenly unction peculiar to such seasons, and feels the very breath, as it **were,** of Jesus to be on their souls, he bids them adieu, saying —"I **thank** God for the grace **and mercy,** and knowledge **of** Christ our Saviour, which **He hath** bestowed upon you, with abundance **of faith and** love; for your **hungerings** and thirstings after further acquaintance **with the Fa**ther, in **the Son; for your tenderness of heart, your trembling at sin, your** sober **and** holy deportment also, before **both God** and men. They are a great refreshment to • me, for ' you are my glory and joy.' "

The holy Gifford, by this time, has **been** taken **to his** rest; and the Church is waiting for **another** pastor, **who shall teach** them **the good way of the Lord. It is a cold winter night in December (1671);** and **the people are** gathered, **in the belief** that He **who** "holds **in his** right **hand the** seven **stars"** has indicated **the choice which will** meet His sanction. "At a full assembly **of** the Church," is the record **in** the minutes still extant, " after much seeking of the Lord by prayer, the congregation do **with joint** consent call forth and appoint **our** brother **John Bunyan** to **the** pastoral office." **An hour** elapses; and the **pris-**

* Cant., v. 8.

oner of Jesus Christ" arrives, on another of his kindly errands. The choice is announced ; and, as **the record** again runs, " he, accepting thereof, gives himself **up to serve** Christ and His Church **in** this charge, **and** receives from the elders the right hand of fellowship, after having preached fifteen years." Commend**ed to** the Lord and to the word of His grace, the pastor, as he rises, says—"My dear children, the milk and honey are beyond **this** wilderness. God **be** merciful to you, and grant that you be not slothful **to go** in and possess the land." He returns to the " den," but " with much content, through grace." Yes, thou **brave** confessor, thou art not forsaken or out of mind.

> " Justice hath her balances ;
> Another world can compensate for all ;
> The daily martyrdom of patience shall **not be** wanting of
>   reward."

CHAPTER XVI.

Scene in the Channel—The **bankrupt** merchant—The landing—Court of St. James's—The audience—"**Six** poor Quakers"—Owen and **the** tinker—The petition—Liberation—The "motto"—The meeting——**Scene in London—The** appeal—Fellowship—The Shibboleth.

OFF Brighton, then a fishing village, a boat is **seen** one night, making for the coast of France. On board is **a** mysterious stranger, very restless and very wretched, whom the sailors believe to be **a** bankrupt merchant, in hot haste **to escape** the bailiffs. One **eye has** recognized **him ; and the** bankrupt trembles **from** head to **foot,** until **a** side-whisper from the mate assures **him** that he is safe in his hands. After a **rough** passage, they reach **the** opposite coast **off Fe**camp: **faithful to his word,** the mate **rows** his **pas**senger ashore ; and, in shoal **water, he carries** him **on** his shoulders to the land.

Twenty years elapse, **and** the **mate** finds himself **at St.** James's, in **the** audience-chamber of Charles II. **He** has just returned from the West Indies, after a long absence; and, hearing that multitudes of his brethren of the " Society of Friends" are in prison for conscience' sake he has agreed to intercede for them with the king, whom he has **never** seen since they **parted** that morning on the shore.

" Ah !" exclaims his majesty, instantly recognizing his deliverer, " why have not you come to claim your reward ?"

" I have been rewarded enough, Sire, with the **sat**-isfaction of having saved life."

" Is there any favor I can grant you ?"

" Sire, **I** ask nothing for myself, but for my poor friends, that you should set them at liberty, as I did your majesty !"

" I will release **any six** you name."

" **What** !" **says the** sailor, bluntly, " six poor Quak-ers for **a** king's ransom !"

" Come back another **day," says the** king, kindly, " and we **shall** see what can be **done."**

The liberations begin ; and another voice **is** lifted at **Court** in behalf of another prisoner.

" **How," said** Charles, a year or two after **this,** one day, **to** Dr. John Owen, " can a learned **man like you** sit down to hear **a** tinker **prate ?"**

" **May** it please your majesty," answered Owen, " **could I** have **the** tinker's abilities for preaching, most gladly should I relinquish all my learning."

Whilst the tinker **is yet** in prison, Owen has read some of his wonderful treatises, and has heard of his godly ways. **A** hint reaches Bedford, that **a** new petition to the king may not now be fruitless. **A** week or two pass ; and, sitting **in** council, his majesty has before him a certificate from the Sheriff in Bedfordshire, that Bunyan's only crime **is** "nonconformity." It is the day to issue the royal deed of pardon, opening the prisons to four hundred and seventy-one Quakers, and to about a score of Baptists **and** Independents. And to the bede-roll **is** added **the** name of John Bunyan. It is on May 17, **1672.**

The "den" is exchanged for a humble cottage; and, to supply the wants of his family, he combines for **a** time with **his pastoral** work the trade of **a** brazier. **"Love not the** world," is his remark one **day to a friend; "for** it is **a** moth in a Christian's **life."** His own simple habits are a daily commentary upon that weighty counsel.

The tinker's words are eagerly sought after by hungering and thirsting souls. Whilst his friends are erecting a large place of worship, **the** earnest **man** is to be seen, like the Master, going everywhere, from house to house, " teaching and preaching." And, **at** its opening, it is " so thronged that, though it is very spacious, many are constrained to stay without, every **one** striving to partake of his instructions."

It is a cold winter morning in London ; and we hasten along in the dim dawn, the oil-lamps still casting their feeble glimmer on a stream of working-men, unusually soon astir and plainly bent on some engrossing errand. We fall into the stream, and are carried with it into a capacious chapel, which, though it is not yet seven o'clock, is already filled to overflowing, with an audience rarely seen on a working-day in such a place. A few minutes pass; and a broad-shouldered, cliff-browed countryman is struggling, amidst a buzz of whispers, up the pulpit-stair. He rises; and as he utters, in his sturdy vernacular, his burning appeals, it is " to astonishment, as if an angel or an apostle had touched the people's souls with a coal of holy fire from the altar."*

Another time, it is the Sabbath; and only a single day's notice has been given of his visit to town. We repair to the spot—it is the "Town's end Meeting-house," holding between one and two thousand persons. The doors are scarcely opened, when the anxious multitude pour in, "half being fain to go back again for want of room." The preacher "himself is fain, at a back-door, to be pulled almost over people to get up-stairs to his pulpit." And oh, how he pleads with these souls! " I have been vile myself," he says, "but have obtained mercy; and I would have my companions in sin to partake of mercy too. A great sinner, when converted, seems a *booty* to Jesus Christ. He *gets* by saving such an one: why, then, should both Jesus lose his glory and the sinner lose his soul, at once, and that for want of an invitation? Come, pardon and a part in heaven and in glory cannot be hurtful to you! Manasseh was a bad man, and Magdalene was a bad woman;

* The authority is the Rev. Charles Doe, who was present.

to say nothing of the thief upon the cross or of the murderers of Christ: **yet** they obtained mercy; Christ willingly **received** them. And **do** you think," **he** proceeds, as every eye is fixed intently and **an** awful stillness pervades the vast concourse, "**that** those, **once** so bad, now in heaven, repent them there because they left their sins for Christ when they were in this world? I cannot believe but that you think they have verily got the best of it. Why, sinners, do you likewise! Christ, at heaven's gate, says to you, 'Come hither!' and the devil, at the gate of hell, does call you to 'come' to him. Sinners! what say **you?** whither **will** you go? Do not **go** into the fire; **there you will be** burned. Do not **let** Jesus **lose His** longing, since it is for your salva-**tion**; but come **to** Him and live." And, closing with another of his touching appeals, the tear-drop already stealing down many a rough cheek, he adds:—"One word more, and so I have done. Sinner, here thou dost hear of love; prithee, do not provoke it by turning it into wantonness. He that dies for slighting love, sinks deepest into hell, and will there be tormented by the remembrance **of** that evil, more **than by the** deepest cogitation of **all** his sins. Take heed, therefore; do not make **love thy** tormentor, sinner! Farewell!"

We return with him to Bedford; **and** how meekly and lovingly he goes in and out amongst his simple flock! "To seek yourself in this life," **is** his observation, one day, "is to be lost." Too intensely has he been refined in the Lord's furnace, **to** be a self-seeking man **now.**

> " That which before was darkened clean
> With bushy groves, pricking the looker's eye,
> Vanishes away when faith does change the scene,
> **And** now appears a glorious sky."

And right joyous is the fellowship **of** the saints in this tried church. " Church-fellowship, rightly managed," says he, " is the glory of all the world. No place, no community, no fellowship is adorned and bespangled with those beauties, as is a church rightly knit together to their Head, and lovingly serving **one** another." And such a fellowship meets us here. All who have " spiritual communion with Christ" are welcomed **to** the table of their common Lord, every detail being **" left to private** judgment." The light is too heavenly, and **the** love **too** genuine, to give place to any human shibboleth. " Consider," is the affectionate counsel with which he closes his last sermon to them, " that the holy God is your Father; and **let** this oblige you to live like the children of God, that you may look your Father in the face an other **day."**

CHAPTER XVII.

The midnight-lamp—Writings—The furrow—The great morrow—The "blind one"—More than half **away—The** ark of God—Argyle—Rumbold—Evil time—The peacemaker—Illness—"Black river"—Beulah—Dying words—Heaven—"Feels the bottom"—Beatifical **vision**"—How **to** pray—Ague—Longing—"Mortal garments"—**"The city"—A look in at the glory.**

AT the little upper-window of that lowly cottage in Bedford is to be seen, of an evening, a faint light, casting athwart the curtain a dark, deep shadow, as if of a man in deep thought. It is Bunyan, with his Bible, and his glowing heart, and his magic pen, "sequestering" himself to his "beloved work of setting forth the glories of Immanuel." Night after night, his studies are protracted far into the morning; for he does not serve the Lord with that which costs him nothing. Within the sixteen years which elapse betwixt his liberation and his death, that midnight-lamp witnesses the production of not fewer than forty-five separate works. During the day his hours are occupied with his beloved flock, and with his evangelistic wanderings.

His iron frame is not what it has been. The twelve years in the " den" have left their traces, in a tread less elastic, and in a brow more furrowed, though not less serene. And his abundant labors since have not arrested the course of the furrow's deepening line. It is the seed-corn of a great to-morrow which he handles, and he may not trifle with his errand.

And one trial visits him, which goes deeper into his soul than all the rest. It is " that poor blind one," smitten by the icy finger of death. It is said of the Swiss, by one of our poets, that

> " The loud torrent and the whirlwind's roar,
> But bind him to his native mountains more."

To this afflicted child—because of the very ruggedness of her lot—her father's heart has clung with a most peculiar love. She is sick now ; and this other self, as she lies there so faint, seems to prostrate him at her side. Day after day, night after night, the harrowed father watches. But she is gone ! And, oh ! what a blank ! " In all these dead," says Vinet, " we ourselves die. A part of our life, and of our heart, is buried in each of these tombs." The stroke Bunyan never recovers. It seems as if already he were more than half away.

His spirit, too, is trembling for the ark of God. The apostate James has been imbruing his hands in the blood of God's holiest saints. Argyle has fallen on the scaffold, " thanking God that He has support-ed him wonderfully." And Rumbold has fallen at his side, "blessing God's holy name" that He **has** "given him grace to adhere to His cause in an evil day," and declaring, that, "if every hair of his head were a man, he would in that quarrel venture them all." "Deliverance," indeed, according to the almost prophetic words of Argyle, pronounced in his closing hours, "is to come in very suddenly;" but the cloud is as yet dark overhead, unrelieved by any silver lining.

In the town of Reading there resides a family bitterly opposed to the work of **God.** The eldest **son** has been at Cambridge, **and, hearing** of the great **preacher,** has **goue one night to** listen. Arrested **by** the Word, he has returned **to** his home " a new man." The father, greatly offended, has determined to disinherit him. Day by day the estrangement grows more painful. At length the thought occurs—" Will not my spiritual father come and mediate ? And his prayers—will not they avail ?"

Bunyan sets out for Reading ; **and,** having earned **the** blessing of the peacemaker, he reaches London on his way home. A drenching rain upon the road has brought on fits **of** shivering; and he is taken seriously **ill.**

From the first, a presentiment seizes him that he **is** nearing the "black river." Calling for pen, ink, and paper, he addresses to his dear flock a few sentences of parting tenderness. "Thus have I written to you," says he, " before **I** die, to provoke you to faith and holiness, and to love one another when I am deceased

and shall be in Paradise, as through grace I comfortably believe."

Already the air of Beulah surrounds him with its fragrant breezes. "In heaven," says he to one kind friend who has come to visit him, "we shall find blessings in their purity, without any ingredient to embitter—with everything to sweeten it." And to another: "Oh! who is able to conceive **the** inexpressible, inconceivable joys that are there? None but they who have tasted them." And another day thus: "How will the heavens echo for joy when the bride, the Lamb's wife shall come to dwell with her Husband for ever!"

Fever comes on; and, in a few more days, the "earthly house," enfeebled by so many labors, shall be "dissolved." But his earnest spirit "feels the bottom, and it is good." And so, with

"A heart at leisure from itself,"

he calmly utters, as from the river's farther bank, sundry parting counsels.

"If you would be better satisfied," says he, "what the beatifical vision means, my request is, that you **would live holily,** and go and see."

"Christ," says he, **on** another occasion, "is the desire **of all** nations, the joy of angels, the delight of the Father: what solace, then, must the soul be filled with, that hath the possession of Him to all eternity!"

And again: "Before you enter into prayer, ask

thy soul these questions : To what end, O my soul :
art thou retired **into** this place ? Art thou come to
converse with the Lord in prayer? Is thy business
slight ? Is it not concerning the welfare of thy soul ?"

In these last hours, this closet-fellowship again and
again he urges. " Pray often," he says, one morning
with great earnestness ; " pray often, for prayer is a
shield to the soul, a sacrifice to God, and a scourge
for Satan." And an hour or two later : " The spirit
of prayer is more precious than thousands of **gold**
and silver." And again, **thus** : **" In** thy closet, consider that thou art but *dust* and *ashes*, and **He the**
great God, Father of our Lord Jesus Christ, **who**
' clothes Himself with light as with a garment ;' **that**
thou art **a vile sinner,** and He a holy God ; that thou
art but a crawling worm, and He the omnipotent Creator." And still again : " When thou prayest, rather
let thy heart be without words than **thy** words without heart. And, remember," he adds emphatically,
" either prayer **will make** thee **cease from sin, or sin
will** certainly entice thee **to** cease from prayer."

The ague grows more alarming ; and, once and
again, **in** the intervals **of its** feverish paroxysms, his
eye **is lifted** upward, **and** the whisper is breathed—
" Oh ! to depart **and to** be with Christ ! **far, far**
better !" **A few** more hours, and the **longing** is
granted ; **he** " leaves behind him **in the river"** his
" mortal garment ;" and from **the humble** dwelling
in Snowhill his great spirit is **wafted upwards,** to
" the city beyond the clouds."

It is on the last day of August, 1688, and in the sixtieth year of his age.

Reader! look in for a moment after him into that glory whither he is gone. See! the city shines like the sun; its streets are paved with gold; and in them walk many men with crowns on their heads, palms in their hands, and golden harps to praise withal. And yonder *he* is! the wayworn tinker—not wayworn now! The bells of the city ring again—he is "with the Lord" for ever!

> "Servant of God, well done!
>   Rest from thy loved employ!
> The battle 's fought, the victory won
>   Enter thy Master's joy!"

II.

The Christian Laborer:

GERHARD TERSTEEGEN.

"Man is all weakness; there is no such thing
As prince or king.
His arm is short; yet, with a sling,
He may do more."

"Let us not be weary in well doing; **for in due** season we
shall reap, if we faint not."—*Gal.* **vi. 9.**

"Let us not be weary in well doing; **for in due** season we
shall reap, if we faint not."—*Gal.* **vi. 9.**

"Flowers, that with one scarlet gleam
Cover a hundred leagues, **and seem**
To set the hills on fire."

" WHEN a tired laborer," says Foster, " **can** repose **upon** laying aside **his work,** that is something.   But *can* the *Christian* laborer ?   How would **a** soldier, who **had deserted in** battle, look **at** his arms ?" GERHARD TERSTEEGEN is reposing now; but **his** battle is fought, his work of service **is** done.

Reader ! here is a life-study which **we** invite you **to** ponder.   **And may you** have grace to go **and do** likewise !   Rest comes after **victory :** *your* final victory **is** not yet.

And take courage !   **The** " Well done !" **will** be pronounced " **in** due season ;" and, **when it** comes, **you will not deem it late.**

CHAPTER I.

Birth—Early struggles—Studies—Earnest nature—Apprenticeship—Scene in the forest—Awakening—The moonlight and the sunlight.

BORN in the principality of Moers, in 1697, the youngest of a family of two daughters and six sons, and losing his father while yet a child, GERHARD was early summoned to that energetic self-reliance which gives tone and force to the will. At school he studied earnestly the Greek, and Hebrew, and Latin tongues; until, in his fourteenth year, at the close of his course, he pronounced an oration in Latin verse with such *éclât*, **that** a magistrate of his native town urged his mother to allow her son to devote himself entirely **to** study. But, destined from the first to a mercantile life, he **was bound, in** his fifteenth year, an apprentice **to** his brother-in-law in Mülheim, for a term **of four** years.

"That man is to be pitied," said the Reporter of **the** Young Men's Christian Association of Paris, at the recent meeting of Young Men's Associations in that capital, "who has never felt enthusiasm—who carries beneath a youthful breast a heart prematurely old." And he added : "Christianity does not fear enthusiasm—it purifies and exalts it. What do I say ? It alone preserves it ; it alone keeps intact— sheltered from the contamination of the world—that fruitful source of generous devotion which has its deepest seat in the human soul." Tersteegen's was a nature which could not waste itself in mere *ennui*. A fire was there which *must* burn. Unsanctified, it will blaze in a consuming ambition—a restless worldliness : touched from heaven, it will become the lambent flame on the golden altar, wafting upward the fragrant incense, a sweet savor before the Lord.

At the age of sixteen, and whilst an apprentice at Mülheim, he was first brought face to face with the great question of his salvation. On his way, one day, through a deep forest to a neighboring town, he was seized with a sudden illness, which seemed to threaten immediate death. Retiring out of the road to a secluded spot, he fell on his knees, beseeching God to spare him until he should be better prepared to enter eternity. The pain left him as suddenly as it had come ; and from that hour began his groping after the heavenly light.

"An ungodly man," we find him saying, long afterwards, "is one who is detached from God, and cleaves to himself and the creature : a godly man is one who is detached from himself and the creature, and adheres to God with all affection." And he adds : "The sole basis of this godliness is an essential union to Christ Jesus ; and the godliness itself is the new life which springs from it, therefore emphatically called in Scripture, 'Godliness in Christ Jesus.'" In search of that godliness his earnest spirit was now darkly feeling its way.

The loving Saviour had wounded him. "My carnal nature," he tells us, "would gladly have expelled the thought from my mind, and would have had me live, the day through, as before, free, and jovial, and merry ; but there had fallen upon my heart such a burden as I could not get rid of—I felt my sins, my wants, my danger. It was the love of Christ which constrained me to feel thus ; although my soul as yet knew nothing of this love, but was only conscious of wrath and condemnation."

For many days, the light around him was but as the moonlight paleness and dimness. "God leaves us," he wrote afterwards, referring to that season of groping, "to exert all our strength, and to weary ourselves, and to become faint, as it were, by our own attempts after holiness and righteousness, in order that we may come weary and heavy laden to Jesus." Tersteegen's earnest nature drew him into a rigid self-denial ;—such as, coarse apparel ; coarser fare, consisting of flour, milk and water, and partaken of only once a-day ; together with the humblest possible lodging. In this way he sought rest ; but, by seeking it out of Christ, he was "only adding (he tells us) day by day to his burden." It was like dragging a lifeless corpse, **or** a man in a swoon: what labor is needed to remove him only **a few** feet from **the** place where he fell down !

At last, in his twentieth year, the sunlight **rose.** The loving Saviour, who had wounded him, now drew near to **heal.** "He took me by the hand," he says, "drew me away from perdition's yawning gulf —directed my eye to Himself, and, instead of the well-deserved pit of hell, opened to me the **unfathomable** abyss of His loving heart."

CHAPTER II.

Augustine— " For thyself" — Dedication—Ribbon-making—" **Artless humility**"—Daily routine—Living sacrifice—" Perfectly **at ease in God**"—Closet fellowship.

It was a favorite saying of Augustine—" Thou, O Lord, hast created us for Thyself; and our heart is restless until it rests in Thee." With a characteristic intenseness, Tersteegen now made this rest his own. "I thank God," we find him writing, " that He has permitted me to live so long as to enable me to become acquainted with Him." And twenty-seven years later, he says, referring to this great crisis—" God graciously called me out of the world, and granted me the desire to belong to Him, and to be willing to follow Him. I long for an eternity, that I may suitably glorify Him for it." And, describing the same deliverance, he wrote, in lines generally ascribed to Wesley, but really Tersteegen's, thus :—

" Thou hidden love of God, whose height,
  Whose depth, unfathomed, no man knows!

I see from far thy beauteous light,
  Inly I sigh for thy repose;
My heart is pained, nor can it be
At rest, till it find rest in Thee.

Thy secret voice invites me still
  The sweetness of thy yoke to prove;
And fain I would; but, though my will
  Seems fixed, yet wide my passions rove—
Yet hindrances strew all the way;
I aim at Thee, yet from Thee stray.

'Tis mercy all, that Thou hast brought
  My mind to seek its peace in Thee;
Yet while **I seek but find** Thee not,
  No peace my wandering soul shall **see.**
Oh, when shall all my wanderings end,
And all my steps to Jesus tend?

My own endeavors are in vain;
  From self-attempts Love turns away;
A gaze too ardent gives her pain*
  And will not suffer her to stay.
Mine eyes against each object close,
And bring me, Love, to thy repose.

Each moment draw from earth away
  My heart, that lowly waits thy call;
Speak to my inmost soul, and say,
  'I am thy Love, thy God, thy All!'
To feel thy power, to hear thy voice,
To taste thy love, be all my choice."

Service now took **another hue.** "Thou, God, seest
me!" was henceforth his master-thought. And that
God was his Father, with whom he felt himself **at**

* Song, vi. 5

home. "I knew," **he** says, "that God saw all that passed within me; I, therefore, laid open my inmost soul to this Sun of righteousness, to be enlightened, warmed and renovated by its beams."

"**Can** these be thy people," he exclaimed one day, "who serve thee only occasionally with their lips, and thine enemies daily in their hearts?" Tersteegen himself, delivered from the fear which hath bondage, was a follower of the Lord as a dear child. "I **am** the Lord's," he wrote about this time to a friend. "Having surrendered myself to Him, I belong **to** Him, with all that I am, and **no** longer **to myself**: by this I must abide, or else **I** must make as solemn a revocation as my previous surrender—from which may the Lord preserve me! I am His, I repeat, and God regards me as such." And he added, in one of his touching stanzas:

> "Is there a thing beneath the sun
>   That strives with Thee my heart to share?
> Ah! tear it thence, and reign alone,
>   **The** Lord of every motion **there.**"

Fearing the distractions of a more engrossing mercantile life, he was led, soon after the expiry of his term of apprenticeship, to adopt the humble trade of a ribbon maker. After laboring from five in the morning till nine in the evening, he would steal out quietly to visit the sick and the needy in some back alley of the town, sharing with them his scanty earnings, and telling them of the Friend of sinners.

"Bear one another's burdens," he used to say, "both of body and soul, as if they were your own. Be ever ready to serve one another gladly and in artless humility, **and** to wash one another's feet (so to speak), **or** in the meanest and most laborious offices."

This "artless humility"—how precious a grace! Tersteegen was daily learning to be "clothed" with **it.** "Do not think so much," he said to a friend one day, unfolding the method of exercising it, **"upon** denying yourselves, upon being faithful, or upon living holily and strictly; but only seek to love, hunger after love, exercise yourselves in love. Love is always exercising self-denial, without tasting its bitterness, and almost without ever thinking of it. Think only **how** you may love Christ—how you may love Him more cordially **than** ever; and do every thing to gratify and satisfy **His love."**

In 1725 he associated with himself **in** his trade **a** young man named Sommer, who was desirous of acquiring the art of ribbon-making. His season of solitude **had** been peculiarly pleasant to him. **"I cannot** express," **he** tells us, "how happy I was during the time I lived alone. I often thought that no monarch **on** earth could live so contentedly as I did." **And now** that he had exchanged, somewhat reluctantly, **the** solitude for the society of his friend, nothing could be **more** beautiful than the daily **routine** beneath **that** lowly roof. Rising in the **morning** at five, **after** their secret devotions, the **friends** sang together **a** hymn, and read a little of the Word. Coffee followed; then a brief prayer; and both proceeded quietly to work. At eleven they rested; and, after separating for an hour for the purpose **of** prayer, they dined together, and resumed their labor at one. At six in the evening they were at liberty, when they again spent an hour in private meditation and prayer. The remainder of the even**ing was** spent in labors of love, either at the desk **or** in the dwellings of the poor.

Even his commonest occupations had acquired a new dignity in his eyes—they were a part of his daily "living sacrifice." "The love of Christ," we find him saying on one **occasion, "enters** voluntarily into all **our** concerns; it will, and must, have its hand, not **only in the** greatest, but even in the smallest things. **By** love all these trifles may become truly great, and a means of serving God. He that (so to speak) picks up a bit of straw from the ground, from love **to** Christ, performs a great work."

And by the same love his **frequent** bodily *sufferings* were transformed **into willing sacrifices.** One **day, as he lay** in **bed very ill, and a** friend was bidding him what **both** thought might be a last farewell, Tersteegen **said,** with **a** pleasant smile, "I am perfectly at ease **in God: I** find him in every way all sufficient: **I can** enter eternity to-night with com**fort."** And another **day he** said, "How many let **their** courage fail when they see **that** Jesus distributes, not bread and wine only, but also crosses!" Tersteegen's whole life was a life of cross-bearing;

but he bore them joyfully, knowing that He **who** distributes crosses now, will, ere long, distribute crowns.

And the **same** love made his *closet* **so** pleasant. "Solitude," he would say, " is the school of godliness. **You** are called—think what grace !—to social converse with God." And again, "To be emptied of everything—to be alone with God in **the spirit, at rest** and in silence, giving place to God and things divine, from which alone result truth, and strength, and life, and salvation ;—how dear to me are the times I can **spare** for that purpose !" Reader ! is **your** closet **a** pleasant place to you ? **What you are** upon your knees, that is the real man.

CHAPTER III.

An awakening—Indian backwoods—Madeira—"Very hungry"—His
trade—The cottage—Its "consecration"—His one theme—"A naked
infant"—The corrective—Where to get Theology—Payson—Luther.

In 1727 there was a great awakening in the
neighborhood of Mülheim. A friend, who for some
time had noted Tersteegen's so singular progress in
the divine life, urged him to speak to the awakened.
But, distrusting his own powers, he hesitated to open
his lips in a public assembly. "I would rather hide
myself from all the world," he said, "than let myself
be seen or heard." The Lord, however, was saying
to him, "Say not, I am a child; for thou shalt go to
all that I shall send thee; and whatsoever I command thee thou shalt speak." At length Tersteegen
yielded. And such words! To the whole-hearted
they were as barbed arrows, and to the wounded as
an excellent oil.

Instinctively discerning in him a heart of intensest
sympathy, the people resorted to him from every
quarter, seeking his counsel and his consolations.

Brainerd tells us, in his Diary, that, when the Divine Spirit was working among **the** Indians, he could scarcely get an hour's rest—so earnest were the people for the bread of life. In Madeira, during the awakening there, the Portuguese used to travel over-**night** many miles; **and an** expression which we re-member Hewitson once told us they were in the habit of using when they came to him, was, " We are very hungry." So also was it with Tersteegen at Mülheim. " The awakening," we find him writing, " occasions me many visits. I am obliged to devote myself, almost from morning till evening, to converse with people, either individually or collectively. I feel I **must** spend and be spent. **It were** a small thing to put health and even life itself into the scale, in order to fulfil the good pleasure of God."

With increasing bodily weakness, aggravated by his nightly studies and watchings, he soon found himself driven to the alternative, either of declining the greater part of these visits, or of giving up his employment. Many generous offers had been made to him by friends who saw that the Lord was calling him to this spiritual work. One, a merchant, had proffered him an annuity for life ; another, a Dutch gentleman, had with tears urged his acceptance of **a** bond for 10,000 florins; whilst **a** third, a Christian **lady** whom he had never seen, had in her will appointed him her executor over a property of 40,000 florins, on condition of his taking whatever he needed.

But these offers, and many others besides, he had declined. It was only when disabled by weakness from manual labor, that he at length consented to accept the love-offerings of a few very special friends. And, his moderate wants thus supplied, he gave his little surplus to the poor followers of Jesus.

Tersteegen did not shrink from labor. "Your undertaking some external employment," he once wrote to a friend, "is needful for you and well-pleasing to God. The idea which some have, that all is temporal and transient, and therefore useless, merely arises from the disrelish and gloom of the constitution. We were driven out of Paradise by **sin ;** and, according to God's wise arrangement, we must now till the thistly ground as a penance, and for our amendment, and be exercised in the performance of things so worthless. It would be folly to doubt on the subject. We ought not, however, to burden ourselves too heavily, but do all that we do to **the** Lord ; they will then, not only not be prejudicial to our spirit, **but** advantageous **to it: so** that, **by this** simple intention of doing all things, whether little or great, to the Lord **and** from **love to** Him, even the smallest things become important, and earth is turned into gold." Tersteegen might still have continued at his trade, and he would have transformed its engrossing cares into a heavenly discipline ; but **the same** single-hearted dedication to God, which would have kept him at his ribbon-making, if such had seemed to be the divine leaning, now constrained him to cast himself into the new and less certain mode of life to which plainly circumstances were calling him.

And such **is** the befitting way for those who are "not their own." One disciple the Lord needs **as** a Christian tradesman ; another as a Christian mer-**chant** ; **a** third as an evangelist ; **a** fourth as a prisoner in the dungeon ; a fifth as **a** martyr at the stake. Each man, in deciding his work, is a law to himself, provided always he is "under law to Christ." The general rule **is,** to abide in the calling in which His grace found us. The exception to the rule is, **for** Peter to leave his nets, and Levi his desk, and William Carey his lasts. Tersteegen found himself in the latter category ; and joyously he "went out, not knowing whither he went." One thing, however, he **did** know—the Lord was on before him.

A friend died, and he rented his little cottage. There he welcomed the many strangers who resorted **to** him in increasing numbers, from all quarters, to hear at his lips the Word of Life. **It** thus became known, and is known to this day, as "The Pilgrims' Cottage."

The "consecration" of the cottage (as Tersteegen called it) was a touching scene. Hoffman, its former possessor, had requested him on his death-bed **to** assemble some friends **a** few days after his decease, **and** give **thanks** for his happy departure. At two hours' notice, one hundred and fifty people gathered ; and Tersteegen was compelled to address them. A deep emotion pervaded **the** meeting—the Word "came with power." It was a true consecration of his humble dwelling—the Lord Himself was there.

And other scenes, not less affecting, were witnessed there from week to week. "There is still, God be thanked," he writes, some time afterwards, "a great awakening and stir among the people here : for some weeks together, from morning to night, they were compelled to wait one for another, to have an opportunity of speaking with me. Many were obliged to return five or six times, before a quarter of an hour could be found to converse with me alone ; and I have occasionally had ten, twenty, and even thirty anxious souls with me at **the** same time."

In these communings his one theme was Christ. "Methinks," he once wrote, "it would be an inexpressible consolation to me, if, in my dying hour, and when I shall have to appear in the presence of God, I could once more proclaim to all the world that God alone is the Fountain of Life ; and that there is no other way to **find** and enjoy Him than the life hid with Christ **in** God, opened out to us in the death of the **Saviour.**" **And on** another occasion he wrote :—" The power and the riches of the merits of the blood of Jesus are seldom recognized in the manner in which they ought **to be.**" Tersteegen so recognized it ;—it was his own life—and it must be the life, he knew, of these anxious souls. "It was once whispered in **my** heart," he used to say, "'Come like a naked infant, and then my bosom **shall** receive thee.'" And another favorite expression was, "I have obvious motives for forsaking myself, and letting myself drop, that I may be found alone in Jesus." Taught thus personally, how could he but speak to these souls the things which he had seen and heard?

This is the true corrective for all the husks, alike **of a** religionised philosophy and of a dry barren orthodoxy. " I everywhere find," says Tersteegen, "**a** *hunger* among the people : the customary food no longer suffices them." Yes, and so is it now. Souls " hungering after righteousness" must have Christ, " the living bread," or perish. The stricken conscience must have rest in Christ's blood ; the vacant heart must have rest in Christ's person. **No** more can **a** hungry stomach be satisfied by the perfumes of a beautiful flower, than an awakened sinner **can** be satisfied with **any** thing short of Christ. When, a century ago, in England, Whitefield, and Wesley, and Grimshaw, **and** Fletcher, and Harris, **and** Romaine, went forth on their errand of **love to** sinners—they all, though taught **in** different human schools, found their theology to be practically **one.** **The** reason was, they all were now sitting at Christ's feet, and received at His hand the living bread for those perishing souls. A poor lifeless orthodoxy, however zealously embraced, finds itself, in such scenes, a mere galvanized " body of death." And **a** brother, who in **colder** times was suspected as heretical, stands forth, in spite of himself, a true apostle of Jesus. It is not disputings we want **in** these days ; it **is** not angry warrings ; it is awakened souls, trembling consciences, " pricked" hearts. We want to " hear the sound **of a** going in the tops of the mulberry-trees ;" and **then we shall** go **up and** " smite the host," " for **then shall** the Lord go out before us." Payson tells **us** that he got his theology "upon his knees;" and Luther tells **us he** got his in the furnace of affliction. It is when alone with God, in **"the** entering in **of** the cave," not amid the tearing " wind," and " earthquake," and " fire" of human wranglings, that we receive the teachings of the " still small voice."

CHAPTER IV.

New fields—Barmen—People in tears—The Barn—Illness—The
Mayor—"Retire into a hovel"—Inquirers—The poor widow—
The little boy—The student—Books and the new birth—The
decision.

NEW fields opened **for** his sickle. A message
came from some awakened souls in a neighboring
principality, desiring him **to** come and visit them.
Distrustful as ever of himself **and** of his own ways,
we find him committing himself **to** the Lord, thus:
—"Jesus! I entrus tmyself nakedly, blindly, and entirely unto thee, assenting willingly to my own nothingness, and desiring, in the artless carelessness of
faith, to live and die with thee, and in thee."   And
again :—"Rather **let** me suffer a thousand afflictions
with God, than walk in my own way, even were it
in the smallest degree."   And yet again :—"I am
myself a poor, ignorant infant, and neither know nor
possess anything except in the Lord, and have no
control over what belongs to another."

"**To the** upright," it is written, "there ariseth
light **in** the darkness." To this upright soul the

light soon shone. **He** went to Barmen, and the Lord went with **him.** So deeply moved were the people under the Word, that he found it difficult (he tells us) to remain firm in the midst of many tears. Wherever he went, the people surrounded **him** from morning till night. " I found myself," **he** says, " once a few miles distant from a certain place; but I was waited for on the way, and conducted into a barn, where I found about twenty persons, most of whom were unknown to me, and were desirous of hearing the Word. The Lord supports me, both **in** body and soul, **and—to appearance at least—vouch-safes** His **blessing."**

On one **of these** occasions, **a** touching incident occurred. His excessive labors having brought on a **severe** cold—aggravated by fever, and an almost total loss of voice—he was mounting his horse one morning, about eight, to return home, when he was arrested by some five-and-twenty earnest inquirers, some **of** whom had travelled several miles to see **him. And, at** another place **on the way,** such was the thirst **for the** Word, **that** the people assembled to **the number of** three or four hundred, "filling the house to the **very door,** and placing ladders against the windows in order to hear." The mayor of **the** little town, like some of our greater authorities nearer at home, attempted to arrest the work; but Tersteegen stood **firm.** " I wrote," **says** the lowly man, " a pretty sharp letter to him, representing to him how inconsistently he would act if he prohibited assemblies of this nature, and at the same time permitted quack-doctors, mountebanks, gaming-houses, and taverns, and asking him how he expected to reflect upon these things on his death-bed. The mayor," he adds, "as well **as** the other magistrates, gave way, and acknowledged that I was right."

Returning home, he found the anxiety as great as ever. Himself almost ashamed that God should take into His hand an instrument so unworthy, he would still have shrunk from the great work. "I have need," we find him saying to a friend, who was commending him **for** his untiring zeal, "I have need to retire **into a** hovel, to weep over my sins." And again :—" O God, thou seest that I know myself **to** be but a poor, weak, and helpless infant." But necessity was laid upon him, and he labored on. "Last Thursday, at eight o'clock," **he** writes, " when I had scarcely risen from my bed, and that with difficulty, in order to answer a letter which **I** had received by express, **I** was **told** that a whole troop of country people were entering the house, anxious to speak **with** me ; and before half an hour elapsed, nearly **fifty** had assembled. I spoke to them on Isa. lv. 10 ; and, whilst speaking, **a** powerful emotion manifested itself amongst the auditory, **and** afterwards I suffered some, who were in great anxiety about their souls, to converse with me in private." So earnest on these occasions were his words, so clear **and** so tender his exhibition of Christ, and so endued withal with power from on high, that the inquirers rarely failed

to obtain real peace. "You have no need," he used
to say, "to have recourse with so much anxiety to
such a poor creature as I am for advice. You have
the best guide and Teacher unspeakably near you."
Tersteegen, like the Baptist, was continually saying,
"HE must increase—I must decrease."

Most affecting scenes were continually occurring.
There was present one day a poor widow, who had
lived a most ungodly life. As the Word was spoken,
she was suddenly wounded with a sense of sin. **At**
the close, she came to him in a state of dreadful agitation, and "began, unsolicitedly," says Tersteegen,
"to confess **her sins to me, which, I acknowledge,**
were very **great. As** she seemed **to** be in such **de-**
spair," he adds, "I encouraged her to tell me all that
lay upon her mind, assuring her I would keep it
secret. 'What!' said she, 'keep it secret! Tell it
to the whole world! I am not afraid of being dis-
graced in the opinion of mankind. I would gladly
bear the severest torments, **and am** willing to be consumed even to **a skeleton, if I may only** find favor in
the sight of God.'"

Another day, a little boy about eleven years of
age, was **brought by** his mother, who had herself re-
cently found Christ, to hear the story of the **Cross.**
With great kindliness he spoke to him of sin, and of
wrath, and of the atoning Saviour; and, taking him
by the hand at parting, he asked him if he would
not that day cast in his lot with Jesus. "He seemed
to wish," wrote Tersteegen afterwards, "not to hear

me. However, on reaching home, he said to his mother, ' The devil wanted to hinder me from attending to what Tersteegen said ; but yet I have heard every word very well, and resisted the devil.' And, since that time, the boy is become very silent, and goes often alone into the fields, or elsewhere, where he can conceal himself, to pray, and weeps in secret over his sins in such a manner that even his father, who was before opposed to the truth, appears to be much affected and struck by it." Among the Indians, Brainerd tells us that little children were frequently thus arrested. On one ocaasion, he says, several, " not more than six or seven years old," were " brought into deep distress." And " it was apparent," he adds, " that they were not merely *frighted* with seeing the general concern, but were made sensible of their danger, of **the** badness of their hearts, and (as some of them expressed it) of their ' misery without Christ.' " So was it under the words of Tersteegen. " Children of twelve, or fourteen years old," he writes, " are awakened." Fathers ! mothers ! what are you doing for **your** children's **souls** ' Children ! what are you doing **for** your own ?

A student was awakened one day as he was speaking to a little company at Duisburg. The young man, engrossed with his books and his studies, had, with a name to live, been living without God and without Christ. " A man," said Tersteegen that **evening, " who** retains his previous habits and infirmities from one year to another, has great cause to consider whether he be not a tree without life—a branch which is not in the vine. **What** are all our virtues, and all our piety, unless fellowship with Jesus lie at the bottom of it ?" The words went to the student's conscience—he was stung with intense alarm. **An**-other evening, he hung on the preacher's lips as he was setting forth the marvels of God's grace. " Be-hold," said he—" and oh ! that every eye was really opened to see it ! behold how God loves us in Christ, and how tenderly He loves us ! How ought all those to be ashamed, who represent God as a tyrant and a misanthrope ! There is no wrath in God, ex-cept against **sin.**" The young man **decided to** come that night with his sin to Jesus, and to lay it on Him, and to leave it on Him. And, finding peace at His **feet,** he went about everywhere, " calling the people to repentance." Young man ! have you found peace ? Then, what are you doing to publish abroad among perishing men the glad tidings of great joy ?

CHAPTER V.

"Speak with thy God"—Prayer and the tempter—A little heaven—
Sect and party—Genial sympathies—"Thy neighbor"—Maxims on
self-denial—Where we live, and how we live—Fellowships—"Eternal love"—Labors.

AMIDST all these labors, Tersteegen took heed most
scrupulously to his own soul. "Speak with none so
gladly," he used to **say**, "as with **thy** God." **And
any** engagement, even in itself holy, which **gave** his
soul a disrelish for HIM, **he** felt to **be a** snare. "Let
us accustom ourselves," he wrote **on** one occasion **to**
a friend, **who** had sought his counsel on this matter,
"the whole day long, **and even** whilst in business, to
the Lord's presence, and **seek, in** simple faith, to make
ourselves known **to** Him, and **to become** intimate
with **Him in our** hearts : but," he added, " we must
have a frequent seclusion in order **to** this sweet and
prayerful exercise of recollection and retiring to God

in our hearts." Yes, young man! if, with Nehemiah before the king, you are to lift up your heart to God in the crisis of each day's emergencies, you must retire with Nehemiah into your closet each day, and there live for some time alone with Him. " A soul without prayer," wrote Tersteegen on another occasion, " is like a solitary sheep without a shepherd. The tempter sees it, and lures it away into his snare."

Next to his God, there were none whose society Tersteegen loved so well as the saints. " He is lovely in Himself," he would say, " and lovely in His children." And the more he saw of Christ in any saint, the more his heart was drawn **to** him.

" How few there are," he remarked one day, " **w**hose fellowship is really a spiritual advantage to us! I can often grieve like a child to see some, even pious people, trifle so much, and not employ their time better." With such he felt little in common. But place him amongst a few brethren who were really devoted to God, **and** it seemed **to him** like a little foretaste of heaven. His eye glistened, and **his** words dropped **fatness.**

Tersteegen lived too **near the Lord** to set much store by **sect** or by party. " **I** ask not whence they come," he would say, " but whither they are going." He loved the saints in spite of their defects ; and, if **a** defect or an error in a brother was to be corrected, he handled it so lovingly that, whether surrendered or no, the sin was felt to be there. " Let us extinguish the fire," he would say, " but *with water.*"

Tersteegen was singularly *human*—of warm affections and of a genial heart. "I do not like," he would say, "the indifference of a Stoic, but would willingly participate in the joys and the sorrows of my brethren." One day, in a family which he often visited, he was speaking a few words of consolation on the removal of one of its members, who had been very dear to him. As he spoke, he broke off abruptly—tears hindering further utterance. "How could you be so childish as to weep?" said some one to him afterwards. "Well," he answered, "perhaps it was childish; but believe me, I feel more and more depressed in the world, when those who **are** so wholly devoted to God take their departure from **it.**"

"Love thy neighbor as thyself," is the Lord's command. Notwithstanding our constant faults and shortcomings, we still care for ourselves. Do we still care for our neighbor, and love him, notwithstanding his errors and deficiencies? Few men ever loved their neighbors as themselves with a steadfastness and a patience like Tersteegen's. "Think no ill of thy brother," he would say; "judge not; be not hasty; **put** the best construction upon everything." And again: "Love those **who** do not walk in all things as thou dost; let every one go his own way; what is that to thee? Follow Jesus."

And nothing could be more wise and considerate **than** the counsels he addressed **to** the troubled and the distressed. "We must not prescribe," we find him saying **to** one, "too many laws of self-denial for peculiarities, but leave grace to counteract them, and chiefly insist upon a complete surrender of the heart." And to another, thus : " You must not be too scrupulous in your devotional exercises : good children do what is given them to perform, as well as they are able, and are desirous of improving every day. May filial love govern you in all things! The picking up of a straw with an intention to please God, is of greater value in His sight, than the removal of mountains without such intention."

And, on another occasion : **" Y**our happiness or unhappiness does not depend upon *the house*, **but** upon the **state of mind.** When it is well within, all **is** well. Consent sincerely to **your** nothingness and misery, and submit to be found such as you **are ;** the Lord is then with you, and will break your fetters." And again : " I repeat—it is not the houses : inwardly wrong, all wrong ; inwardly well, all well—everything and everywhere well. It is alike to the Lord where we live, but not how we live. **A** royal palace is too narrow **for** him who lives to himself; and a little cot**tage is** large and beautiful to him who lives **to the** Lord."

To a friend who **was in** danger of another **snare,** he said one day : " Avoid all unnecessary intercourse with those who make great pretensions to reason. Suffer not yourself to be detached from simplicity in Christ, by any pretence of superior knowledge and wisdom. Nature seeks room, and avoids confinement. The poor and simple life of Jesus is offensive to scornful reason, which sophisticates until it has found a convenient middle way which just terminates in a point with the broad way. With respect to us, let us be affectionate children; dying, praying, loving shall be our wisdom. Let reason scorn us as long as she pleases; we shall see who fares the most peaceably, and to whom the heavenly Father will reveal His mysteries."

And a growing brotherliness drew him nearer and nearer to fellow-pilgrims. "If we only detach ourselves more from all secondary things and notions," he writes, indirectly indicating his own way in this matter, "and exercise ourselves in that which is alone needful, seeking how we may be truly faithful, in dying to the world and to all false life, and in remaining near to God in simplicity of heart—our spirits then flew together, as of themselves, in delightful unanimity and unity. In this way eternal love delights to dwell among us, and to bless us, as the dew which falls on Hermon; and we evermore deeply experience the unknown blessings which are to be enjoyed in the *true fellowship of the saints.* Seeing that we have cast out the world, and the world has cast us out— let us therefore give each other the hand, and, as strangers and pilgrims, brotherly and courageously go forward, in one mind and spirit, to the happy land of inward and eternal fellowship with God in Christ Jesus."

The earnest man continued his labors. "Since my last," we find him writing, April 9, 1751, " the people scarcely ever let me rest. I try occasionally to withdraw myself by force ; but it is of no avail. Last Sunday, I had scarcely risen from my bed, when I was obliged to address more than **sixty** persons, who had thronged into the house, which **I** accordingly **did** from Matt., xxv. 5. After **I** had done speaking, **I** had to converse with various individuals **until** evening. **And** yesterday morning, after I had passed the whole night in a fever, at least two hundred and fifty people assembled in the corn-loft and in **the** room adjoining, to whom **I** spoke, with the Lord's gracious assistance, from Gal., i. 3–5. I have also been obliged to speak this morning, early, without knowing of **it a** quarter **of** an hour before. But now I feel myself quite exhausted. I spoke to-day on the last words of the Lord Jesus, ' It is finished !' and comforted myself with the hope that my toils and troubles would also soon be finished."

CHAPTER VI.

The Furnace—"Self-made heroes"—Lessons in the fire—The "one thing"—Last address—The wood—New sufferings—Reproaches—Backsliders—The angels' praise, and Job's—"Something noble."

The Lord was refining him in His **furnace-fire.** "Up to the present moment," he writes, March 20, 1753, "I can scarcely use my head or my eyes, and my hand trembles very much; the little rest I have had, owing to the concourse **of** people, may have been the principal occasion of it. I cannot think what the people seek from such a poor creature. A **short** time ago, a person totally unknown to me, but a true Nathanael, came nearly two hundred miles on foot, in bad weather, **to** visit me; but who, on such occasions, can withdraw himself entirely?"

And these trials and labors were not unblest to **him.** "**If** we **have** already tasted and experienced much," he said, **one day, in the** autumn **of 1755,** "**and have** passed **through many** trials, the result ought to be a lovely, artless, and childlike spirit."

And another day he said :—" The Lord lets us feel our weakness in the season of trial, in order that we may be no self-made heroes, but creep the more helplessly into His strength, and that He may be all things and alone in us." And another day, **a friend** was remarking how much trouble God had in bringing up His children. "Yes," said Tersteegen, "and in bringing them down !" These were the lessons which the mellowed saint was learning in the fires.

And another lesson which, amidst his incessant labors and deep trials, he was learning was, **the** necessity of waiting upon God **and** of checking the restless and impatient "flesh." "When we cease to **care** and labor," he would say, "then **God** begins, **and will be** all **in** our nothingness." And again :— " Our Lord Jesus was silent and kept Himself concealed for thirty years, in order that, by His example, He might inspire us with a fondness for a truly retired life ; and scarcely did He spend four years in a public manner. It **is a secret** but common temptation of the enemy, and **a subtle** device of **the** flesh, by which the tempter would allure us from **the** only thing needful, and weaken our strength by the multiplicity **of** the objects in which we engage." And, on another occasion, thus :—" All you have to do, is to love Christ, to abide in Him, and **you** shall bear much fruit. Does the branch of **the vine** find it difficult to bear sweet grapes ? Is it necessary to compel it to do so, by commanding, threatening, and rough usage ? Oh, no ; the whole process takes place very quietly, easily, and naturally; the branch merely abides in the vine, and imbibes its precious sap, and then it flourishes and bears fruit without any further trouble. It is thus that we ought also to act."

It was in the spring of 1756 that, for the last time, he addressed the assembled people. So many had come together, that he was obliged to fill with his voice five or six rooms of his house. The bow, so long stretched, was at length broken. From that day, he was unable **to** do more than take an occasional short ride into the country, or saunter into a neighboring wood, where, in company with a few friends who had come from a distance to see him, he would enjoy a simple repast, savored with the salt of his own meek and heavenly converse.

New sufferings came on him. His whole life had been little else than one painful illness; but now the furnace was heated seven times. "A week ago," he writes, "I was attacked by catarrh in the head causing such acute pain, night and day, that my head throbbed convulsively every moment." And again:—"On Friday morning before Whitsuntide, in writing an urgent letter, I was seized with a trembling from head to foot. In the evening I was attacked by fever, and by a pain **in** the limbs so acute that I knew not where to put myself." And another time:—"I have an eruption over **my** whole body, and my **back** is so sore that my shirt adheres to it." And during these latter years his stomach was so weak that he had a repugnance to every sort of food. "I am always sorry," he would say, " when my dinner is brought up, for **the** lightest food causes me much difficulty and pain."

Added to these trials were sufferings of another kind. One blamed him for doing too much, another for doing too little ; a third, envying him for his gifts, spoke evil of his work. And, of all his griefs, none penetrated his soul so deeply as the unholy walk of a disciple. " Oh, what a load of anxiety and care," he exclaimed on one such occasion, accompanying the words with a mournful sigh, " do those occasion me, who, divinely **called, yet walk** unfaithfully **before** the Lord ! It gives me so much pain, **that I am** often obliged to **throw** myself on **my face** before God."

But he was made " more than conqueror, through Him that loved him." " Is it anything wonderful," he said to a friend, who came to him one evening in great distress of spirit, " that the angels praise God ?" " No," replied the sufferer ; " for if we were in their place, we should do likewise." **"That** is also my opinion," rejoined Tersteegen ; **" but** when Job praised God whilst sitting in the ashes, that **was** something noble, and his praise pleased Him better than that of angels." Such praise he himself was offering now, in his own " great fight of afflictions.'

CHAPTER VII.

'Breathing of the holy soul"—Sinking into Christ—The sick child—
"Gladly weak"—"Always poor"—Going Home—Death-bed—"Thou
all, I nothing"—Conclusion—"Entirely God's."

A HOLY man once said, writing to a deeply tried friend—" How blessed, that, when the soul is in a holy frame, the exertion of prayer is so little felt as not to oppress even the languishing body! The natural breathing of the holy soul is prayer, which enters into the ears of **the** Father." And another departed saint, at the time sorely pressed by weakness, said :—" We can sink into Christ, though we cannot rise to Him." Gerhard **was** tasting this joy. "On account of the weakness of my head," he writes, "I am often unable to think either of God or of my own soul; but I know that 'God is'—that He is the great, the good, the ever-blessed God. The mere recollection of this is unspeakable rest to me." And **again** :—" Just as a sick child upon its mother's lap causes the pain it feels to be understood only by the moving expression of its eyes—so **endure in the presence** of God, simply looking up to Him."

As he hastened onward, the simplicities of faith grew more and more precious to **him.** "Our life," he remarked one day, " is **an** infancy and commencement of an eternal life." And it seemed as if, **in** infancy of heart, he was daily gaining more distinctly the lineaments of the " little child," who alone can enter the kingdom. " I am like a poor man," he writes, " who has nothing in reserve, and would **be** always like a poor child, who desires neither to know nor to possess anything." And another day : " I feel I must do nothing, and desire nothing ; and, letting God do what seemeth **Him good, be** as a child, **contented.**" And again **: " I am** gladly **weak,** in order not to run without God—that His **glory and** power may be perfected in my nothingness." And once again : " I am lost in adoration when I reflect that God has selected such a way to eternal glory as takes away everything from the creature, and gives it all to God, and, consequently, sweetly compels us to cleave most closely to Him—to abide and live **in** Him and upon Him—and **to** continue always poor, **that we** may in reality possess all things—a way for children, but only for naked children—a way which the wise overlook." And, in one feature of his trials, this growing childlikeness solaced his heart peculiarly. " Seek to become," said he one day to a friend, desiring to comfort him with the abundant consolation with which he himself had been comforted **of** God, " seek to become inwardly a little innocent child, that finds fault with nothing, and lets all the world act and speak of it, even in its presence, as they please, without once regarding it, or letting itself be troubled **by it."**

"The end of all our lamentations is—going home." So said Tersteegen one day in the spring of 1769, and that home he was now speedily to enter. Towards the end of March, he was seized with an asthma, which obliged him to sit forty-seven hours together in his arm-chair, sometimes leaning **backwards** for a few minutes on the chair, and then again forward on **a** cushion upon the table. Friend after friend came in ; and, whilst they were overwhelmed at the sight of agony so acute, he spoke to each, according to their peculiar circumstances, in **a** manner **so edifying** and so comforting that they were all affected even to tears. "Oh, sister, the way is a good way," he said to one; "follow the Lamb with cheerfulness whithersoever He leads you." And **to** another : "I commend **you,** through **grace,** to the love of Jesus ! Let the present moment induce you to surrender yourself entirely to our dearest Saviour." And to a third : "Ask His grace, like the woman of Cana : ask it without regard to temporal things, which are of less value than **is** generally supposed. What a happiness it is, when obliged to part with them, to have a gracious God in Christ !" And to a fourth **he** whispered : "Outwardly **very** weak, but inwardly overflowing with love !"

On the morning of April 2, the pain somewhat abated ; **and,** during all that day, he had successive fits of slumber, deepening and lengthening as night drew on. "Yes, Amen!" he said, as he awoke out of one **of** them; "Thou all! I nothing!" And at another waking moment, "O God! O Jesus! **O** sweet Jesus!" They were his last whispers; and at two in the morning of the 3rd April, he passed upward into His presence, to wait with Him for "that day."

A life like this is its own interpreter. Who will arise and follow Tersteegen, **as** he followed Christ?

"Oh, how seldom," **he once** exclaimed, "do **we** meet with those **who are** *entirely* God's! Alas! on every side we see scarcely anything but dead bones, **dead** hearts, **dead** formalists, dead words, dead works, **a** dead walk, dead worship!" Were Tersteegen amongst us, would he have any reason to utter the same lamentation?

Reader! you yourself best know whether *you* are now ENTIRELY God's. **You** that **are** hesitating to **be** wholly on the Lord's **side**; oh, **that we** could **per**-suade you how willingly the Lord would become **to** you **"your treasure,** your **portion,** your **all!"** It **is** not head-notions, **however** captivating, **which will** here avail **you.** "Nature finds it easier," **said Ter**-steegen, on one occasion, "to amuse herself with **ideas,** than to suffer and **to** die." Your religion must have **power** in it, not **only** to carry you **along** the path of sunshine, but to carry you up to cross-bearing, and through it. And, if **you are** to have this power, you must get it at the BLOOD—you must be accepted in your crucified and risen Lord. Are you so accepted? Is the blood on your conscience?

And then, if accepted in Christ, what are you doing for Him? "Keep this truth," said Tersteegen one day to a Christian young man, "firmly and unshakenly, with the help of God—that your heart, and inmost love, belong wholly, undividedly, and eternally, to God alone ; **and** remain devoted **to** Him, come what may. Regard Him as I do, as your only treasure, comfort, support, and salvation ; and you shall experience peace and blessedness wherever and howsoever you may be, both now and for ever." Yes, grasp that truth—grasp it firmly—and you are girded for all labor and for all trial.

III.

The Christian Man of Letters:

JAMES MONTGOMERY.

" The love of Nature, **and** the power
   To **read her** glowing page ;
The pleasures of each passing hour,
   In youth, or riper age ;
The buoyant, bounding pulse of health ;
   The strength for **duty's** task ;
Bright thoughts, **and** garnered mental **wealth**
   More than thy soul didst ask ;—
These are the gifts of God—Rejoice ! **rejoice !"**

" The hope **of** better things to come,
Of higher joys in store;
The vision of a brighter home,
Where change shall vex no more;
All that the present brings to thee
Of blessings in their bloom ;
All that the great Eternity
Can yield beyond the tomb ;—
These are the gifts of God—Rejoice! rejoice!"

IT is recorded **of** Count Zinzendorf, that in his boyhood he would sometimes **write a** little **note to** his Saviour, telling **Him** how his heart felt **toward** Him, **and would throw it** out **of** the window **in the** hope **that He** might find **it. And in** his **manhood,** casting aside **the** boyish romance as to the channel **of** the fellowship, but realizing even more intensely the fellowship itself, he would often, in his **missionary** travels, be found diverging into **some solitary** path, **that** he might **converse more** unreservedly **with** Jesus, **speaking** to Him face **to** face, as **if He were** personally **at his side.**

JAMES MONTGOMERY "learned **Christ" in the same** simple, heart-touching school. "Whatever we did," he writes, referring **to his** ten-years' residence at the **Moravian** Seminary **of Fulnec,** "**was** done for the **sake of** Jesus Christ, **whom we were** taught to regard in the amiable and endearing light of a Friend and Brother." The Gospel, as the glad tidings of God's wondrous love to sinners, is comprehended **only** by the heart; **for** only **love** can comprehend **love.** **It** is such a religion of the heart which we **are now** to contemplate, in the Christian Bard whose name we have just pronounced.

CHAPTER I.

The Moravian settlement—Its Founder—"A hardy worker"—The
father—The lad behind the plough—The birth-place—The voyage—
" The faith of that child"—The missionary—Fulnec—The sunshine—
" That tincture"—The poetic fire—The " Coal ass"—The hedge—
Stolen interviews—School-days—Wakefulness—Epic—The prayer.

ABOUT the middle of last century, in a rustic spot
in the county of Antrim, there was founded a Moravian settlement of earnest, praying men—who,
awakened by the same divine visitation **as** had stirred the stagnant waters by the hand of **W**esley and
of Whitefield, used to traverse **all** the surrounding
country, preaching in simple fervor the message of
grace. **"He was** truly a great soul," said Whitefield,
on one occasion, speaking of John Cennick, the
founder of the Settlement, and its presiding spirit—
" one of those ' weak' things' which God hath chosen
to confound the strong. Such **a** hardy worker with
his hands, and such a hearty preacher at **the** same
time, I have scarce known. All call him a second
Bunyan."

There comes one day to a village-preaching, where this " second Bunyan" is holding forth the Word of life, a young man of the neighborhood who earns his daily bread by hard field labor. John Montgomery is observed to be unusually grave that evening, as the preacher proclaims his simple but telling message. Moved into anxiety, and, by and bye, finding rest at the feet of Jesus, he enters the ministry; and, after divers wanderings in England and in Germany under the guidance of his Moravian brethren, he ultimately settles in the town of Irvine, a sea-port on the western coast of Scotland, having previously married, in 1768, an estimable member of the little community in Antrim, who is destined to be the mother of JAMES MONTGOMERY.

Some dozen miles distant, on a small farm owned by his father, there might be seen in those years, " whistling behind the plough," a rustic lad, who was already beginning to feel those poetic inspirations which were one day to immortalize " the land of Burns." In the humble dwelling of the Moravian pastor—still extant in Irvine as a weaver's shop—is ushered into the world, on November 4, 1771, another bard, who is to sweep his lyre to a more heavenly symphony.

Returning a few years afterwards to Ireland, his parents send him in his sixth year to Fulnec, near Leeds, in Yorkshire, to be trained after the fashion of the Brethren. On the voyage across there arises a terrific storm, which so agitates the captain that he gives up all for lost. "I would give," says he to John Montgomery, after the crisis has passed, "a thousand pounds for the faith of that child." It is the youthful poet to whom he points; for the child has sat all through the tempest calm and composed, as if a more than mortal faith already possessed his heart. "I was, as might be expected," remarked Montgomery long afterwards, alluding to the scene, "afraid at first; but my father told me to trust in the Lord Jesus, who saved the apostles on the water. I did so, and felt composed." In 1783, John Montgomery proceeds as a Missionary to the West Indies; and his son is left at Fulnec, with a patrimony more enriching than gold or than broad acres—the blessing of the self-denying disciple's God.

On a pleasant eminence, some six miles from Leeds—once surrounded by a desert of rough moorland, but now the centre of a tract of richly cultivated soil—stands a range of buildings, known to this day as the hamlet or "settlement" of Fulnec. Though exposed in winter to a biting wind, which comes sweeping up the valley from the south—it is delightful in summer, the sun seeming to repose on the side of the hill, and in front of the Seminary. These genial sunbeams, like Bunyan's "sunny side of the hill" in his waking dream of the three saints of Bedford, are but shadows of a brighter sunshine within. James Montgomery, in his riper years, always lingered in fond remembrance over that scene.

" Hither," we have him writing, in his " Departed
Days,"

> " From this my native clime,
> The hand that leads Orion forth,
> And wheels Arcturus round the north,
> Brought me in life's exulting prime.
> Blest be that hand! it is the hand of God."

What law and custom ordain elsewhere, is done here
as an act of Christian sacrifice. Work, play, study,
recreation, going out and coming in, rising up and
lying down—all is perfumed with " that tincture,
'For thy sake,' " which

> " Makes drudgery divine."

It is within these walls that our poet first joyously
lifts **a** prayer, which **a** protracted life of service is
never to rob of its fragrance—

> " Teach me, **my** God and King,
> In all things thee to see ;
> And, what I do in any thing,
> To do it as for thee."

The earliest scintillation of the poetic fire is
kindled by hearing one **of the** masters one day,
under a hedge, read Blair's " Grave." " Driven like
a coal-ass" through the Latin and Greek grammars,
distinguished for nothing but indolence, and always
asleep when he ought to be awake, he listens to the
master's recitation that day with an ecstasy which
fires his whole soul—though, before the rehearsal is

half over, his companions are already all asleep. "If ever I become a poet," is his secret whispering to himself, "I will write something like this." Like the child born inland, whom Wordsworth describes as listening to the shell's low murmuring sound of its native sea, it seems as if on that summer day, whilst the future poet sits beneath the shade of that hedge, the music of the spheres is awakening for the first time the kindred harmonies of his genius.

Books are his daily, hourly joy. The forbidden, however, rather than the sanctioned and authorised, are chiefly coveted. "All mankind," we find him writing, "are made of the same **clay** : my curiosity **is** insatiate ; and **the pains which** are taken to con ceal certain **things from** us, only makes us more anxious to explore them." The favorites, **in** those stolen interviews, are the great English poets. With these, up to the age of thirteen, he is almost entirely unacquainted—though he has already filled a little volume with his **own** sacred rhymes. A habit **is** contracted **in** those school-days, **which** remains with him **to** old age. He will frequently retire to rest with **a** half-finished poem on his mind, resolving not to close **his** eyes till **it is** completed. This wakefulness, he tells us, so grew upon him, that **for many** years he never enjoyed one peaceful night.

At the age of fifteen, he conceives the idea of an epic poem, to be entitled "Alfred ;" commencing with the Anglo-Saxon hero **in** his disguise of a peasant in the Isle of Athelney, and proceeding to exhibit a scene in heaven—the Almighty upon a throne looking down in pity on the ruins of England, when suddenly there appear in His presence the spirits of a host of Englishmen who have just perished in battle, bewailing the condition of their country, and imploring God to deliver it. The idea is truly a " boyish daring; but it is the daring of a boy of genius." The epic, however, is not executed; for, whilst his soaring wing is trimming itself for such flights, his heart will be arrested by such words as these, in the Moravian Litany—" Keep us, our dear Lord and God, from untimely projects, from all loss of our glory in Thee, from unhappily becoming great."

CHAPTER II.

"Away! 'Tis time my journey were begun."

"Whether is it better with the many to follow a beaten track,
  Or by eccentric wanderings to cull unheeded sweets?"

The setting out—"A business"—The village inn—The visitor—Wentworth—The "store"—"No **vulgar** boy"—The missionary—Life's battle—London—Goldsmith—"The Row"—The "sixpenny volume"—**The presentiment.**

It is the desire of the Brethren that young Montgomery shall devote himself to the ministry; but a habit of abstraction, gradually withdrawing him from exact studies into that excursive freedom through which minds **like** his are ordinarily ushered into their future, at length induces his teachers to seek for him some other line of service. Accordingly, it is resolved **to "put** him to a buisiness, at least **for a** time." For **a year** and a half, he stands behind the counter of **a** "Fine-Bread Baker" in Mirfield, a village near Fulnec—feeling, like Foster at the **loom, "a** stranger in **the** place," but dissevered finally from that sacred calling to which his parents, ten years before, had devoted him. With little to occupy him, and craving, like some pent-up flower, another ele-

ment of life—he breaks loose one morning, determined

" To view

The world, which yet by fame alone he knew."

With three shillings and sixpence in his pocket, and
with a suit **of** old clothes on his person (for, though
he has just got **a new suit** from his master, he leaves
them behind, not thinking his services have merited
them), and with a single change of linen—here he
is, at the age of sixteen, with the world all before
him, and his spirit at last free.

That night he rests at Doncaster, and the next in a
village near Wentworth, the seat of Earl Fitzwilliam.
As he sits in **the** humble **inn,** wearied and downcast,
a lad comes **in,** and, seeing him with his little bun-
dle, enters into friendly converse. " My father," says
he, " keeps an establishment at a village not far off;
and as he is wanting an assistant just now, probably
you may suit him." The wanderer is thankful ; and
the **next** day he repairs to Wath, and engages himself **to** this new master. Writing **to his** friends at
Fulnec, and also to his late employer at Mirfield, he
obtains a warm recommendation from them, coupled
with an affectionate entreaty on the part of the latter
to return to his service. Meanwhile he ventures into
Wentworth Park with the hope of meeting its noble
owner, and of presenting to him a copy of his verses.
Scarcely has he **entered** the domain, when Lord Fitzwilliam **comes up on** horseback, and, affably accept-
ing the proffered gift, and reading the verses on the

spot, presents their author with a guinea—the first patronage and the first profit which his poetry has yet received. At a future day, he is to be welcomed there as the honored Christian poet.

Behind the counter in a " General Store" in the rustic village of Wath, is to be seen a slender youth, about the age of eighteen, serving with a scrupulous fidelity from morning to night the simple villagers, who find in that universal repository the flour, the sugar, the tea, the cloth, the shoes, the hardware, the all of their humble homes. But there is something about the lad which even their **eye can detect—a** certain grave thoughtfulness which, as he paces the street on some business-errand, will suggest the whisper—" Surely he is no vulgar boy." Of an evening, he saunters to a neighboring village, where the stationer's shop of the district finds in the youthful poet a stated visitor. Into no other ear can his longing spirit pour its irrepressible aspirations.

But though at Wath he meets **no mental sympathy, his heart is** too full of the love **of Jesus not to** spread abroad in his humble dwelling the fragrance of His **name. A** prayer remains which he wrote for his master's sick wife, and which indicates indirectly and very affectingly the tone of his own inner life. " O Father of Eternity !" is one of its impressive sentences, " we adore thy undeserved love **in** giving up thine only **Son out** of thy bosom **to be** a sacrifice for us, when we were aliens **to** God and rebels against our Creator. We thank thee for His hard, uncomfort-

able birth in a stable among the beasts ; for His mer-
itorious life ; for His watching and fasting, His praying and preaching ; for His every action, every thought,
every word.   For us He agonized in the garden of
Gethsemane ; for us His **blessed** head was crowned
with piercing thorns—His sacred back was ploughed
with scourges ; for us **He** was spit upon, buffeted,
abused, blasphemed.   The flaming sword of Justice
was quenched in His heart and blood ; **and** Mercy
opened the gates of Paradise to us His redeemed.
May He see in us the travail of His soul !"

"Nature," says Lord Bacon, in one of his Essays,
" is often hidden, sometimes overcome, but never extinguished."   James Montgomery, in the "Fine-
Bread Baker's" at Mirfield, and in the "General
Store" at Wath, seems in as fair a way for having his
poet-nature extinguished **as** one is able well to con-
ceive. But man is led by a way which he knows not;
and **often it is** not till after many uncouth experiments
that his destiny is at length reached.   Our poet's
next trial **of** life's buffetings is in London. His friend
the bookseller of Swinton, having forwarded to a bib-
liopole of the " Row" a manuscript volume of his poetry, the youthful author in a few days follows—literally, like the pilgrim-father of Mesopotamia, "not
knowing whither he goes."

Washington Irving, describing Goldsmith's first
essay **in** the same direction, speaks of him as launched
on the great metropolis, or rather **as** drifting about
its streets, at night, in the gloomy month of Feb-

ruary, with **but a few halfpence in his** pocket—the deserts of Arabia not **more dreary and** inhospitable than the streets **of London at such a** time, and **to a** stranger in such **a** plight. **The young Moravian** has a heavenly compass **in his** hand, **which poor** Oliver never knew ; but scarcely less friendless does he feel in that vast wilderness. The magnate **of the Row** gives him a humble situation in his shop—Goldsmith's first refuge was among " the beggars of **Axe** Lane ;" but, like Oliver and his rejected " tragedy," Montgomery finds **no** patron for his prized **volume** of verse. Recommended to turn his hand to prose, **he** hies him, one morning, with **a** production entitled **" Simple Sammy," to a** publisher whose special vocation is " Books, bound and gilt, at one half penny." It is his first prose-work, and is to be a sixpenny volume ; but Marshall put him off, saying as he leaves—" You can write better than this, you are more fit to write for men than for children." A few more essays, scarcely more successful—and the disappointed youth is on his way back to **W**ath again, but feeling within **him** an inextinguishable presentiment that one day **he shall**

> " Strike the lyre
> To nobler themes."

CHAPTER III.

The missionary's grave—The slave—" Son of a missionary"—Solitary hours—" A clerk"—Sheffield—First fibre—Patriotism—The " Iris"—Castle of York—His "den"—The Muses—Discipline—Pensive lyre—" A farewell blessing"—Sympathies—The little dog.

IN a grove of tamarinds, in the island of Barbadoes, a humble tablet meets you—it is a missionary's grave ; and, in a secluded spot in the neighboring island of Tobago, there lie the remains of another good confessor, who, sixteen months before, had been summoned to her heavenly home. They are the earthly resting-places of John and Mary Montgomery, the parents of our youthful wanderer.

Arriving in the West Indies in 1784, they had entered buoyantly, amidst a population of slave-owners, and slave-drivers, and slaves, upon the blessed office of making known the glad tidings of the liberty which maketh free. The negroes they had found so sunk and degraded, that the message of life was but coldly welcomed. " O that I knew but one soul in Tobago truly concerned for his salvation," the missionary **had written,** after being some time in the island **" how should I rejoice !"**

" By Satan more than man **enthralled,"**

the negro would not listen.

At length Mary Montgomery is seized with fever. On the fifth day, the physician expresses some anxiety. " Are you going to leave me alone on this island ?" says the missionary. " Indeed I **should** wish to remain longer with you," replies his **dying** wife, " knowing how much **you want my** assistance; **but the** Lord's **will be done."** " **But if** it should **please Him to call you** home," **he** says tenderly, **" can** you go with **full** confidence into His presence **as a** ransomed sinner **?"** " **O** yes," is the immediate rejoinder; " He indeed knows my weakness and unworthiness, but He knows also that **my** whole reliance is upon His death and merits, **by** which **I, a** poor sinful creature, have been **redeemed;** and I am assuredly convinced that **I shall be with** Him alway." Two **days afterwards, she calmly** falls asleep in Jesus, a **minister of the Church of** England who is present exclaiming, **" God is truly** present here !"

> " From **lip to** lip, from heart to heart,
> Passed the few parting words—' We part !'
> But echoed back, though unexpressed,
> ' We meet again !'—rose in **each breast."**

The meeting **is not long postponed.** A year **later,** John Montgomery **also is** called away. " They finished well," said the poet one day, long afterwards, the tear of filial tenderness rolling down his manly face. "I am the son of a missionary," was his remark on another occasion, as he appeared on a missionary platform. **And,** indicating how truly he had caught that missionary spirit which elevates a man above the littleness of sects **and of** *isms* into the purer and loftier region of God's own light, he added:—" I know but of one mission—the mission of the Son of God—the propagation of our common Christianity throughout the world by Christian missionaries of every denomination."

The tidings reach him during his second sojourn at Wath; and deeply do they move his affectionate heart. Again in the service of his old employer, and his chief occupation the delivery of goods and the collecting of accounts in the surrounding country —he luxuriates in the solitude of the grassy lanes, indulging his poetic fancies, **and** enjoying a graver and a holier fellowship than mortal heart **can** furnish. But another field **is** now to open.

In one of his rounds, he takes up for **a** moment a Sheffield newspaper, when his **eye** falls on an advertisement from **a** house in **want** of a "clerk." It is " **a** Printer, Bookseller, and Auctioneer;" and, **after** sundry preliminaries, Montgomery is engaged. Entering Sheffield in April, 1792, and now in his **twenty**-first year, he finds in the home of his new **employer, Mr.** Gales, the first fibre **fixed by** which he **is** to be firmly rooted during his remaining sixty years.

At this period, the **whole country is** stirred **to its** depths by the political **agitation** originating in **the** French Revolution. **A fervid** spirit like Montgomery's, especially in such **a** scene as Sheffield, is not likely to escape the contagion. At a vast assemblage of several thousand persons, convened **in** February, 1794, by the " Friends of Peace and **of** Reform," a hymn of his is sung in full chorus, three of its stanzas running thus :—

> " O Thou, whose awful word can bind
>   The roaring waves, the raging wind ;
> Mad **tyrants tame,** break down the high,
> Whose **haughty foreheads** beat the sky ;
>
> **Make bare thine** arm, great King of kings !
> That arm alone salvation brings ;
> That wonder-working arm which broke
> From Israel's neck the Egyptian yoke.
>
> Burst every dungeon, every chain ;
> Give injured slaves their right again :
> Let truth prevail, let **discord** cease ;
> Speak—and the world **shall** smile in peace."

Drawn **into this vortex of** political excitement, **not** by a **mere unbridled passion for** change, but **by a** generous **patriotism, which,** like charity, **beginning** at home, goes forth from that centre everywhere **in** search of objects whom it may love **and** bless—he is not the man either to be browbeaten **by** threats, or **to be** cajoled by tempting bribes. Accordingly, no sooner has his employer been compelled by stress of weather to quit **the** helm, than our poet starts a

new enterprise in the shape of the "Sheffield Iris"—
a weekly newspaper, to which for years to come the
energies of his vigorous mind are to be dedicated.

Whatever Montgomery does, he does courageously
and **well.**   **In** those days of political excitement, an
earnest spirit like the editor of the "Iris" is not
likely to go unscathed.   In 1795, he is sentenced
to three months' imprisonment for uttering words
which in calmer times would have secured him a
niche among his country's most leal-hearted and
worthiest citizens.   Accordingly, whilst "cheerfully
resigning himself to suffering," he enters the Castle
of York, " not blushing for his intentions."   A human
verdict may pronounce him " Guilty ;" but it cannot
make him guilty.   "I do feel," he writes from the
prison ; " but I will not sink.   Though all the world
should forsake me, this consolation can never fail me,
that the great Searcher of hearts, whose eye watches
over **every** atom of the universe, knows every secret
intention of my soul ; and when, at the bar of eternal
 justice, this cause shall again be tried, I do indulge
the humble hope that His approving voice shall confirm the verdict which I feel His finger has written
upon my conscience."   **A** second time—not long
after his liberation—he is indicted for libel, and is
found guilty ; and a second time he is incarcerated at
York, his conscience still unburdened.   A few weeks
before **the six** months' imprisonment expires, he for-
wards from his " den" to the " Iris" some verses, in
which he writes :—

SHEFFIELD MANOR LODGE.

Previous to the Storm of March 2, 1793.

Life Studies.

> "Blest with freedom unconfined,
> Dungeons cannot hold the soul:
> Who can chain the immortal mind?
> **None** but He who spans the pole!"

And again, thus :—

> "I know—and 'tis my proudest boast,
> That conscience is itself a host:
> While this inspires my swelling breast,
> Let all forsake me—I'm at rest!
> Ten thousand deaths in every nerve
> I'd rather *suffer* than *deserve!*"

But, notwithstanding these **valorous** contendings and patient endurances, he **does not** feel at home in politics; his mission is poetry. "**In** early life," he remarked, one day, long afterwards, "I sometimes dipped into political controversy; but politics become more and more disagreeable to me; I enter no further into them than my duty, as an editor of a newspaper, compels me to **do:** frequently **do I** wish **I** had nothing to do with them." And **on** another occasion :—"Surely never was moon-struck lunatic more vexatiously haunted by **the foul** fiend than **I** have been through every **nook and** alley of **life by** the Muses!" The Manor-Lodge, an ancient building, since removed, was a favorite haunt in his meditative hours; and it was here that many of his earlier poems were conceived or constructed.

And his inner life is passing through a discipline, tempering his poetic genius into that calm pensiveness which is to **be** the characteristic tone of his lyre. "In no situation of life"—we find him writing from Scarborough, where, after "the narrow circumferance of a prison," he enjoys for a few weeks "the boundless immensity of the ocean"—"have I ever met with unmixed happiness. But shadow relieves the glare of light; the bitter corrects the sweet; and solicitude softens the tone of bliss. And, issuing some months later, in a collected form, a series of poetical effusions which have appeared in the "Iris" during his imprisonment—he speaks of them as "composed in bitter moments"—"the transcripts of melancholy feelings"—"the warm effusions of a bleeding heart." The subdued, chastened brokenness of his spirit, is indicated in some simple lines sent by him to his brother at this period, in reply to a request made, after a long silence, as the latter is leaving Fulnec for the original Moravian settlement in Ireland :—

> "A blessing, brother, ere we part,
>   A farewell blessing you require ;
> **Oh,** if there lives in this cold heart
>   One spark of all our Father's fire :—
> That spark, an humble sacrifice,
>   In prayer for you I send above
> 'Twill bring a blessing from the skies,
>   The blessing of THE GOD OF LOVE."*

And the discipline is quickening his sympathies for the distressed. "As a token of God's remembrance," he writes, with a rare tenderness and de-

* October 15, 1804.

livery, to a humble friend **who** is suffering from loss of health and **of** employment, " I have enclosed **a** five-pound Bank of England note, **which** I hope will be seasonable and **servicable to you in** your present **low estate.** Accept it, Henry; not from **me,** but **from Him** who, though He was rich, yet for **our** sakes became poor, and, by suffering all the ills of poverty (for He had not whereon to lay His head), sanctified them to His people. For His sake, and in His name, receive it; for His sake, and in His name, I send it. I assure you, my dear friend, **that** I feel far more pleasure **in** being, on **this occasion,** the minister of His bounty **to you,** than **I could possibly derive from any** other **disposal of** this small sum, **which I considered to** be **as** sacredly your property, from the moment when He put it into my heart to send it, as it had been mine before."

A little incident of another kind reveals the genial warmth of his tender nature. "The little dog," he writes, describing a visit he has just paid to the " place of his captivity" at York, " who forsook his friends and amily in the **city to come** and live with me, happened to be **in the** yard with his master when I entered; he recognized me in a moment, sprang into my arms, and almost devoured me with joy." The canine instinct is **a** trusty interpreter of a kind, loving nature.

7*

CHAPTER IV.

———

Napoleon—The moon and the laurel—Lady Huntingdon—" Man's
chief end"—Indecision—Fitful gleams—Lights and shadows—" A
coal from the altar"—The " Wanderer in Switzerland"—His " apos-
tasy"—Grave thoughts—Brighter day—The prism—New poem—
Besetting sin—" A new thing in the earth"—The Lord's Table—
Fulnec.

ALLUDING one day to Napoleon's passage of the
Alps with his army and artillery, Montgomery char-
acterized it as "worthy of the daring genuis of a
man who would scale the battlements of the moon
to gather a leaf of laurel." The poet himself has
sought, for many days, the laurel-leaf with what he
calls "a mad ambition;" and a "burning fever"
it has been to him. But there is dawning on him
now, after a season of backsliding, a brighter and
more joyous morning; and its returning light is re-
vealing to his heart a juster estimate of life's great
business. "Man's chief end"——so runs the empha-
tic formula of Christian duty, which, suddenly starting into her memory one day, awoke the late Count-
ess of Huntingdon out of her dream of self-pleasing,

" is to glorify God, and to enjoy Him for ever;"* and these magic words stimulated her to a life of self-denial. James Montgomery, now awakening as from a trance, begins anew to gird up his loins for the Christian race. "It is hard," we find him writing, in March 1807, " to renounce the world and all those pleasures which the world deems not only innocent, but useful and commendable; and yet, methinks, that Christianity requires the sacrifice of them." Not willing to take up his cross and follow the despised and rejected Man of Sorrows through poverty, reproach and tribulation, he yet feels the guilt of indecision hanging heavy on his heart, and outweighing all those little joys for which he is unwilling to relinquish the world. But a "cheering ray of hope, of Christian hope," will break at times through "the pagan darkness" of his mind, "opening heaven to his desiring view;" and the period is now come, when that cheering ray is to be more than a fitful, flickering visitant. " O my friend," he exclaims, describing to a correspondent the return of a brighter season, "how does my heart expand, my soul aspire !"

Yet painfully fitful still are those gleams of sunshine. At times, he will trace with his poetic pencil the lights and shadows of the scene, thus :

> "There is a winter in my soul,
> The winter of despair;

---

* The words occur at the opening of the Westminster Shorter Catechism, which she had been taught in her early youth.

> O when shall Spring its rage control?
>   When shall the Snowdrop blossom there?
> Cold gleams of comfort sometimes dart
> A dawn of glory on my heart,
>   But quickly pass away:
> Thus Northern-lights the gloom adorn,
> And give the promise of a morn
>   That never turns to day!"

And again, he will write, in the way of apology for not sending to a friend a "methodistical hymn"— "I seldom dare to touch holy things. My lips and my heart want purifying with a coal from the altar." Then the cloud will brighten once more; and he will rejoice, though tremblingly, in the hope of final deliverance from his besetting sin—despair; "for it *is* a sin," he will add, "to despair when God proclaims Himself to be Love—despair gives Him the lie."

This condition of heart it was, which gave its pensive tone to the poem which he now published under the title of "The Wanderer in Switzerland," and which at once placed him in the front rank of the poets of his age. But the arrow is infixed too deeply in the heart of the awakened backslider, to suffer him to be lulled again, even by Fame's syren strain, into any repose save that calm rest which is found at Christ's own feet. And such rest, after his protracted wanderings, he is now once more to enjoy; "sitting down under His shadow indeed with great delight."

These years, preceding 1806, he used to describe as the period of his "apostacy." Not that he had lapsed into any outward immorality; but business, and bustle, and exciting scenes had insensibly **drawn** him away from his former habits of godliness, **until** holiness had lost its " beauty," and his spiritual sensibilities their fine edge. But He who once said—" I will restore that which the caterpillar hath eaten," is now drawing near to him in tender mercy; and, though the eminence to which he has risen as a poet imperils his returning brokenness of spirit, the poetic laurel is not to adorn a vain-glorious brow, but to **be** consecrated to God as **a** part of his daily " living sacrifice."

Grave and **earnest** are **the** thoughts which now possess him. **"Here I am,"** we have him saying, for example ; " **and** what **I am** finally here, I must for ever be." And again—

> "I stir the ashes of my mind,
> And here and there a sparkle find,
> That leaps into a moment's light,
> Then dwindles down again in night.
> **Yet** burns a **fire** within **my breast,**
> Which cannot quench, **and** will not rest:
> O for **a** sudden, secret **rent,**
> **In this hard** heart to give **it** vent!
> O for **a gale** of heavenly breath,
> **To** quicken life again from death!"

And another day, alluding to a **visit to** Sheffield **by** Henry Steinhaur and sixteen pupils from Fulnec, most of them introduced into the school by Montgomery himself, **he** says : " Who knows what eternal consequences may result from so many boys and girls hearing the simple Gospel of 'Christ crucified' preached faithfully to them among the Brethren. It warms my cold, and melts my hard heart, sometimes, when I think that I may thus, accidentally, have been the cause of promoting the everlasting welfare of some of my fellow-creatures in this neighborhood, where I came an outcast, and in which I have lived a stranger."

Montgomery has " a temper made for happiness ;" and though, for a time, it has worn a somewhat sombre hue, it begins to brighten under the genial beams of that Sun of righteousness which now again shines down upon him. Writing to his brother, who has been bereaved of a beloved child, he ministers the comfort wherewith **he** himself has now been comforted of God, thus: **"This providence** of God you both feel **has** drawn **you** nearer to Him ; and, the nearer **you have** been drawn to Him, have you not been **the** more strengthened, and comforted, and submissive to His will, till, at length, you had no will of your own, and were enabled to rejoice amidst your affliction, **in** the hope of **the** glory which shall hereafter be revealed ?" And, **in** God's light seeing light, **he is** learning to assign **to** things God's own proportions— God's great things growing great, and God's little things little. " In the Bible Society," said he, one day, in November 1813, at a large meeting in Sheffield for the formation of a Methodist Missionary Society, " all names and distinctions of sects are blended till they are lost, like the prismatic colors, in a ray of pure and perfect light: in the Missionary work, though divided, they are not discordant; but, like the same colors, displayed and harmonized in **the** rainbow, they form an arch of glory ascending **on the** one hand from earth **to** heaven, and **on** the other descending from heaven to earth—a bow of promise, a covenant of peace, a sign that the storm of wrath is passing away, and the Sun of righteousness with healing in his wings breaking forth on **all** nations."

Another poem **now** issues **from his** pen—"The World before the Flood;" and the fresh fame which it brings to him **he** feels to be a new temptation. "How worse than worthless," he writes to the Rev. Dr. Raffles, "how profane, were the exercise of my powers on sacred and solemn themes for my own glory! Yet such is the deceitfulness of the human heart, that in **its** holiest offerings (I speak from the experience of mine), it cannot forget itself and its own merits, **nor** help being pleased in the **eyes** of man to divide with its Maker **that** glory which its language ascribes to Him. This is the peculiarly-besetting sin of poets as well **as** of preachers: **I** said sin, though I should have said temptation; for it is impossible to avoid the temptation, **but it** *is* possible to avoid the sin by continually watching unto prayer against it."

It is a touching utterance which one of our poets has given to the heart's longings in certain of its phases:

> "Behold, Thy dust doth stir;
> It moves, it creeps, it aims at Thee.
> Wilt Thou defer
> To succor me,
> Thy pile of dust, wherein each crumb
> Says 'Come?'"

And again, thus:

> "Lord JESU, hear my heart!
> Which hath been broken now so long,
> That every part
> Hath got a tongue.
> Thy beggars grow; rid them away,
> To-day.
>
> My love, my sweetness, hear!
> By these Thy feet, at which my heart
> Lies all the year,
> Pluck out thy dart:
> And heal **my** troubled breast, which cries,
> Which dies"

James Montgomery, though still sad and downcast in moments of self-inspection, is already enjoying unconsciously the light and the life of God. The man who has learned on his knees to crucify that besetting "temptation," is once more in confidence at the feet of the Crucified, "begging himself rich." At a Missionary festival, held in Sheffield (May, 1814), he spoke with great fervor. "The Lord," said he, "has created 'a new thing in the earth'— the disciples of Christ not only loving as brethren, but those who from some difference of opinion before acted separately, now uniting in one purpose to promote their Master's cause among men." **And,** very solemnly he added :—" There is danger in running with the multitude **to do** evil, when, amidst the **con-**tagion of example, and the tumult of publicity, the sinner seems to lose his personal responsibility in **the** crowd, and the guilt, divided among thousands, appears to attach to none, though, in truth, it attaches to each as if each acted alone ! There is danger also in running with the multitude to do good—danger in trying to escape from *ourselves* among **the** people of God. We may have a name among Christians ; we may be affected by the external solemnity of **divine worship; we may** delight **in the joy and** animation of meetings like this ; and yet be devoid of the spirit and power of godliness." At the close of the festival he was persuaded so far to overcome his anxieties as to sit down with the assembled friends and brethren at the Lord's Table. And, when it was over, he was not ashamed to write in the " Iris" concerning it :—" It **was a** season of humble and **holy joy, such as will be** remembered **even in** heaven with gratitude." The words were evidently the expression of his **own** personal thanksgiving. At the end of the year he was formally **re-**admitted into the Moravian fellowship at **Fulnec,** rejoicing once again to " devote himself to **the** Lord and to His people."

CHAPTER V.

IN one of his sonnets, George Herbert thus articulates the Christian heart's desire, the Christian's missionary yearnings :—

> "Lord, I will mean **and** speak thy praise,
> Thy praise alone !
> My busy heart shall spin it all my days."

And again :—

> "Wherefore **I** sing. Yet, since my heart,
> Though pressed, runs thin ;
> Oh, that I might some other hearts convert,
> And so take up at use good store ;
> That to thy chests there might be coming in
> Both all *my* praise, and more !"

With **James** Montgomery the missionary enterprise **now takes its** place **as** "the greatest **and the** best work in the world—the work of God **himself.**"

"Pray, do not disappoint **me**," **he** writes, urging the attendance **of a** speaker at **a** missionary meeting; "I am **not alone in this** request; I **am the** proxy of six hundred millions of pagans—and how many Jews, Mahometans, and Christians, verily I know not."

And, some months later, in a literary Review, **he** writes :—"It is a fact awfully illustrative of the essential depravity of the heart, that, while the greatest energies of the greatest minds—the utmost means of the most enlightened nations—are, more or **less,** continually exercised in **achieving the** destruction **of** their species and **the** desolation of nature, the labors of the missionary are by numbers treated as visionary, and by others deemed expensive." And he adds :— "In Greenland alone—a country overlooked by all the philanthropists of Europe, except by a few Danish or Moravian missionaries—more good **has** been done to mankind, and, certainly, more glory **given** to God, than has been directly accomplished **by all** the **wars** of Christendom, **from the** days of Gustavus Adolphus **to** those of Napoleon Buonaparte."

His clear head **and sound** heart give to his trumpet a not **uncertain** sound. "The wisdom of **man,**" he writes, "**says, '** first civilize barbarians, and then Christianize them ;' and the wisdom **of man has** proved itself '**foolishness**' in every experiment **of** the kind which it has made, though it must be confessed that it has been too prudent or **too** selfish to make many. The wise counsel of **God is** very different

No motives less powerful than conviction of sin, fear of hell, faith in Christ as a Saviour, His love shed abroad in their hearts, and the hope of everlasting life, can command attention from fierce, obstinate, sensual savages, to plans of civilization—much less **wean them** from their roving, indolent, cruel habits, and make them stationary, social, self-denying beings." And, urging the necessity of a consecration of every energy to the work, he adds :—" We are commanded to love the Lord our God *supremely*, and to serve Him *only;* it follows that we must serve Him in the same manner as we love Him— with all our heart, and soul, and mind, and strength —with all our corporeal and intellectual faculties, with all our affections, and all our attainments."

Cowper, in his "Task," speaking of "the free- man whom the truth makes free," has written :—

> " He looks abroad **into** the varied field
>   Of Nature, and, though poor perhaps, compared
>   With those whose mansions glitter in his sight,
>   Calls **the** delightful scenery all his own.
>   His are the mountains, and the valleys his,
>   And the resplendent rivers. His to enjoy
>   With a propriety that none can feel,
>   But who, with filial confidence inspired,
>   Can lift to heaven an unpresumptuous eye,
>   And, smiling, say—' My Father made them all !' "

Only by the Cross can a *sinner* ascend to God: **then,** having reached Him, and found Him recon- ciled, the sinner descends to God's Nature. Montgomery had an exquisite eye for the beauties of creation; and nothing grieves him now **so much as to** find a poetic interpreter of these beauties standing in Nature's Temple as her priest, and bringing in his hand **a** Cain-like offering. In a critical review of Wordsworth's " Excursion," after the most generous appreciation of its real merits as a " work which *would* live," he boldly, though with tenderness, places him at the Gospel-bar, thus :—" The love of Nature is the purest, the most sublime, and **the sweetest emotion of the mind, of which** the senses are the ministers ; **yet the love of Nature** *alone* cannot ascend from **earth to heaven, conducting us, as by** the steps of **Jacob's ladder,** to the **love** of God ; nor **can** it descend **from heaven** to earth, leading **us,** by **similar** gradations, **to** the universal love of man; otherwise, it had not been necessary for Him, who ' thought it not robbery to be equal with God,' to take upon Himself ' the form **of** a servant,' and die ' the just for the unjust, that **He might** bring **us to** God' by **HIMSELF.**"

Cowper's maxim is one never to be forgotten :—

> " Acquaint thyself with God, if thou wouldst taste His **works.**"
> "So reads he **Nature,** whom the lamp of Truth Illuminates."

7*

CHAPTER VI.

Instinct—"Love in the Spirit"—"Feeble in Splendor"—Plying the oar—The Iris—A scene—Holding the candle—The Sunday School—The little group—Prayer—Greenland; Privations and self-denial—Appeal—Wild Arab—Compassion—Public affairs—Holy walk—Robert Hall—Vicarious sacrifice—Christ's divinity—"Songs of Sion."

VINET has **somewhere** said, **that** the attachment which does not become " a love **in** the Spirit" is **to** be classed with those instincts **which** man shares with **the** lower animals. Montgomery's heart, **now warmed and** purified by **the** grace of Christ, expands year **by year** into a wider, and intenser, and **more** Christ-like **love.** After "enjoying the holy communion" at Fulnec, and, though " staggering sometimes **in** bearing the cross up **the** rugged steep of Calvary," **yet.** " borne **up** by the **right** hand of Him whom he **has accom**panied there"—**he goes** forth into the midst of **his fellows, his** face **shining** with **a** certain **divine halo, and** speaks to them thus :—" What **is the** bond of this Association ? Love—Christian love—

the love of God shed abroad in our hearts, and endearing us to each other. This love is not like gold, which, being expanded under the hammer, exchanges solid weight for feeble splendor! It is **not like** water, spilled out of a vessel, and spreading over a large superficies, but promptly **absorbed** into the earth, or exhaled into the atmosphere. No—

> " 'Love is a spirit, all compact with fire;
> Love is a spirit, and will to heaven aspire:'

Yes; and, in proportion as it rises above, it spreads below, increasing in splendor and intensity precisely according to its elevation and diffusion."

Though the turmoil of politics grows less and **less** congenial to him, **he** continues manfully to ply the oar. "Politics," he writes in September, 1816, "I hate with so perfect a hatred, that I meddle **with** them no more than I can help. And, if I could dispose of my newspaper for its value, I should rejoice to be at peace from **them, at least** with my hands and my head, for ever. Meanwhile, however, I shall not disguise my sentiments, whenever it seems **my** duty to **avow** them." And, in announcing, **some** months **later,** the **accession** of a partner, he adds:— "The independence of character which this journal has ever maintained, through evil report and good report, shall never be forfeited, whatever **other** changes may take place in the editor's years, in his person, or **in** his circumstances—so long as **he has** the fear of **God** before his **eye, and** the love of his country in his heart. Engaged in an enterprise, honorable, but hazardous—we are determined, to the best of our knowledge and ability, to do our duty : if we succeed, well ; if we fail, we have done our duty ; millions succeed with doing less—who can do more ?"

One day in a public meeting in Sheffield, there stands upon the platform an aged woman of sixty, reading a chapter of the New Testament. She has begun her alphabet a few months previously in a Sunday-school ; and, " with spectacles on nose," she plies her task before the assembly—a kind, joyous face " cheek by jowl" with hers, for she needs a candle to be held up to her as she slowly, but surely, deciphers the words of life. " It has been my lot, at various periods," says James Montgomery, as the venerable dame resumes her seat, " to be exposed to the effects of malicious slander and detraction, and to the still more dangerous temptations of praise and flattery ; but never, during my whole life, have I felt myself so deeply humbled, or so honorably exalted, as during the time I have held the light for my venerable sister, and have listened to her voice. She has read the words of eternal life, which are able to make her, as well as every one else who heard them, wise unto salvation. You will naturally ask, ' Why do not I become myself a Sunday-school teacher ?' I have no doubt I could adduce reasons which would satisfy you ; but I must honestly confess that they do not so fully satisfy myself." From that day the poet takes his place as a religious instructor in the Red-Hill Sunday-school.

A Christian poet has described prayer as

"A kind of tune, which all things hear and fear."

And, again, he calls it

"God's breath in man returning to his birth:
The soul's blood:
The land of spices; something understood."

Week after week, in that lowly room, is Montgomery to be found on his knees, amidst those poor girls and boys, praying **with a fervor, and a** simplicity, and a confiding affection, which not seldom melt **to tears** the little group of pupils. And, if the veil could be lifted which conceals from all eyes save ONE the *closet* and its lonely exercises, the same heart would be seen in a very peculiar nearness of converse with Him who delights to dwell with the man who is " of a humble and a contrite spirit."

Greenland, with its " icy mountains," **was at** this period the scene **of a** missionary self-denial such **as** modern **days have** rarely witnessed. Resolved to **do** the work **of** evangelists among its degraded people, at whatever cost of personal sacrifice—the Moravian brethren did not hesitate **to** eat seal's flesh, **and to** prepare with train-oil their scanty stock of oatmeal. A crisis of destitution has overtaken **the** natives, and Montgomery publishes in Sheffield **an** appeal in their behalf. " The wild Arab in the desert," says he, in his own graphic **and** touching way, " sitting down to his meal of black bread and salt, nevertheless, gives God thanks, and, before he begins, calls aloud to any hungry wretch who may be within hearing, to come and partake with **him.** In Britain, where thousands sit **down** every day **at** plentiful tables, so far as his voice **may be** heard through the circuit of this paper, the present advocate of Greenland widows and orphans would remind the truly charitable **of** the words of their Redeemer, when he had counselled those **who** made feasts to 'call the poor, the maimed, the lame, the blind'—' *they* cannot recompense thee, but thou shalt be recompensed at the resurrection of the just.'"

In the space of three weeks, and within the comparatively limited circle of the readers of the " Iris," the appeal produced 130*l.*; and, in acknowledging **it,** the poet wrote : "These gifts have been altogether **volun**tary, in the best sense of the term; they have been such as the givers could not withhold, from the impulses of genuine pity. The purest produce of the olive **is** the oil which distills freely from the gentlest pressure of its fruit; the most precious juice of the grape is that which flows from the thick clusters heaped abundantly together, without any other compulsion than their own ripe weight and bursting fulness. The wine and oil which 'the dear English people' have thus poured into the wounds of the poor Greenlanders, perishing by the wayside, are the purest and most precious of their kind." The lips which so speak have been touched by the seraphim with a live **coal from the** brazen altar. A noble poem, entitled

"Greenland," and published the same year, proves still further how deeply engraven on his heart are the missionary sympathies of his divine Master.

Public events necessarily continue to occupy a large share of his thoughts; and no easy task does he find it at once to uphold popular rights and to moderate the popular zeal. But, in the **midst of all** the turmoil and the excitement, he is enabled to maintain the fervor and the simplicity of his Christian walk. "Your letter," we find him writing to **an old** schoolfellow—John Edwards, **of Derby, a** correspondent of Wordsworth and of Coleridge, "pleased and affected me much, as the first I had received from **any one,** except **Brother** Ramftler, belonging to the Brethren, since my re-admission. I hope that henceforth we shall be brothers in heart as well **as** in name and profession—brothers by our common relationship to our only Lord and Master, whose poor disciples it is our calling and elect**ion** to be. May it be the first and last **concern of our souls to make** these sure, and **to love and seek other** things **only in** reference or **in subor**dination to them!—for all our temporal **duties and** affections may be so sanctified, that we **may remain** *in* the world without being **of** the world, through that liberty wherewith Christ makes His people free."

One day, in the summer of 1822, **he** is listening **to** Robert Hall. **The** preacher's **subject** is Christ's vicarious sacrifice. Speaking of **the** rarity of such sacrifice, **he** utters a thought **which** Montgomery greatly relishes. "He wished," is the poet's remark afterwards to a friend, "to impress his auditory with the importance of Christ's death, as an event standing alone in the annals of the world, without a parallel, agreeably to that passage of Scripture, 'For scarcely for a righteous man will one die; yet peradventure for a good man some would even dare to die. But God commendeth His love toward us, in that, while we were yet sinners, Christ died for us.' Then it was that he burst forth, first employing the word *monument*, and then *column;* next trying the weaker word *plain*, till at length he rushed upon *champaign*—when away he went, and bore us away with him, contemplating the sacrificial death of the Saviour as 'a single monument, a column standing in the champaign and wilderness of the universe, inscribed with characters found on none other!'" And, on the same occasion, our poet gives utterance to an article of his heart's creed, which ever formed the very corner-stone of all his hopes as a sinner. "It is the Divinity of Christ," he continues, "which stamps the sacrifice of His humanity with infinite importance. These were admirably connected by Mr. Hall; and they must be really connected by us. For my part, I cannot conceive in what any alleged efficacy of the atoning sacrifice of Christ could consist, abstracted from His Godhead; and the opposers of the one—very consistently, because necessity is laid upon them—relinquish the other. The doctrines stand or fall with each other ; **and, before** Socinians can hope to get rid of the **Divinity** of Christ, **they** must burn the Bible—and even **then would** that doctrine be seen rising out of the **ashes of the** imperishable **Word of** truth."

Alas ! it is not professed Socinians only who are lapsing into this twofold error. Scarcely a man amongst the rejectors of the sacrificial sense of Christ's atoning death, who are so rife at this day, continues beyond a few years to uphold His Divinity. And the transition is simple **and** easy. The denier of the necessity of **a divine** Saviour **to** atone, passes **of necessity to the denial of the fact of a** divine Saviour **at 'all.** Montgomery clings to the doctrine **of a** Substitutory Atonement, as the very sheet-anchor of his faith.

In his "Songs of Sion," published about this period, he strings his sweet lyre to the same heavenly melody. "It is far from popular," said he one day to a friend, who was inquiring if the book was making its way, " to become the champion of the Cross, even **in** this way ; but it must be an honor to any poet to furnish words in which sincere Christians may appropriately express their joys and sorrows, **their hopes** and their fears."

8

CHAPTER VII.

An hero in humble life—One talent—" How does he use it ?"—A sick-
bed—Heart not older — A traveller — Impressions—Retirement—
Ovation—" Humble under all that glory"—Triumph of truth.

THERE lived in those days, in a humble room in
Sheffield, a Christian shoemaker, who, after calling
one evening on Montgomery for a subscription " in
aid of one of those many works of mercy in which
he was engaged," was suddenly summoned, a day or
two afterwards, to his heavenly rest. Samuel Hill
was very poor—so poor that he could not always
afford to pay to a Tract Society, of which he was a
member, his subscription of six shillings a-year ; but
so rich was he in faith, so ripe in religious experience, and so mighty in prayer, that Montgomery
tells us, that for the sake of being present at the
society's monthly private meeting for prayer, he
many a time, notwithstanding his constitutional indolence and weakness, " left his warm bed on a cold
winter's morning." " I declare to you," is his remark at the first meeting after the shoemaker's sud-

den departure from this life, " that I never stood in
the presence of *any* man with such trembling as I
used to feel beside that humble individual. Let the
weather be as cold as it would, our hearts were sure
to be warmed here. O God! I thought—thou hast
given to that man perhaps only one talent ; but how
does he use it?" And on the evening of his inter-
ment the poet adds, in another assembly :—" Could
I now be reinstated in the heyday of youth, with the
promise of fifty additional years of life, in which I
might enjoy all and more than **all** the honors I have
received from man since the period when I first set
up in my heart that **vain** and delusive idol of human
applause, which **I** have so long and so intensely wor-
shipped at the peril of my soul—I say, rather than
voluntarily incur the dreadful risks arising from the
repetition of such popular praise as even I have experienced, I would prefer to occupy that grave in which
the remains of our friend are now for their first night
sleeping, 'in sure and certain hope of the resurrection to eternal life through our Lord Jesus Christ.' "
An incident like this reveals, as in the light of a sunbeam, that growing lowliness which adorns him in
these ripening years.

Another glimpse into his inner life occurs **on** one
of those scenes of tender friendship which his genial
heart and warm spiritual sensibilities so often brightens. " I sometimes returned from visiting you," he
writes one day in January, 1823, to a dear friend,
who has been unexpectedly restored to convalescence,

"with feelings as if we had parted for the last time in this world. On those occasions, however, I wept rather for myself than for you, fearing that, when my heart and flesh should fail, **I** might not have that clear, simple, scriptural confidence and hope—though humble, full of immortality—which I saw, and rejoiced **to** see, in **you.** '**So** might **I** live, so may I die, in the faith of the Son of God, who loved me and gave Himself for me!' was the constant prayer with which I closed your door. You had been peculiarly endeared by our frequent association in the most delightful labors in the cause of Him whose service is perfect freedom; and therefore I thought **I** had a right—I will not call it a claim—to be peculiarly interested in your sufferings and in your consolations. Thanks be to God, the latter now abound."

A glimpse of a different kind we have in a letter of this period thus :—" You may think that I forget you, because I so seldom tell you on paper that I remember you, both with gratitude and esteem, for many kindnesses shown to me, especially in former days; but the truth is, that my letter-writing age is gone by—never to return—unless youth, the season for correspondence, comes back again. *That*, however, **cannot** be : childhood, I believe, does sometimes **pay a** second visit to man—youth, *never*. The heart, however, when **it is** right, is always young, and knows neither decay **nor** coolness : I cannot boast of mine in other respects ; but assuredly, in the integrity of its affections, it has not grown a moment older these five-and-twenty years."

One evening, in July 1825, a traveller from New York paid a brief visit to our poet, and published afterward his impressions of him. Introduced into a parlor in which is "a table set for tea," the stranger soon finds himself at home. "The poet," he wrote, describing the interview, "is now at the age of fifty-four. In his person he is slender and delicate, rather below the common size. His complexion is light, with a Roman nose, high forehead, slightly bald, and a clear eye, not unfrequently downcast, betraying a modest degree of diffidence. In his manners, the author manifests **all** that mildness, amiable simplicity, and kindness **of** heart, so conspicuous in his writings. His flow of conversation is copious, easy, and perfectly free from affectation. His sentiments and opinions on all subjects of remark were expressed with decision and frankness, but at the same time with a becoming modesty. His language is polished and select, betraying occasionally the elevation of poetry, but exempt from any appearance of pedantry. While the merits of all his cotemporaries were freely discussed, and the meed of discriminating praise **lib-**erally awarded to each, not the slightest allusion **was** made to his own productions, although they are quite as much read in our country as those of any other living poet. It would have been a breach of polite-**ness** in me to have told him how many generous sentiments he has instilled, and how many hearts he has made better, beyond the Atlantic. He appears to be universally respected and beloved in the place of his residence."

In the autumn of this year, the poet finally surrenders into other hands the "Iris," on which he has expended so many years of toil, and through whose columns he has given forth to the world so many earnest and noble thoughts. "From the first moment," are his farewell words, "that I became the director of a public journal, I took my own ground; I have stood on it through many years of changes; and I rest by it this day, as having afforded me a shelter through the far greater portion of my life, and yet offering me a grave when I shall no longer have a part in anything which is done under the sun. And this was my ground—a plain determination, come wind or sun, come fire or flood, to do what was right. I lay stress on the purpose, not on the performance; for this was the polar star to which my compass pointed, though with considerable ' variation of the needle.' "

Montgomery's religion is a sterling thing, moulding his whole commercial transactions, and regulating his whole life. And now, retiring from public life, he receives from his fellow-townsmen, through the lips of their chairman, Lord Milton, a verdict of approval, which draws forth from him these words: —" There is a splendid Italian sonnet by Giovanni-battista Zappi, on Judith returning to Bethulia, with the head of Holofernes in one hand and the sword which had smitten it off in the other. The populace hailed her at the gates, through the streets, and from the roofs, as the deliverer of her native city; the maidens pressed around, to kiss her garment, 'but not her hand;' while a hundred of the sons of the prophets went before, proclaiming her achievement, and foretelling her glory 'from the sun's rising to his rest.' The poet adds—

" ' Stavasi tutta umile in tanta gloria.'

There is an untranslatable idiom in the original, which gives exquisite point to the idea; but the simple meaning may suffice us—

" ' She was humble under all that glory.'

And this is the frame of mind which becomes me on the present occasion. Since I came to this town, I have stood through many a fierce and bitter storm; and I wrapt the mantle of pride tighter and tighter about my bosom, the heavier and harder the blast beat upon me: nay, when I was prostrate in the dust, without strength to rise, or a friend powerful enough to raise me, I still clung to my pride, or, rather, my pride clung to me, like the venomed robe of Hercules, not to be torn away but at the expense of life itself. However haughtily I may have carried myself in later trials or conflicts, the warmth and sunshine of this evening, within these walls, compel me irresistibly, because willingly, to cast off every incumbrance, to lay my pride at your feet, and stand before you modestly, yet uprightly in the garment of humility."

Such is the attitude of all " true men." He who in his closet was heard whispering—" I have in my-self no might. O God, help me, Amen. O God help me, Amen !" met the remonstrances of timid friends with this resolve—" Though there were as **many** devils in Worms as there are tiles on the houses, **I** would enter the mouth of this Behemoth."

" Erect before his fellows; on his knees before God."

This ovation of Montgomery's was hailed by his Christian friends as something more than a mere personal triumph. "Your muse," wrote **one of** them, " **has** been persecuted for righteousness' sake; and, after having passed through much tribulation, she now appears, like the saints before the throne, clothed in white raiment, and holding in her hand the emblematic palm. I have contemplated the honors with which you have been arrayed as the fruits of a victory, a glorious victory, in which the whole Christian world should participate. It is the triumph of truth, and virtue, and piety, over error, and vice and impiety."

CHAPTER VIII.

Mellowed heavenliness—House of mourning—"The price of wealth"
—His "moderation"—"Lake School"—Offence of the Cross—"Too
vile"—Heaven's joys—A welcome—Indian backwoods—Advancing
years—"Working materials"—Mount Sion—An aspiration.

NOTWITHSTANDING these outward honors, his **inner**
life is acquiring daily a more chastened mellowness.
"Oh, it is a blessing, beyond all the mere enjoyment
of good things under the sun," we find him writing
to his nieces in the summer of 1826, "to know that
we are sinners, and **that** Christ came into the world
to save sinners. I entreat **you, my** dear, dear nieces,
that **you** will employ **some** portions—a little at a
time—of **every** day in reading the New Testament,
especially **the** four Gospels, and more particularly
that of St. **John,** in which you will find refreshment
for **your** minds **when** they are languid, comfort for
your spirits when they are troubled, **and** peace for
your souls when you are willing to hear what your
Saviour has done and suffered **for you.** And pray,
each for yourself, **that God** would bless you and fulfil

in you every purpose of His mercy, for which He has **sent** your present trials; and if you can find freedom, **pray** *together* in your own simple language, and your prayers will be answered, for the Holy Spirit will help your infirmities."

And **the** same mellowed spirit would indicate its heavenly tastes in such utterances as these :—" I take your offer very kindly, and should have been very happy to avail myself of your hospitality, had I been at liberty to visit York during the musical festival; but duty calls me another way. I must go to the house of suffering—though I cannot call it the house of mourning, because there is joy and hope in tribu**lation** there."

And, in another direction, thus :—" I am not rich —I never took the means to be so; I have often said that I could not afford to pay the price of wealth, and that, as there was neither a law of nature nor an Act of Parliament to compel me to become rich, I would not sell all my peace of mind, nor consume my time, in gathering what I might never enjoy. I do not despise money; I love it as much as any man ought to do, and perhaps something more at particular times: but a small provision is enough for my few wants, and the Lord has made that provision for **me.** I owe it all to Him; I cannot say that my **skill,** or industry, or merit of any kind, has acquired it: **I have** received it as a free gift at His hands; and to **Him** I would consecrate it, and every other talent, as an unprofitable servant at the best, and too often as a slothful and wicked one." It is a fitting commentary upon these words, that, when the writer sold his paper for £400, he allowed the money (which was considered a very moderate price for the paper) to remain in the purchaser's hands—intending, should the paper not succeed in strange hands, to remit the whole sum agreed upon for copyright. If every disciple of Christ " made his moderation known unto all men" as unmistakeably as James Montgomery, the Christian name would not have its fair escutcheon stained in these days with so many grievous blots.

It was the failing of Wordsworth and of **all** the " Lake School," that their poetry ignored the peculiar doctrines of the Gospel, and especially man's total depravity. Montgomery, as he advances in years and in the divine life, instead of modifying his earlier belief respecting our fallen nature, is constrained to darken the picture even into a deeper hue. For example, **in a** new poem, called " Pelican Island," which appeared **in** the autumn of 1827, **we** find him apostrophising man thus :

> " **Man,** in the image of his Maker formed ;
> **Man, to** the image of his tempter fallen !
> **I** saw him sunk in loathsome degradation,
> A naked, fierce, ungovernable savage,
> Companion to the brutes ; himself more brutal."

" It is the ' offence of the Cross,' " was the poet's remark one day to a friend, who was mentioning a complaint of a critic that he had made man " too vile."   "Any direct allusion to the state of the poor heathen—their barbarity and immorality on the one hand, or their religious experience and their hopes of salvation on the other—is generally unpalatable: I have long had to endure a good deal for my sentiments on these points, as well from the open pity as from the secret contempt of some of my readers."

Hastening onwards to the Celestial City, his soul seems oftentimes rapt into a very peculiar fellowship with its holy joys. "Prayer," for example, is his remark on one occasion, "is not only the sublimest expression of the Church on earth, but there seems to be something very like prayer among the souls of the martyrs in heaven itself—'How long, O Lord, holy and true, dost thou not judge and avenge our blood on them that dwell on the earth!'"

And, on another occasion, addressing, on her birthday, a friend under whose roof he is sojourning on one of his brief occasional tours on behalf of the Bible Society, he writes :—

> "When suffering life—Shall end its strife
>   In death's serene repose ;
> Be Sabbath rest—On Jesu's breast,
>   Its everlasting close ;
> Your daily cross may you lay down,
> To gain an everlasting crown !"

And, welcoming home a beloved friend who, during an absence of five years, has, on a missionary errand, circumnavigated the globe :—"May you long enjoy the blessing of a heart right in the sight of God, which shall render all his His dispensations, afflictive or joyous, *right in your sight!* This is the Christian's secret of happiness; may you ever be in possession of it in this world of trials, where faith is perpetually put to proof, and often staggers, not at the promises only, but at the wisdom and goodness of God, from our frailty and ignorance in judging of His works and ways!"

And, on still another occasion, referring to Brainerd in the Indian backwoods, and to his suffering **and** solitude, he reveals indirectly **his own** heavenly tone of soul, thus :—" **Was there** at such **times,** on the face of the inhabited earth, **an** object lovelier in the sight of heaven, **than** that lonely man, in the depths **of** immense **forests, reading the** words of eternal life for himself, or pouring out his soul, amidst the silence of the desert, in prayer for the salvation of the heathen ? Yes, there was an object yet lovelier— the same man, after he had been thus hidden in the secret pavilion of the Most High, coming forth from under the wings of the Almighty to teach wondering savages among **whom God was** unknown and Christ was not named, the lessons which he had learned **in** his retirement. **Brainerd,** thus occupied, presented a spectacle to the eyes of angels which **they might** behold with delight, and even long to be **partakers** with him in the honor and felicity of ministering to those heirs of salvation."

Advancing years are beginning **to tell** upon his never very robust frame. "I have not been able to accept," we find him writing, March 16, 1830, to the secretary of the Manchester Wesleyan Missionary Committee, " one invitation of this kind, though I have had many—not because my *heart* has changed, but *I* am not even the man that I was: the bruised reed grows weaker and weaker with handling, and **the** smoking flax dimmer and dimmer with blowing upon, while the ashes scatter to the wind." And, on another occasion, he says :—" I sometimes seem to myself quite worn out, or so fast wearing, as if, atom by atom, **I** were falling into dust; thought, feeling, fancy, memory, invention, fear, hope, affection—all exhausted: and yet there are working materials and working power in me which eternity can**not** exhaust."

But his Christian zeal and boldness freshen into **new** fragrance. **At a** local festival, attended by a host of political and literary celebrities, he rose to acknowledge the cordial words of Lord Morpeth (now Earl **of** Carlisle) who, in proposing his health, had spoken of " the genius and virtues of the bard, who, having scaled the height of Parnassus, had, with equal success, directed his poetical footsteps toward the holier elevation of Mount Sion." " And **I am** not ashamed," were Montgomery's closing words in reply, " in this festive meeting to say, with **reference** to that place which has been the subject of my **later** themes—God grant we may all meet there !"

CHAPTER IX.

> "If we conld see below
> The sphere of virtue and each shining grace,
> As plainly as that above doth show;
> This were the better sky, the brighter place.
> God hath made stars the fire
> To set off virtues; griefs to set off sinning."

In heaven, the saint, walking in God's own immediate light, shall interpret perfectly the (as yet) indistinct hieroglyphics by which now he reads God's leadings; and the hallelujah which celebrates them **shall be** one **of unmin**gled thanksgiving—"Just and **true are all thy ways, O thou** King of saints." Of all those leadings, none shall **seem** so blessed as the sojournings **at Marah** and in Baca.

> "I scarce believed,
> Till grief did tell me roundly, that I lived."

James Montgomery, now nearing **heaven** in spirit, is already singing **in** the wilderness some of heaven's melodies of praise. "Though **it is** true," we find

him writing to a friend at this period, " that certain
exceedingly great and bitter disappointments of my
hopes and schemes in former life left a burthen and a
gloom which have never ceased to make the remainder of my way more or less dreary, yet I dare not
say at this hour, much as I lament many things which
I have *done*, that I wish anything which I have *suffered* in the course of providence, and which has not
befallen me from my own fault, had not happened.
Miserable I may have been made by such events as
we usually call *misfortunes* ; but that I should have
been less so, if they had not been permitted to remind me that here is not my rest, I dare not even
suppose, much less assert. I have actually lived long
enough to see that some of the most afflictive of these
were the means of preserving me from far greater
evils.   I see wisdom, and goodness, and mercy,
guarding and guiding me, and overruling, for my
good, things which almost broke my heart when
they came upon me, and which seemed at the moment to cut off hope altogether."

What words can utter the accession of strength
and of calm joy, which a tutorage in the truly
heavenly art of " in *everything* giving thanks" brings
to life's daily conflicts and labors and cross-bearings ?

"Then do those powers, which work for grief,
            Enter thy pay,
            And day by day,
    Labor thy praise and my relief;
    With care and courage building me,
    Till I reach heaven, and—much more—THEE."

One of his sorest trials at this period is " an oppression and an obstruction in all the faculties of mind and body," which often brings with it " a cloud which falls in no showers of refreshment, but seems to stagnate in the heavens, and to chill and darken his very soul." But " natural feeling" will again " begin to creep along his nerves, and to quicken his whole frame ;" and existence, from being a burthen which he dares not lay down, but finds harder to carry as the length of the way to the grave grows shorter, will once more become a delight, and, with returning bodily vigor, **a fresh** " dawning of life and warmth of reviving **hope rouses** him to new exertion." These seasons of gloom, however, have their own solacement. " I am **not** aware," we find him writing, September 23, 1833, " that you are much tried in this peculiar way ; but you cannot expect to escape entirely this thorn in the flesh, otherwise you will never have the perfect manifestation that His ' grace is sufficient for you, and His strength made perfect in weakness.' **By any** way—by every way—which He is pleased to appoint, may He purify you, till, like gold **seven** times passed through the fire, you are meet to **receive** the ineffaceable stamp of His **image** and superscription !"

Now, " three-score years and one," he has **gathered** upon him an air of almost apostolic **sanctity.** It is not unusual for him, for example, **to** commence a platform-address at a missionary meeting, thus : " The grace of our Lord Jesus Christ, and the love of God,

and the fellowship of the Holy Ghost, be with us all.
Amen." On another occasion, alluding to those same
words, he remarks : "I have no more doubt of 'the
communion of the Holy Ghost' than I have of ' the
grace of our Lord Jesus Christ,' or of ' the love of
the Father;' but I do not enjoy it as I ought, as I
might, and as I pray daily that I may." It is because
he is gradually realizing more intensely the Spirit's
indwelling, that his outward walk, and even person,
are contracting a more heavenly hue.   Like that
" hope" of which the poet so beautifully sings, he
almost literally,

> " With uplifted foot, set free from earth,
>   Pants for the place of his ethereal birth,
>   And crowns the soul, while yet a mourner here,
>   With wreaths like those triumphant spirits wear."

A friend who was with him one morning in a
large circle, when Montgomery was invited to lead
the devotions, felt " the fervor, the simplicity, and the
sweetness" of his breathings, as if already foretastes
of heaven.

But it is only in momentary moods that the burthen of the mortal coil oppresses him.   " Montgomery is now," **wrote a** Sheffield friend, in August 1835,
" not only a poet **in full** possession of fame, and commanding the most extensive circle of readers that any
poet can boast, but he is justly appreciated as a good
man, of extraordinary capabilities, **by** his townsmen,
and the country at large ; and Nature, as if seconding
the tardy justice of man in redeeming the past, has

rendered him the very youngest man of his years
ever beheld, for had he not been known to the world
as a poet thirty years, we really think he might at
this time pass for thirty—such is the slightness of
his figure, the elasticity of his step, the smoothness
of his fair brow, the mobility and playfulness of his
features when in conversation. This circumstance, it
is true, makes a great difference; the lighting up of
Montgomery's eye in the moment when he is warmed
by his subject, or induced to smile to others, is abso-
lutely electrical." But it is

"Heaven **in his eye**,"

which gives to him the choicest charm—to those,
at least, who can discern that peculiar characteristic.

Nothing could be more simple than our poet's
manner of life. "With the world, as to its goods
and luxuries," writes the same friend, "he has nothing
to do; but with its sorrows, ignorance, and want, he
is continually engaged; and, **when** Sir Robert Peel,
to his own immortal **honor,** marked the sense which
himself and his **countrymen** entertained of Montgomery's merit, **by placing** him **on** the Civil List **for a**
pension of **150l. a year,** he only added to his power
of benefitting his fellow-creatures, for of personal **in-**
dulgence in expenditure he has unquestionably no
idea."

One afternoon, in the autumn of 1836, Montgomery is sitting with a friend, poring with intense emotion over an album which a daughter of Wordsworth

has forwarded to Sheffield for a contribution from his pen. The page on which the friends are gazing so intently, is an autograph-sonnet, by Sir Walter Scott. Tremulously penned in the minstrel's last days, and with some of the lines unfinished, it has a melancholy tone about **it** which painfully affects his heart. " Here," is his remark to Mr. Holland, as he closes the book, " we have almost the last written testimony of one of the most active and vigorous minds of the age, made in the very prospect of death ; and yet there is not **the** slightest allusion to the promises of the Gospel, or to the prospects of the Christian : but, instead, an equivocal allusion to ' enduring the stroke of fate.' " It is Montgomery's own happier lot, to be hastening onward to life's earthly " bourne" under a joyous hope. " May the Lord compensate him," he writes this year to a friend, solacing a bereaved disciple, **" in** that way which to infinite wisdom and eternal goodness shall seem best, for the removal to His own glorious presence of her whom, for a brief but lovely season, He permitted to **be** at his side as **a** life-companion, at a time when her life was so far spent, that its twilight on earth, while he walked amidst its sweetness, was to herself the dawning of immortality—as sunset to us in the East, is sunrise **to** them in the West! It was a sudden ' translation' **(because,** like Enoch, she ' walked with God') to the kingdom of glory and **of** bliss, of peace and assurance for ever, from sin, sorrow, and death."

CHAPTER X.

Voltaire's death-bed—The "Encyclopædists"—"Wretched glory!"—
Scott's death-bed—Sheffield poet—Earthly laurel—A crown of glory
—"Natives"—"At home"—A bereavement—"Passed on"—Dickson
of Irvine—"Strive to steal away"—The Cross—New bereavement
—"Not here"—"Died for me"—Thankfulness.

It is recorded of Voltaire, that on his death-bed he
was visited by D'Alembert and some twenty others
of the French "philosophers," but that, as they
crowded one after another into the apartment, he
cast on them a bitter reproachful look, and exclaimed
—"Retire ! **It is you that have** brought me to my
present state ! Begone ! I could have done without
you all, but you could not exist without me ; and
what **a wretched** glory have you procured **me !"**
And, as they withdrew, and lingered about the **pas-**
sage, they could hear him alternately cursing and
supplicating God, and then in a plaintive tone crying
out—"Oh, Christ ! Oh, Jesus Christ !" It is said of
poor Walter Scott that his death-bed was scarcely less
appalling. Genius unsanctified was his ruin, and,

though not to be classed with the Frenchman as an open blasphemer, he is reported to have died in the most heart-stricken horror. The poet of Sheffield is **not** ashamed of Christ and of his cross. "From the time," was **the** remark of the Rev. J. Angell James at a missionary meeting held that year at Birmingham, "that the distinguished individual who has addressed **us** baptized his **muse at** the Christian font, and made her a member, not of any section **of** the Christian community, but of the whole Catholic Church—he has never written a line over which truth or holiness might blush, or which charity might not love to own." And therefore, when death approaches, and plucks the earthly laurel from his **brow,** the Destroyer of **death is** there with a better laurel—the "crown of glory, which fadeth not **away."** Like "the man in the picture," he continues meanwhile to live as an earnest, self-denying happy pilgrim—that crown **of** glory hanging over his head. "There is another country," he writes one day this autumn to a friend in New York, with whom he has enjoyed some pleasant interviews during a recent visit to this country, "of which all, of every land on earth, who are *born* of God, become by that very fact *natives*—even a *heavenly* country : *there* may **we,** and all we have known in the flesh, as of one spirit with us in the Lord, find ourselves at home, and **for** ever with **Him, at the end** of our pilgrimage !"

The following winter a bereavement visits him,

which lifts his heart nearer than ever to his heavenly home. "One light," we find him writing, "which has long cheered, and, I may say, accompanied me through one-third of my way **of** life, is now gone out —no, no, not *out ;* it has passed *on* before through the shadow of death into the splendor of eternity : but I shall miss it ; and, oh ! how many more **whom** its mild beams were wont to bless will miss it, **too !** But the Lord liveth—He gave, and He has taken away—blessed be His name ! To none but him would we have surrendered it."

Like all who have been drawn into a close fellowship with the Lord, **Montgomery** is learning to lean with **a** fresh simplicity **of** faith upon the arm of his beloved **Lord.** Alluding **one** day **to** the authorship of the hymn, "Jerusalem, my happy home" he describes the writer as " a man of God indeed,"—adding :—" His last words, in answer to an inquiry concerning the hope that was in him in the hour of death, were these—' I have taken all my good deeds, and all my bad ones, and have thrown them together in one heap, and have fled from them to the " foot of the Cross for **mercy.**' Oh, my dear friend what a confession of faith ! Let us *go* and *do* likewise, that **at** our departure we may be enabled, through Almighty grace, to leave the same testimony behind us."

And he does go and do likewise. " I strive to steal away," says he, "from this poor world's business, to sit with Mary at the Master's feet—my constant prayer being to have the mind and the power to ' choose the better part,' and to attend to the 'one thing needful,' without entirely neglecting the many things which are necessary." And, on another occasion :—" I feel my place of safety to be that to which I do **know** I am permitted to come—the foot of the Cross."

Another bereavement, touching him to the quick, reveals, **indirectly**, yet even **more** affectingly, the same simple and joyous faith. It is one of three sisters, who **have** lived under the same roof with him " more **than** forty years." He writes :—

"She went as calmly as at eve
    A cloud in sunset melts away,
  While blending lights and shadows weave
    The winding-sheet of dying day.

No;—the day dies not; round the globe
    It holds its flight o'er land or main :
  Morn, noon, **and** evening are its robe,
    And solemn **night its** flowing train.

So **when to us she** seemed to die,
    And left a shadow in her shroud,
  'Twas but the glory passing by,
    And darkness gathering round a cloud.

We gazed upon the earthly prison
    From which the enfranchised soul had fled;
  ' She is not here, for she is risen ;—
    Seek not the living with the dead.'

  For, by no sophistry beguiled,
    She loved the Gospel's joyful sound :
  Received it as a little child,
    And in her heart its sweetness found."

And a year later, alluding to a venerable disciple, **who** had unexpectedly been raised up from what seemed to be his dying bed, he writes :—" The turning-point of his disease seemed to occur **on the** Saturday before Easter. He said then, ' To-day I am seventy-seven years old, and yesterday my **Saviour** died for me.' Oh, my dear friend ! though you do not call **a** certain day *Good Friday*, **you** love to remember, on that day and every other day of the three hundred and sixty-five, that wonderful event (which the annals of the whole **creation cannot** parallel) which so **many** Christians commemorate on that day **; and I know that the most** cheering, animating, glorious, heart-breaking, heart-healing **reflection** which can come upon you at any time, in any circumstances, is the thought of our suffering friend Roberts, when you can say with him, ' My Saviour died for me !' He did, He did ; and He died for me, too ; then let us live to Him—live wholly to Him—that when we die—as **soon we** must—we may die unto the Lord, and that, where He **is, we may** thenceforth **ever be."**

And, referring to the death of the " Martyr of Erromanga," he adds : " Alas ! for *us*—the **removal of** Mr. Williams : I cannot say, Alas ! for *him*. But his death, like Samson's (in the **reverse of** the **nature** of its issue), must surely be the **means of more** life, faith, zeal, and labor, in the missionary cause, than has yet been shown."

Link after link is being severed which binds him

to this vale of tears. In the spring of 1841 he loses a beloved brother—beloved at once in the flesh and in the Lord. A pastor of the United Brethren, he "found grace," writes the poet, "to prove himself a good and faithful servant, through long labors, and longer sufferings, **and he now has** entered the joy of his Lord at the age of sixty-five years." "There were yet visible in his countenance," **he** adds, after taking a last look at the corpse, "some traces of that placid resignation which had always marked it in life—the lingering twilight which followed the shining of that Sun of righteousness amidst which the spirit had passed into a better world."

It was a longing of a poet in another age—

> "Thou that hast given so much to me,
>   Give one thing more—a grateful heart!"

And again, thus:

> " Wherefore I cry, **and** cry again;
>   And in no quiet canst thou be,
>   Till I a thankful heart obtain
>   Of thee:
>
> Not thankful, when it pleaseth *me;*
>   As if thy blessings had spare days:
>   But such a heart, whose pulse may be
>   Thy praise!"

In the brother he has lost, nothing affects our poet so tenderly **as** his " childlike, humble, fervent expressions of thankfulness." And no grace does the survivor continue himself **to** cultivate so anxiously. " Among the ' thousand thousand precious gifts,' " **we** find him writing to a friend, " which, during that long period **of** changes and trials, of mercies **and** chastenings, you have received of God's free bounty, in providence **and in** grace, I am sure you feel that ' *not the least*' is that *one* which Addison so emphatically records in his admirable hymn,

" ' **A grateful** heart to taste those gifts of joy.'

Ah ! indeed, without that, **all the** temporal and spiritual benefits with which **the** good Lord daily loadeth **His** people would be **bestowed by** Him in vain, **or** would be remembered **only in** judgment against them. In that tremendous summing-up **of** the sins of the heathen world—in which the world called Christian is hardly less criminal—contained in the first chapter of St. Paul's Epistle to the Romans, there is a very remarkable clause, ver. 21 : ' Because, when they knew God, they glorified Him not as God, *neither **were** thankful.*' "

CHAPTER XI.

In the autumn of 1841, "for the first time after a lapse of three-score years," Montgomery "appears on his native soil," at a missionary meeting in Glasgow, and is hailed with a singular enthusiasm. "Lofty powers of genius," says the now deceased Dr. Wardlaw, in introducing him, "unconsecrated to the praise of that God by whom they were bestowed, have always appeared to me like lamps of pure oil gleaming in the midst of sepulchral darkness and corruption ; but we rejoice to know that these powers have been devoted by our friend to the service of God and to the promotion of all that is connected with the present and everlasting happiness of mankind. We rejoice, therefore, in having him among us; and we rejoice because we regard him as a Christian poet, and **one** belonging to our own land. When first I had the happiness of becoming acquainted with him personally, I found him, I may be allowed to say, in the most unpoetical place it was possible for a poet to occupy—in the very centre of the dark, dusky, smoky town of Sheffield; and it seemed to me as if he had chosen that particular place to illustrate the **words,** '*E fumo dare lucem!*' He has now changed his residence—he is now **on** 'The Mount,' the very place where a **poet** ought to **be.**

"But **he is** now among us," the speaker adds, "in another capacity. He is the son of missionary parents, and that is no small honor—of missionary parents, too, who, after having submitted so terrible calamities, sleep, as the poet has told us, where the sun

"'Shines without a shadow on their graves.'

I cannot **help** being **struck with that** line, not only from the fact **which it** states, that his parents sleep under **a vertical** sun, but because associated **with** that fact **is** the pleasing thought that all is light over that hallowed spot, far away,

"'Where rest the ashes of the sainted dead.'"

Montgomery is deeply affected by the cordiality of his welcome to Scotland. "I feel it," says he, "to be a high and humbling privilege to be permitted to meet you, and to make my public appearance as your countryman, in a place where, in one of the first sentences of our opening prayer, the name of Jesus was mentioned. That is the name in which we meet ; that **is** the name which is peculiarly preached **as** ' Jesus Christ, **and Him** crucified'—as the only hope, the **only** ground **of the hope, of salvation** for perishing sinners."

A day or two afterwards he visits Irvine, where the corporation awaits his arrival and makes **him a** burgess of the ancient and royal burgh. "I cannot say more," he himself writes, describing the scene, "**than** that the heart **of** all Irvine seemed to be moved on the occasion ; and every soul in it, old and young, rich and poor, to '**hail**' me to my birth-place. My heart was moved almost beyond feeling by the overpowering kindness which oppressed it, and by the overflowing gratitude which could scarcely find vent in **words or** in tears." **One incident** affects him **more** than all the rest—his visit to the humble **cottage** where first he drew breath, his father's chapel, now converted into a workshop, and strangers sitting beside the hearth which once was his mother's ; but the birth-place is not forgotten there—fixed in the wall is a small **tablet,** intimating that in that lowly cottage was born "James Montgomery, the poet."

Not long after this Northern tour, a feebleness of health returns, and with it, at intervals, such an arrestment on his whole mental energies as makes

him feel "as if in the course of an irrevocable de-
cline." It is in allusion to this, that at a meeting in
Sheffield at the close of 1842, he quotes from his
" Pelican Island" the affecting couplet—

> "No snow falls lighter than the snow of age;
> And none lies heavier, for it never melts."

And some time later, using another figure, and **referring** to another symptom, he writes :—" The feeble
and diseased state of my hands seems to paralyse all
my faculties ; and **the** difficulty **and** pain of writing
makes **the** process so languid, **that** such thoughts and
feelings **as** I have, **in the** effort of composition, effer-
vesce and exhale **before I** embody them in fit words.
There is as much music in the fiddle as ever ; but the
hand has lost power over the bow, and cannot call
the spirit out."

The poet's remaining years are like the calm setting of a summer's sun,

> "Sinking down in its tranquillity."

Another of " four friends," whom once he apostro-
phised so touchingly in one of his sweetest sonnets,
is removed ; and Montgomery is " left **a solitary**
unit." " Four and twenty years ago," **he** writes,
alluding to the new bereavement, " towards the
close of the ' Pelican Island,' **I said**—

> " 'The world grows darker, lonelier, and more silent,
> As I go down into the vale of years.'

You will understand this better four and twenty years hence, and also find out that there is something to a living man darker than darkness, more lonely than loneliness, more silent than silence. What is that? The space **in our** eye, our ear, and **our** mind, which the presence of a friend once filled, and which imagination itself cannot now fill. **Infi**nite space, invisible, inaudible, dimensionless, is not more inapprehensible than that remembered range in which to us he lived, moved, and had a being. 'Absent from the body' is a far different separation from that which the earth's diameter interposes between two breathing, conscious beings, *each present with himself* and contemporary with the other, but as utterly beyond personal communication as the living with the **dead, or** as the dwellers in the dust, each resting **in** his **bed, side** by side."

And as his earthly horizon is thus yearly contracting, **and the** horizon of his eternity is expanding its brightening circle, **a** " tremblingly-alive **agi**tation," incident now to all public appearances, **with**draws him into the comparative privacy befitting his advanced years. Young, in his " Night Thoughts," describes the soul at such a time, as

> " Walking thoughtful on the silent, solemn shore
> Of that vast ocean she must sail so soon."

In 1849, Montgomery has **a** slight threatening of paralysis, which leaves upon his mien a yet graver and more heavenly solemnity. **He** recovers ; but

" how faded ! how infirm !" is the involuntary observation of his townsmen as he once more appears out of doors. And, a year or two later, he writes :— " An eightieth birth-day can occur once only, once in a life, though this were prolonged to the age of Methuselah ; and, having now reached the last milestone distinctly marked on the pilgrimage (Ps. xc. 10) from the cradle to the grave, beyond which there is no track except over stumbling-stones and among pitfalls, to the end of all things **on earth,** I am necessarily looking onward **and** backward, around and within me, to ascertain **where I** am, what I am, and **whither I am** going. Of the past, I may say, ' Goodness and mercy have followed me all the days of my life ;' and of the future, my heart's desire and prayer **is,** that **I** may, **in my last** hour, have the blessed hope **in** me to realise the fulfilment of the remaining clause **of** the text (Ps. xxxiii. 6), ' I will dwell in the house of the Lord for ever.' "

One afternoon, in the summer **of** 1853, three travellers from America call at " The Mount." " Scarcely had I entered," writes one of them, " when the venerable bard stepped from his library into the hall, and received us with a greeting which went to my heart." " You were known in our country," remarks one of the strangers, after they are seated in the parlor, " and loved before we were born." " Few men," says another of them, "have lived, as you have, to hear the verdict of posterity." " Yes," replies the poet, " I **have** survived **nearly** all my contemporaries."

And "this led," says the visitor, "to a religious conversation, in which he spoke of that peaceful but trembling hope he had, that he should soon enter upon the promised rest; his lips quivered, his voice broke, and big tears dropped from his eyes, as he spoke of his unworthiness to be accepted, but of his trust in the Saviour, whose grace is sufficient for the chief of sinners. **We rose to** take leave, and, as we shook hands in silence, Edwards repeated **one** of the poet's own stanzas from ' The Grave'—

> " ' There is a calm for those that weep,
>   A rest for weary pilgrims found.'

And he had strength to say, ' I hope we shall meet in heaven ;' and, following us to the door, bade us an affectionate farewell."

The weary, but not unjoyous, pilgrim is now to " find" his " rest."

A fortnight previous, **he is** proposing to revisit once more the loved scene of his boyhood at Fulnec. " I should have indeed been happy," he writes to his niece, explaining an unexpected hindrance, " to make an Easter campaign, and especially to spend another Maundy-Thursday, which then was (I may frankly own it) to me the happiest day in the year ; the evening reading in the chapel, of our Saviour's agony and **bloody** sweat in the garden of Gethsemane, was almost **always** a season of holy humbling, and affecting sympathy of my soul with his, who then was wont to make His presence felt."

Into that presence he is now speedily welcomed, to walk no longer by faith, but by sight. One evening —it is Saturday, April 29, 1854—he hands to Miss Gales the Family Bible, saying, " Sarah, **you** must read !" And, after himself leading the family devotions with **an** unusual tremulousness of voice, but with **a** heavenly pathos, he retires to rest at his usual hour. In the morning **he** is worse ; but **in** a few hours he revives, so that it seems as if he once more may rally. At half-past three, however, as he lies quietly asleep, **his attendant observes in** his countenance **a** sudden and startling change. The clay **is** there ; but the **man** himself is away. **Like** " a shock **of corn fully ripe,"** he **is** already gathered into the heavenly **garner.**

"O death ! what art thou ? strange and solemn Alchymist,
Elaborating life's elixirs from these clayey crucibles !
O death ! what art thou ? antitype of Nature's marvels,
The seed and dormant chrysalis bursting into energy and
glory !
Pass along, pilgrim of life ! go to thy grave unfearing ;
The terrors **are** but shadows now, that haunt the vale of
Death."

IV.

The Man of Business:

FREDERICK PERTHES.

" Placed for his trial on this bustling stage,
    From thoughtless youth to ruminating age."

" Some men make gain a fountain, whence proceeds
    A stream of liberal and heroic deeds."

HAMBURGH.

Life Studies.

CHAPTER I.

"Custom is most perfect, when it beginneth in young years: this we call education, which is, in effect, but an early custom."—LORD BACON.

In the busy town of Hamburgh, some sixty years since, there might be seen, **in a** book-shop in one of the busiest of its streets, a slender, **but** firmly-knit German, whose genial heart draws around him the sympathies, as his energetic decision in business secures the respect, of the most worthy of its citizens. "Little Perthes," they will say, **"has the** most manly spirit of us **all." "** He is the king of booksellers," remarks one **day** the historian Niebuhr. And another writes: "Perthes is **a man** to whom I feel marvellously attracted: I could not withdraw my eyes from him—the charm of his outward appearance I could **not but regard** as the true expression of his inner nature."

This soul—so firm, yet so delicately strung—has **been** reared amidst rude storms.

Born at Rudolfstadt, April 21, 1772, FREDERICK PERTHES finds himself, at the early age of seven, a solitary orphan. A maternal uncle—kind, but poor—welcomes the boy to his humble home. Till the age of **fourteen, his** chief mental food is such books as "Don **Quixote,"** and some quarto volumes **of** Travels, which captivate **his** boyish fancy, but nearly unnerve his native energy of intellect. Two years spent at **the** close of that period **at school** leave him **in** possession **of little** more than the store **of** miscellaneous ideas and fancies gathered at his own hand in his passionate zest for reading.

In his fourteenth year, resolved that, come what **may,** he and his beloved books must be companions through life, he sets out for Leipzig book-fair in search of a master. The tall, gaunt figure of the bookseller, **to whom** the printer of his native town, who **has him in charge,** conducts **him, so** alarms the boy, **that, not being** able to utter **a word, he is** pronounced **to be "too** shy for the book-trade." After some tossings **to and** fro, he **is at** last engaged by another; but **"he** must go home for a year—he is too delicate yet for work."

On September, 11, 1787, **he** arrives again in Leipzig—to begin life's earnest struggle. The youthful apprentice though welcomed kindly enough in his **new** home—especially by Frederika, one of his **master's** daughters, **a girl** of twelve, **who** has the art of "driving **away his** fancies and whims"—finds the discipline and labor not a little **trying.** Beginning work in the morning at seven, he is on his feet till eight at night, with an interval of half an hour at mid-day for dinner ; and, during his **first** winter, **he** has to stand so long on the cold stone-flags, collecting orders, that his feet are frost-bitten ; and for nine weeks he lies in his bed in his little attic-chamber. This is stern training ; **but,** like **the** stormy blast which fixes the rising oak more **firmly in** the soil, it inures his spirit **for** the sharper struggles which are yet before him.

The years of apprenticeship, however, **are** not an unmixed misery. His vivacious and kindly temperament turns them into " happy years of earnest striving." They expire in 1793 ; **and he** betakes himself to **a** wider **and** more congenial sphere **in** Hamburgh —his apprenticeship **to** the book-trade finished, but not his apprenticeship to life.

CHAPTER II.

Inner life—Moral martyrdom—" A philosopher"—Human perfectil il-
ity—" My dignity"—The dark shadow—The struggle—Longings—
" A friend"—The seven Swabians—Goethe—Schiller—" Enthusiasm
in me"—Sunday-trips—" A necessity"—Three friends—" Verge of
destruction."

In these early years, Perthes knows but little of
the struggles of the inner life. Shrinking sensitively
from all impurity and coarseness, he has found himself, among his fellow-apprentices of Leipzig, a sort
of martyr; for " men here," he wrote, " must live
like others, or make up their minds to be persecuted." But his spiritual cravings have not yet intenseness enough to rise above the earth. The order
of the day in Germany for all young men is " philosophy." Perthes must be in his turn a " philosopher ;" and deeply does he study the favorite books
of the day, till at last, in his nineteenth year, after
poring for months during his hours of leisure over
a translation of Cicero " De Officiis," he believes he
has found true satisfaction."

His ideas, it may be supposed, as to **his real** relation to God, are of a kind the most crude and romantic. Regarding life as " a vast institution of the Creator for leading individuals, and the whole human race, to an ever-increasing perfection"—he does not believe in evil, since every occurrence is only fitted to improve us. And he writes :—" I frequently believe that I can say with deep conviction, and with honesty, that, in the struggle after perfection, I have made some progress. Often have I had bright hours, when, conscious of my dignity as a **human** being, and meditating on the perfection of God **and** of His works, I enjoyed **a** foretaste of my **destiny.**" But, not seldom, a dark **shadow** disturbs this pleasant dream. " My principles," he writes to his uncle, " are so interwoven with my whole being, that I have no power to think of myself as without them ; but, as to allowing them to actuate my life, that is quite another matter. I should be a hypocrite, if I were to tell you that they had been the never-failing guide of my conduct. Now passion **triumphs ; now** habit ; again a constitutional levity, which is quite at variance with the results **of my** reflection ; **and** then I find that perfection cannot be reached **by** a bound, **but** must be slowly and painfully worked out."

Mounting the hill Difficulty without having first **got** rid of his burden, no wonder **he** finds the task **a** painful one. " **I** must, indeed, struggle hard," he writes, " if I am to expel from my heart all that disturbs my peace ; for, alas ! when I feel tranquil, it is but the sleep of evil inclinations, which are gathering strength for a more violent outburst. **Ah!** my want of firmness, and my hot blood, often destroy in one hour what it has been the labor of weeks to build up; and then I am the victim of a remorse, which is not soon succeeded by the unreproaching self-possession of a **heart** at peace with itself." And he adds :—" How often have I, with tears, deplored my perverseness, when, after some steadfast resolution to cling to the good, I have fallen, because too weak to overcome some passion !"

But this disquiet is not a heart-piercing thing. " You see, dear uncle," he will write, as if sporting with these convictions, " that I have made a good beginning ; for the being dissatisfied with myself is **a sure** proof of this." And the methods he takes **of** calming his disquietude indicate the same fact. There is **a** void, and it caused him discomfort ; but he is content to fill it with the creature. " The most earnest wish of my heart," we find him writing, " is to have a friend to whom I might freely unbosom myself, who would strengthen me when I am weak, and encourage **me** when I begin to despair : but, alas ! I find no such friend, and yet I feel an irresist-**ible** necessity **to** unburden my heart ; and so overpowering is this longing, that I could press every **man** to my breast, and say, ' Thou, too, art God's image.' " There *is* a heart into which all his longings, **and** aspirations, and sorrows may be poured— the heart of HIM who, when here on earth, never cut short one tale of woe, or blighted with a cold frown one rising hope ; but that heart Perthes does not yet know, nor is he earnest enough as yet to seek it.

To various lower fellowships his frank open nature successively clings. One is the sprightly, joyous girl, who so often has cheered him in his lonely hours. "She is still most kind to me," he writes; "she knows how, by a few words, to comfort me when I am troubled and depressed." Another is, the intimacy formed at this period with seven young Swabians—young men of great mental activity and high moral character, in whose society **he** now spends all his leisure hours, giving **him his** first enjoyment of youth's springy activities. "Never," says he, "have **I** had such pleasant, heart-quickening hours, as now in the society of my beloved new friends. The moment I enter, I read my welcome in their eyes." And another attraction which these Swabians have for him, is the introduction they give him to the friendship of such men as Goethe, Herder, and Schiller.

To Frederick's intellect these latter fellowships are like the morning sun rising on the closed petals **of the** flowers. "When I saw other young men of my own age," **he writes,** "setting about everything with a sort of sprightliness which I never could command —I was grieved at heart, because I was convinced that nothing great or noble could be accomplished without ardor or vivacity. But now I feel that there is enthusiasm in **me.**" And, as he is leaving Leip-

zig, he adds :—"I am astonished at the transforma-
tion I have undergone. I have had seasons of trial,
but they have brought forth much good. My mind
has here begun to develope itself, and to apprehend
the greatness of humanity."

But there is nothing **in all** this to subdue the
guilty sinner. " How highly," **we find him** writing,
with a kind of pagan searedness of conscience, " is
man still favored by the gods ! **how love** exudes
from me at every pore !" And again :—" I have
just returned from a solitary walk, which has done
me much good ; I was penetrated by the glory of
Nature ; certainly I never was better in soul than
now. Dearest brother, be it what it may that now
inspires me—God, Nature, Heart—do not grudge it
me, but rather rejoice with me."

And the joys he seeks **are of the** earthly kind, in
which only such a heart can rest. Working at his
business the half of each alternate Sunday, the **remainder is** devoted **to** the most trivial and unholy
engagements. " Thirty of us," he writes, describing
one of **his** Sunday pleasure-trips, " ladies and gentle-
men—some old, some young—floated yesterday down
the Elbe, to the sound of kettle-drums and trumpets,
and enjoyed ourselves to the full." And, on holi-
days, the theatre, concerts, and masquerades, present
to him the most pleasurable attractions.

A gracious Lord, however, does not suffer him to
go wholly to sleep. " I have tasted," he writes, two
years after he had settled in Hamburgh, " the in

toxicating pleasures of a world, in which all is collision and opposition : I have had my experiences ; but I am not the better for them, and not to become better is to become worse."

Once and again, he repeats the endeavor to find a resting-place in intellectual joys. " My heart," he says, " yearns for the society of cultivated men. Such society is a necessity for me ; and I must compass **it, unless** I am to sink entirely." And Hamburgh affords not a little of such society ; his rising **energy** in the publishing **trade** gradually opening **it up to him.** " I am **now," he** writes, **for example, "** enjoying to the uttermost all that a quick **and ardent sen-** sibility **can** enjoy. I have found three friends, full **of** talent and **heart, of** pure **and** upright minds, and distinguished by great and varied culture. When they saw my striving after the good, and my love for the beautiful—when they perceived how I sought and endeavored—they gave me their friendship ; and oh, how happy I now am ! **I** am like a fish thrown from **the** dry land **into** the **water."** And, at these moments, **he will write in** self-complacency, thus :— " It **does one so much good** when **one can come be-** fore God and **say, ' Thou,** O God, knowest **that I am** good.' "

But, at other moments, the illusion **vanishes.** " I am still too often," he will write, " the **slave** of passion and of habit. And again : " Every frail old man, whose appearance indicates inward tranquillity, is an object of envy to me ; a thousand times a day I wish myself in his place, though involving the extinction of all the pleasures of youth. I would fain possess that cold-blooded calm—that dullness of nerve, if I could thereby **be** set free from this struggle betwixt passion **and** duty, which drives **me** to the verge of destruction."

CHAPTER III.

"Let thy tossed mind anchor upon HIM."

The dawn—Sin and conscience—The mirage—"Trainer-in-chief"—
Play of nerves—The virtuous ideal—"Internal anxiety"—"A poor
sinner"—The Sin-Forgiver—The God-man—"Centre of my being"
—German subtleties—God reduced to man's level, not God become
man—Goethean paganism—The victory—"Religious certainty."

A NEW light now begins to dawn. "It was through
the consciousness of SIN, in the forms of sensuality
and pride," he wrote, many years afterwards, referring
to this turning-point of his inner life, " that I came to
recognize my need of redemption, and the truth of
God's revelation in Christ. Whoever disdains this
way," he added, "will, if he be intellectual, wander
through speculation and mystic symbolism to panthe-
ism ; or, if he be superficial, will take the convenient
way of progress to perfection, Jesus of Nazareth being the trainer-in-chief."

One day, a friend who has already been taught the
more excellent way, whispers to him—" Perthes !
your present love of good is a mere play of nerves,
which assumes the appearance of a nobler passion,
but is merely the result of a sensitive and susceptible
temperament." " Ah ! you are right," replies Frederick; "you have exactly hit my case ; for, even

when all else is lulled to sleep, the spirit of evil, I find, is ever wakeful."

The root of the evil is daily growing more apparent. "**It** is so difficult," he writes, " to continue good, and so much more difficult to become better, that it **has** often occurred to me to doubt whether we were **born good."** And to **another: "So** long as **I** believed that our improvement was dependent merely on the rectification of our understanding, and that men must necessarily become better and happier as they became more enlightened, the future perfection **of** our race upon earth appeared probable to me ; but now that daily experience shows me the fallibility **of** the wisest of men—shows me men whose theories of life are unimpeachable, given up to the practice of vice—I have lost all faith in the realization of this virtuous ideal. If our evil deeds flowed from wrong principles, our errors might then be traced back to misconceptions, and we might improve as these were rectified. But can a more enlightened understanding strengthen **the** feeble will, restore the unsound heart, or change the unnatural and artificial into nature and simplicity? Nay, assuredly ; goodness is no necessary result of enlightenment of mind—this may, indeed, eradicate follies, but not a single vice."

Another friend, whom he meets at this period, speaks to him of " sin as itself the cause of our departure from God." Sin, therefore, must be pardoned before there can be any confiding fellowship with Him. "Salvation," says his friend to him, "**is** to be found, not in feelings listening to the voice of God within, but in the historical fact of the Redemption, and in its converting power on the heart of man."

But still he "timidly draws back" from the Cross. Indeed the Cross, even as a doctrine, is as yet but dimly comprehended. "My internal anxiety," he writes, "calls for some one who in my stead may give satisfaction; and undefined feelings come across me, which seek after a God who, as man, has felt the agonies of man. I have leaned," he adds, **"on many** a staff which has given way, and have seen many a star fall from heaven."

A better "staff" now is in store **for** him. "I am a poor *sinner*," we find him writing one day, "in myself helpless and comfortless." And, on another occasion: "Again and again, the all-important question recurs—Can God forgive sin? and will He? He who does not understand the full force of this question does not know himself." Perthes sees his *sin*, and he *begins* to see the *Sin-Forgiver*.

Still there is not peace. "The time," says he to a friend one day, "when these facts are to become vital to me, and the measure **of** their vitality, depends **on** the grace of God." But his soul is now too earnest **to** suffer this conviction to lull him into a stupid repose. "I want," he says, on another occasion, giving utterance to his heart's intense longing, "I want to grasp the uncreated Son of the Father as in reality my God. I want this God-man **to** become the very centre of my being."

In Germany at that time, as in England at this day, Christianity is paraded by certain thinkers in a certain subtle philosophic guise, which, to a mind like Perthes', has not a little attraction. Talking glibly of the "mysteries of godliness," they affect familiarity with a literally personal God, and complacently boast of their growing assimilation to His earthly life of self-sacrifice. But the Christ they worship is not God become man, but God reduced to man's level; and the God they worship is, not the just and holy Lawgiver, magnifying his law in the Cross, **but** an indulgent and feeble father, who, forgetting the claims of law, has retired from the seat of justice, and has begun to " clear the guilty." Perthes, however, must have *sin*—HIS sin—*forgiven*; else no peace, no rest. " For my part," he says, " I entertain **a** sort of horror for the mode in which the great mystery of godliness is treated in these circles ; they insist **on** being so very comfortable, so much at home with their religion."

And of one of them, Jean Paul, he writes :—" He longs indeed for truth, and for a settled faith ; and yet he cannot abstain from representing **the** God-man as a mere creature of human imagination." And, on another occasion, resolving **into a mere** paganism this deceitful perversion of the only real Gospel, he says :—" In Winkelmann's Letters I find the Goethean Paganism more beautifully and forcibly developed than anywhere else, as the opposite pole of Christianity, The one is all nature ; and every creature, as if self-created, **is to stand only on** its own feet—man is to enjoy **all** things, **and to** resist or endure all unavoidable evil, with **a** strength whose origin **is** in himself; the other is a free-gift investiture—all given by grace and received by love. Heathenism and Christianity exhaust everything; **and** that which lies between, call it by what name you please, is a mere inconsistent fragment—mere patchwork and vanity—resulting either **in** despondency **or** in pride."

The victory comes **at** last. **"How,"** we find him writing **to a** friend, in the spring **of** 1805, "can I **ever** sufficiently **thank you, who have been** the means of **giving a** fixed direction **to my** longings? It is through you that I have attained to the religious certainty which I now enjoy, and shall enjoy throughout eternity." And, years afterward, he thus describes the way by which he reached it:— "My trouble on account of selfishness and impurity drove me to seek reconciliation with the God before whom I trembled. Christianity was not forced **upon** me, but **I** upon Christianity; I was thrown by **an** inward necessity into the arms of the Saviour." And he adds:—"**For** him who in the anguish **of** his heart, cries out, '**I** am a miserable **sinner**,' and stretches out **his** arms to the Saviour—for him, I **say,** 'Christ died.' How closely then **is** faith in the Redeemer allied with a realization of one's own sinfulness!" He has reached the landing-place, and is safe.

CHAPTER IV.

PERTHES is not a mystic, gauging frames and feelings. " I am **more than ever** persuaded," he writes,
" **that** my destiny **is** an active, masculine career—
that I am a man born to turn my own wheel, and **that
of others, with energy."** And right manfully he turns
it on many a trying scene. " How can **I** ever thank
you !" **he writes to the** friend already indicated;
" you it is **who** have strengthened **my** young heart,
and have opened up for **me a new** moral career."
Up to this time **he** has mistaken a planet (as **he** expresses it) for the polar star—the aurora borealis for
the dawn of the coming day. The battle of life now
is to be fought with other weapons ; **and he** fights it
not in vain.

When he first entered **on the** book-trade it was as
the means of a mere livelihood, and ultimately of acquiring **an** independence. **But** now he **is** possessed

with a conviction so intense of its **bearing** on the people's entire intellectual life, that the mere question of gain has henceforth scarcely any weight with him. " I know," says he, one day, " that the book-trade can be managed mechanically, and as a way merely of making money—just as I see, among priests, and professors, and generals, some who, in giving their services, think only of their daily bread. But a shudder comes over me, when I find booksellers make common cause with a crew of scribbers **who** hire out their wits for stabling and provender. Germany is deluged with wretched publications, **and** will be delivered from this plague only when **the** booksellers shall care more for honor than for gold."

And his zeal does not evaporate in vain regrets or reproaches. " Dear Campe," we find him writing to a brother in trade, " in order to bring about all that is possible and desirable, let us first see that we ourselves are, what we ought to be ; let us also increase our knowledge, and strive as much as possible to win for our opinions friends and advocates among the young people of our own standing. There are now five of us ; and what may not five accomplish, if only they are in **earnest ?** Let each strive **to** diffuse a high tone over his peculiar circle ; **let** each seek out some choice spirits ; and, if we persevere, and **God** favor us, what may we not achieve ?" He proceeds, with characteristic energy, to carry his thoughts into action ; and few men ever accomplished so great a work.

Turning aside for an interval from the tumult **and** throng of business, he finds, in the daughter of the distinguished Claudius, " a help from above such as his soul required"—one in whom are " peace and stability, devotion and truth." "My Caroline," **he** writes, " makes me unspeakably happy She is pious, faithful, true-hearted, and submissive; her inward course she shapes for herself, and pursues it with a steady step." And to herself, on one of his business-journeys :—" Can you, then, believe that my restless labors, my activity and energy, can be detrimental to you? Rather let us thank God that He enables me to take pleasure in things which might have been to **me a** burden and a weariness. Believe me, I under-stand your present feelings thoroughly. While you **lived in** your father's house, you maintained a con-**stant** walk with God. You had had but one thought, **and but** one path. But then your walk with God was the walk of **a** child who knew sin and the world, and life, not at all, or only by name. Now, however, simply because **you** are in the world, this condition must be disturbed. Would you live apart from everything? No, we are not to drift away from **the** world. God demands not the sacrifice of natural ties, but the submission of our will to His. The sor-**row** and annoyances which may be our lot in the world **where** He has placed us, we should bear with **inward** tranquillity, rather than seek to escape from them."

These are wise counsels, and they are not lost upon

her. "Caroline does not find life easy," he writes at **a later** period to **a** friend; "in spite of her calm temper, and her rich and lively fancy, she feels it hard to have to do with the ever-changing and finite things of the world and of time. And yet, when **I** see her holding fast by her inward life in spite of the annoyances which the tumult and distractions of her daily existence too often cause her, and also fulfilling the outward duties of her position in a manner **so** self-denying, kind, and noble, she imparts strength to me, and becomes truly my guiding angel. Her lofty spirit, **her** life-heroism, her humility of bearing, her pure piety, constitute the happiness and blessing of my life."

The war breaks up his pleasant home. Hamburgh is for months in the hands of the French; and, with a true patriot-heart, he forsakes all rather than be a slave. Most trying hardships follow; but Perthes stands firm. "May God enable me to do what is right without exultation," writes the brave man, as the trial is at its height: "I will preserve my integrity; I will look upon my fatherland **with a** good conscience, and will return to our city **with an** open countenance and head erect."

Seldom has a family been overtaken **by a** calamity more stern. "There are seasons," **he** writes to his wife, who has fled with the children for safety to Gotha, "in which the whole weight of the anxieties which await us in the future, and **of the** sorrow which is involved in the present, presses heavily upon me.

Your task is, indeed, a hard one; but mine is not **light.** Have patience; be calm and self-possessed, **my** beloved Caroline: trust to my sense and prudence, and leave the event to God. I trust to your wisdom, your energy, your affection; and I pray God to give you what you want, and that **is** tranquillity." And in another letter :—" Thank God that you, my darlings, and my only earthly treasures, are well. **Dear** Caroline, what a vast wilderness the world becomes when man has no home! The sight of little children always brings tears into my eyes."

But Perthes breasts the surge nobly. "Ought we not feel ourselves great," he says, one day, "just because we are born in such evil times?" But it is not Roman greatness. "What the highest greatness **is** without love," he remarks, on another occasion, "we may see in the devil." That greatness Perthes covets no more; but the crisis proves him truly great. "God will help me," he writes; "I dare not leave what I have undertaken. **It** is my business to lift up my voice for truth and justice as opportunity offers, and to show that the will of God is not altogether forgotton, in spite of the sinfulness and weakness which everywhere impede its clear and perfect recognition. That in times such as these, when the struggle betwixt good and evil, truth and falsehood, **is** so fierce, a man cannot hope to achieve anything without risking much—that, in order to do homage to truth **and** right, a man must be ready to give **up** heart, and life, and fortune, and estate—*that,* **my**

noble wife, you know as well as I. I have courage,
and energy, and moderate desires ; and **I** am at peace
with God, and with myself. I **can** pray **now as** I
never prayed before, **and** I pray much. **My much-**
loved Caroline, take courage and be calm ; **God** will
help you, and **me** also." Perthes' Christianity is not
a hot-house plant—it can brave and can outlive the
storm.

3

CHAPTER V.

German mind—Erratic tendencies—Perthes' "plough"—New **era in**
publishing—Claudius—"Tried wrestlers"—Unselfish **in business—**
—Social sympathies—" Family Egotism"—Neighborly—Loving and
being loved—Battle of youth past—Heart not old—"Truth and
Spirit-love"—Christian phrases—"Breath of the age"—"Organ-
grinders."

THE war has ended ; and **his** desolated home is re-
stored, and his business is once more resumed. Not
content with half-measures, he sees that the time is
come for giving **to** the book-trade of Germany a fresh
impulse ; and right well does **he fulfil his** mission **in**
the momentous era which, during **the** next twenty
or thirty years, marks the German mind. Scarce a
single peril besets **the** faith, at the hands of his erratic countrymen, which Perthes does not hasten at
once to meet. **" I have** the gift," we find him writing, respecting one **of** his great publishing enterprises,
" of uniting the dispersed, bringing the distant near
together, and tuning any discord **of** heart and mind
amongst right-feeling men. **This** is the plough I
have ploughed with, all my life." And he does not
miss his mark. The undertaking obtains the cordial

adherence of the leading minds of the day. A new era dawns on the publishing business **of** Continental Europe.

"It does a wrestling man good," says **he,** on **one** occasion, alluding to a picture of Claudius which he has been hanging up in his room, "to be surrounded constantly by tried wrestlers." Not memorials only of departed wrestlers, but living athletes in life's **great** struggle, does he always seek to gather round him. "Remember," is **one** of his maxims, "you **are** not alone in the world." **And worthily** does **he** fulfil the maxim **in his own** daily **life. Not** selfishly jealous of rival **competitors, but aiming only to m**ultiply the **channels of** blessing, **he initiates into his own** great thoughts one and another, and another, in whom his eagle eye discerns a capacity to rise to greatness. "The majority of men are common-place," he writes, "and carry on their calling in a common-place way, whether it be spiritual, or worldly, mercantile or military."

If all Christians were like Perthes, the name **of** Christ would be less often blasphemed in the counting-house and in the busy mart. "We **have now,** dear brother," **are** his words to one **of** those men, who have owed **to** him so much, "worked together for a quarter of a century, carrying **on** one and the same concern in troublous times. **Not** once have we taken different views as to 'meum and tuum;' not for one moment during all these years have we ever felt it possible to waver in our mutual confidence.

Let us thank God that at the hour of parting that confidence is as firm and pure as it has been during our long-associated life."

Thomas Chalmers often notes in his "Diary" a tendency to "hide himself from his own flesh." A warmer or more genial heart never throbbed within a human bosom; and yet he needed to set a daily watch upon his spirit, lest he should be pleasing himself by shutting himself up in his study, or in the privacy of home, instead of going out among his fellows, or welcoming them to his social board. Perthes is continually watching, and stimulating others to watch, against this snare. "Do not shut up your house from your friends," he writes to one of his married daughters—"it is perilous, and leads to family-egotism, and brings its own punishment. Communicate freely with others, and show that domestic happiness does not estrange you from them. The earth is God's house, and we may not live only to ourselves. I know that you will not let any needy person whom you can help go empty away; but neighbors and acquaintances wish to talk of their affairs, their joys and sorrows, and those of their friends, and nothing is so offensive as cold reserve, as though we were beings of a superior nature, able to live, and suffer, and rejoice alone." And to his wife, during her residence in Gotha: "Only make the attempt; let your heart speak in truth and confidence, and you will find that what comes from the heart goes to the heart; you will be met more than half way, for the necessity of loving and being loved is common to us all."

His sun is **now** past its meridian ; **but** his heart does not grow old. "The battle of youth," we find him writing, "is over and gone, and evening **is at** hand. Time may blunt the nerves, and stiffen the limbs, but it has no power over love, which is the life of men—the core of their personality. Despite my half-century, I feel no diminution of love."

And this freshness of the heart gives to him an ever-freshening zest for truth. "Love," we find him writing, "is the sum-total of life ; and **it** is only according to our measure of it, that **we** are accessible to truth. Man has part in the eternal, only in so far as he cherishes in himself the Divine Spirit-love."

Nothing is so perilous to the soul as familiarity with evangelical phrases, coupled with deadness of heart. Never in any age was this peril more menacing than in our own. One **day** Perthes, warning a young man **in whom he** feels a **deep** concern, **writes :** "The **hurry,** characteristic of **our** age, appears **in the** development **of** its religious life. Dangers **which,** years ago, **it would have** been ridiculous to **think of,** are already **at hand.** Our youth, who have any spiritual life, complain **of** Rationalism as cold and barren, and make use of Christian phrases, and an orthodox Biblical terminology, which the breath of the age— not the Holy Ghost—has blown in their way—without, however, being convinced **of** their own sins, or longing for deliverance from them, or humbly accepting justification **by** faith. The spirit of the age may, indeed, imbue **a** generation with Christian doctrine; but Christian faith can arise only from that sense of need for deliverance from sin which makes a man stretch out his **arms in** humble supplication. Christian knowledge without Christian faith is a dangerous thing, both for the individual and for a people."

"Organ-grinders" he used to designate those retailers of Bible-terms and evangelical phrases—"a weariness to themselves and to others." And is not the Church groaning at this hour beneath the burden of such? Cant utterances, but no commanding power—is not that the caterpillar which is devouring the freshness of the trees in the Lord's garden? O **God**! arise, and renew our waste places. Hast not hath said, "I will restore that which the caterpillar thou eaten?"

CHAPTER VI.

"Such as one seemeth as superior to the native instability of crea-
    tures:
 That he doeth he doeth as a God, and men will marvel at his cour-
    age."

"Fight to the end"—"Only figure among ciphers"—Neander—Strauss
—"Salvation of souls"—"Energy"—A model for publishers—Gotha
—Secularism—His son at college—A snare—Besser—Consolations—
Yearnings—"A dark web."

EARNESTLY does Perthes continue to ply his vocation. "To withdraw one's self entirely from contact with the world," he writes to his son, urging on him his own healthful religious life, "is impossible under the conditions of time and space. But, if the attempt to lead an exclusively inner life be hopeless, we have the comfort of knowing that such a life is not ordained of God, but devised **by** man's own deluded will. We may, indeed, with the loftiest sentiments and the sublimest ideas, imagine it; **but** we **are deceived** by Satan. Behind the lofty sentiment **lurks** sloth, which hopes for the crown without the conflict; and behind the sublime idea lurks pride, which, in its independence of the world, would fain assume Divinity. We can do nothing but fight to the end. If we have conquered the grosser and ruder forms of temptation, we have hourly to guard against more subtle and gentle attacks. This world is not made for rest after victory : fight on, love, and trust God's grace."

Bacon remarks somewhere, that "he who plots to be the only figure among ciphers, is the decay of a whole age." It is not among ciphers that Frederick Perthes takes so marked a place. The leading minds of the age owe to him a directing energy. "I think," we find him writing, for example, regarding the method adopted by some Germans to confront the infidel Strauss, " our divines might have shown a greater respect for themselves than they have done in encountering Strauss. They have simply taken up their position in the arena of scientific theology, which is common to him and them—whereas they, whose vocation it is to defend the truths insulted, might well have manifested indignation against the man who *con amore* and audaciously routs about among the events and truths on which the whole Christian world believes its eternal salvation to depend." And, writing to the great Neander, he says :—"I do not think that much would be gained by discovering scientifically the weak points of Strauss, Vatke, and the like. When it is merely science against science, I tremble for theology. The matter on hand is, not the solution of a scientific problem, but the salvation of souls. Whoever would make the saving truths of revelation his own, or would lead others to them, must start from facts coming within his own imme-

diate knowledge. The depravity of **all** mankind; **sin**; **our** double nature (after conversion); wrestling, weakness, and death in every individual; and the ardent longing of the whole man for deliverance from such evils;—these are facts, and they form a basis for faith in the salvation revealed by Scripture. To every one in whose soul God has established such a basis of faith, the life of Jesus and of the apostles becomes the keystone of the world's history, even scientifically regarded; and **it** was this evolution of sacred history from facts within our immediate ken which **I meant, when** expressing my joy that, in addition to your critical history, you contemplated also a positive treatment of primitive Christianity."

Perthes is not the man to suffer this flood of destructive error to go forth over the land unchecked. " A miscellaneous rabble," he writes, " are now rifling Strauss' works, with a view to their popular interpretation and universal diffusion. A sharp eye should be kept on them, as they evidently have high intellect at command. Whoever, like me, has seen parties rise and **fall** during **half a** century, is not startled at the up-blazing of a meteor. Straussism, **however,** may become a power for ten years; just because in ten years the devil can destroy many **souls,** it is not to be overlooked." These words reveal the secret of his many trade-undertakings;—he is not a mere panderer to the taste even of the really religious, hoping thereby to make money;—he lives for a nobler end—his mission is to circulate truth, and, worthily does he fulfil it.

"We are now beginning a common enterprise," he writes to a professor at Heidelberg in 1825, on commencing a religious periodical, "by which we desire to forward the cause of truth and God's glory. I say a common enterprise, because I will employ in it my time, my energies, and my substance in order to procure for worthy men an opportunity of influencing the age. I do not expect any return, the difficulties with which such a periodical would have to contend being very great."

It is Perthes who at this period induces Neander to commence his immortal "History of the Christian Church." "Your challenge," writes Neander to him, "will not have been in vain." And, after receiving a visit from him at Gotha, at which it is decided that he shall undertake the great work, Perthes writes :—"God give Neander health and strength to finish it! Perhaps there is no one who, at this present time, can do so much as he for Christianity." If Perthes had never done any other service than this, he had not lived in vain.

The poet Cowper, tracing the aberrations of the sceptic to their real source, has written :—

> "Faults in the life breed errors in the brain,
> And these reciprocally those again.
> The mind and conduct mutually imprint,
> And stamp their image in each other's mint."

And again, he says :—

> "Thus men go wrong with an ingenious skill,
> Bend the straight rule to their own crooked will;
> And, with a clear and shining lamp supplied,
> First put it out, then take it for a guide."

It is because Perthes has himself been driven **upon** truth by the inward necessities of an accusing conscience and of a vacant heart, that he feels so intense a compassion for all who are out **of** the way. "On one side," we have **him writing,** "is secularism, dead to all but earthly things; and, on the other, a restless agitation, which spends its strength in unsettling all that has hitherto given peace to the soul." And again :—"I am convinced that you will soon discover **that** all mere philosophy is vain, and will gladly avail yourself of Revelation; if, indeed, any true religious feeling be awakened within you." And to another :—"Strauss' work will shake all who have not been brought, by personal experience and inward struggle, to Christ."

His eldest son has left home for the University; and **the** father, it **may** be supposed, is not without his anxieties. "When a man," he writes to him, "**has** passed through the season of wayward minority and stands erect in manhood, he asks himself, 'What means all this?' his reply must be—'All below is **vain** and fleeting; true joy and peace are only to be found in spiritual life.' I have done many things, and perhaps well; but where **is** the fruit of the blossoms which looked so promising? The ideals have disappeared, but not the faculty **of** labor ; and therefore, clothed with humility, 'Forward,' I say, 'to **suffer** and to do.' This is to become a master in the business of life ; but it is vain to expect that this **can** be attained without passing through an apprenticeship. Here it is that so many well-disposed youths of the present day make shipwreck. They affect a simplicity, plainness, and stoutness of heart, which almost look like the repose and dignity of age."

And others share his tender sympathies. "It is your body which again inflicts upon you the well-known 'grey season,'" we find him writing to his friend Besser, whose failing health has brought on fits of deep melancholy ; " and no one is perfect master over bodily moods. You might very often scare away the 'grey' mood, by calmly considering how trivial are the causes of your anxiety, and with what ease you have overcome such before. But, indeed, I know only too well how it is with the man : the head may be weary and the heart full of love and devotion ; or, on the contrary, the head clear, and the heart cold and barren ; but sorrow weighs down head and heart alike, just as joy brightens both. 'Take courage till life's phantasmagoria are over.' You **say** that life becomes a burden ; and so it must **to us** all, as we grow old : but we should try to accustom ourselves to a new race of men, or rather to the same **men** differently dressed. While we live, we must put up with novelty ; but I shall be glad to

die—one gets tired of evermore picking off one husk
after another from the kernel of truth. Here nothing
endures; what most we love, is torn away; all is
brittle and perishable, and we ourselves are **but**
broken reeds. Our heart overflows with love to
some dear object; and yet, how imperfect the union,
how weak the sympathy! And even he who knows
that love to God **is** the only enduring love, and that
it is the only anchor of the soul—how deeply he feels
that he can but seldom draw near to his Father with
perfect resignation and sincerity!"

And, again, to the same friend:—"Your bodily
frame is not in unison with your loving nature, your
lively fancy, and elastic activity. You have been
weaving again **a** dark web of feeling and thought,
which holds you fast, as though it were of iron
strength, while in reality it is but a spider's web."

4

CHAPTER VII.

"Vegetating" and "Living"—Instinct of activity—"Hard work"—A "serious" dream—"Common-places for the invisible"—"Bibliolatry" —The shell and the kernel—Symmetry of truth—Bible's unity— Luther—Rationalism—Pietism and Christianity—Tauler—Theological strife and religious life—Not the ideal of Christ, but His person —Life in God—"Polite society"—Pillory—"Understands erection of a stake"—Party-wrangling.

As years pass **on,** Perthes does **not** "turn the wheel" less energetically. "'All is vanity,'" he writes, "does indeed come home to the man of ripe years, when he reflects upon all that **in** life's vicissitudes has charmed **and enchained** his heart **and** mind ; but **he** who, because **all** things are vain, should cease to take a part in them, would merely vegetate, and no longer live. An entirely contemplative life is an impossibility ; the instinct of activity is innate ; at all events, hard work is **to** me a habit with which I cannot dispense. **He** who should attempt nothing on earth but to meditate on God, and feel His presence, would soon cease to do either. The Christian **is set in the** midst **of the** world ; and, let **him stand where he** may, he will always be called on **to** fulfil various external duties : in these **he is to act** as skilfully, expeditiously, and energetically as his faculties will allow ; and he may not extinguish his earthly nature or his senses, for he needs them all in order to be God's faithful servant and steward."

Perthes continues to urge upon all his friends, with a growing earnestness, the grave responsibilities of this brief hour of probation. "Life," we find him writing, "is a dream, but a very serious one ; and our dreams are solemn truths veiled in airy fiction. People here are taken up with the visible, and have only a few trite common-places to bestow upon **the** invisible." Perthes himself has "learned," as **he expresses it, "to deny** himself without self-annihilation, and to renounce the **world** without living **a** monkish **life."**

There is a delusive religious system in England at the present day, originating in an "inner life" not implanted by God, but self-developed, deriding and pitying with a kind of condescending scorn the lowly Christian, who, cleaving to his Bible, lives day by day upon "every word which proceedeth out of the mouth of **God.**" Surrounded in Germany at this period by that pestilential and deceitful atmosphere, Perthes writes : "What we need, to equip us for **the** battle of life, is—Christ and the holy Scripture." And on another occasion :—"I find that the benefit **I** receive from Scripture in a great measure depends upon myself. How often, on turning to it to clear up some historical sequence or some obscure doctrine —to find material for imagination or ground for hypothesis, I only get at the shell instead of the kernel! **or,** again, if in high-wrought moments a clearer insight be afforded, how prone we are to seek to improve and define it by our own strength, and so to bring to light human fictions instead of divine truth! The mysteries of holy Scripture are only revealed to us when we are seeking for nothing else but for the way of reconciliation with God, and for **help** in our battle with selfishness and sin." And again: "God gave a revelation to men, not to increase **their knowl-edge,** but to deliver them from sin."

The Bible is to him not a multitude of discordant fragments, but a divine and majestic whole; and for this symmetry of truth he is peculiarly jealous, because he feels that it bears directly and immediately upon the symmetry of the Christian life. "The earlier theologians," we find him writing, about the Bible's charactreistic as an unbroken unity, "have perhaps too little remembered that God has spoken in the Bible, not immediately, but through John, Peter, and Paul. At the present time, however, we **are** certainly in danger of overlooking the unity of the Scripture, while dwelling on the individual writings of Paul, John, and Peter. In short, the trees prevent our seeing the forest, and we forget that it is not with a collection of separate writings that we have to **do, but** with the Bible as a whole, as being the Word which, during the course of the world's history, God wrote down for man's salvation; and which contains nothing more, indeed, but still nothing less, than is necessary to reveal the mystery of godliness. It **is** not so much from the individuality of the writers of the Epistles and Gospels that we are to understand their writings, as from the relation of these to the whole."

His favorite author is Luther; and one of his chief projects, in these his latter days, is to give Luther again to his country. "As a whole," he writes, broaching this subject, "Luther belongs to all times —so great, so **pure, so** powerful, was his knowledge of eternal truth, that we may always find in him a guide to God. But who is acquainted with him now-a-days? Few guess what he was and what he effected. Were he better known, his mighty mind and heart-piercing words respecting sin and repentance, faith and the atonement, would smite, like a flaming sword, the dry and unbelieving mass of Rationalism; while others would hear, with surprise, how Luther insisted upon knowledge and reflection, and, with all the energy of his healthy nature, opposed a weak and sickly pietism. To try at the present time to bring Luther as a whole before his **na**-tion, were indeed a noble and blessed undertaking."

But, whilst disrelishing mystic pietism, Perthes is **too** intent on living the heavenly life to be drawn away, by this disrelish, from a holy, self-denying walk. "What the Rationalists call pietism," Neander has written to him, "is nothing but Christianity itself." And he himself writes : "With these people, the Christian is but a pietist, and the pietist is but a

hypocrite."   And again, alluding to an author whom
many denounced as a pietist, he says: "That which
Luther aimed at making openly known, had already
been announced, centuries before, by Tauler. In this
exalted man we find humility, fervor, and sincerity,
united with vigorous inquiry and a free use of human
reason. Luther called him a man of God—a teacher
such as there had not been since the days of the
apostles. At the present time, all may find in him
what they need—CHRIST."

His ripening spirituality shrinks with an intense
sensitiveness from mere theological disputations.
"On both sides," he says, "springs up a hard feeling,
which should least of all find place in holy things.
Theological strife brings, if not gall, at least worm-
wood, into religious life." And to another, he writes:
"Even **if** to-day we argued with the devil down into
the abyss, he would rise from it to-morrow with a
more subtle analysis and **a** more seductive tongue.
You say that many can hardly attain faith till certain
difficulties are solved for them scientifically. I doubt
if any one was ever led through science to faith, till
his very bones and marrow quivered under this question—'Oh, wretched man that I am! who shall deliver me from the body of this death?'"   And he
adds: "Now-a-days science is at once the starting-
point and the goal of Protestantism. Even with the
best among the theologians, Christianity is but a stage
on the way to science; and, whilst they are anxiously
ferreting out scientific results with which to prop up

their faith, the age is demanding, not Christian theology, but the Christian Church—not notions, but deeds—not the ideal of Christ, but His very living Person."

And how he himself is realizing this living fellowship, we may gather from such words as the following :—" Being, the only real being, consists in giving one's self up to God—is to be found only in the life in God. You say that to live with God can only mean to have intercourse with Him, and that he who has such intercourse must needs be conscious of it. Now, the latter proposition is true, but not the former ; for intercourse supposes strangers who seek to become better acquainted—intercourse is, indeed, but a repetition of attempts to abolish an existing separation. Friends and acquaintances have intercourse with one another; but who would use that word to express the relation betwixt mother and child ?"

A Christian like Perthes is not likely to escape the reproach of a lukewarm age. "There are few places in Germany," he writes, " where a man could speak of Christ in polite society without being covered with derision and contempt. A man who confesses the Saviour is pilloried ; the whole public is against him." And elsewhere, reading with a keen glance the real spirit of the times, he says :—" Our age, with all its humanity, understands the erection of a stake." And, on another occasion, alluding to some young men who, for their earnest zeal for Christ, have begun to be reproached as " of a sombre mood," he writes :—" If the zeal of the young men be sincere, you need not alarm yourself about their gloom."

The wranglings of party-strife grow more and more distasteful to him. " Whoever is convinced of sin," he writes, " and believes in redemption through Christ, is a Christian, no matter what be the colors of his party. Wherever Christians are divided into parties, truth and its opposite are mingled in them **all.** The solution must come from within—from the power of truth and love reconciling all things. That all should repent, and humble themselves sincerely before God, is the thing needed—not the battle-cry **of** embittered parties."

CHAPTER VIII.

At the head of the German trade—Secret of success—Incident at the book-fair—Holy walk—"Pray and work"—Daily communion—"Use as not abusing"—Friendship—Constancy—The immortal—Abasement—Aspirations—"More simple"—Rustic retreat—Life in the woods—The cottage—Tholuck—Olshausen—Doctor of Philosophy.

As a publisher and a bookseller, he has risen into the very foremost place in Germany. "I behold with surprise," writes a learned countryman to him in 1835, "your professional activity. By the publication of such solid works, and by the carrying out of so many bold undertakings, you are raising a memorial to your name which will not soon pass away." And another writes:—"Perthes always knows what he wants; he understands people's tastes; and whatever he does, he does with his whole might: in that lies the secret of his success." And a professional brother we **find** saying of him :— "**No** one ever occupied **so** prominent a position amongst us, or influenced the book-trade as a whole,

and its individual members, so powerfully as he."
And himself we find writing in 1842, thus:—" In
the long life, full of chequered experiences, which
now lies behind me, I have almost invariably found
that God's special providence favors human activity
and foresight."

So trusted is he, and so necessary to literature has
he become, that not fewer than two thousand propo-
sals from authors were found among his papers at
his death. And never does he issue a single work
from his press without a fixed belief that he is thereby seeking God's glory.

An interesting incident occurs one year at the
Leipzig book-fair, which illustrates his decisive energy, and also his moral weight. A German bookseller has published an immoral book: the trade are
assembled, to the number of two hundred, and
amongst them the publisher of the obnoxious book.
After the other business has been transacted, Perthes
rises. "The honor of our national book-trade," says
he, "is sullied by such a production; the publisher
of such a work is a most dangerous character; and
every one of our shops is degraded by the mere sup-
position of circulating it. I demand that it be condemned in the name of the German book-trade, and
that all copies of it on which we can lay our hands
be publicly torn." The assembly is silent: a pause
ensues: smitten with a sense of their responsibility,
they assent as one man; and, the next day, all the
copies which can be procured are formally and

solemnly destroyed. A prosecution follows ; but the publisher is condemned, and **Perthes** is honorably acquitted.

He has become the centre, indeed, of the whole book-trade of Germany. "Such is the respect accorded to his Christian integrity and energy," writes Frommau, one of the trade, " that for many years he has been really, though always declining to act as President of our Exchange, the central point in all our deliberations and decisions."

But, notwithstanding this **rude** contact with life's daily struggles, the fine edge of his **holy** bearing is not blunted. "**If I have** gladly and actively used my physical **energies,**" he writes, "that is no contradiction **to my** Christianity ; but if I have failed to sanctify them, and employ them as in God's sight, then I have been untrue to my convictions." Perthes is a true man to the end. "I can be pious in spirit," he says, " and humble before God and Jesus Christ, and at the same time be free and cheerful in **life.**" And on another occasion :—"Pray and work is **the** great maxim for young and **old.** In the **conflict** with my spiritual foes, the best method I find **to be** an unvarying habit of devoting daily a certain portion of time to communion with God. Moments of glow-**ing** aspiration, **and** occasional attempts to command religious emotions, will not do."

Old age is not freezing his genial sympathies. "Go forward," he writes, encouraging a youthful convert, whose progress in the heavenly life seems arrested by contact with life's daily trifles; "Go forward with hope and confidence: this is the advice given thee by an old man who has had a full share of the burden and heat of life's day. We must ever stand upright, happen what may; and for this end we must cheerfully resign ourselves to the varied influences of this many-colored life. You may call this levity—and you are partly right, for flowers and colors are but trifles light as air; **but** such levity is a constituent portion **of** our human nature, without which **it** would sink under the weight of time. While on earth, we must still play with earth, and with that which blooms and fades upon its breast. The conciousness **of** this mortal life being but the way to a higher goal, by no means precludes our playing with it cheerfully; and, indeed, we must do so, otherwise our **energy** in action will entirely fail." And one **of** the many young men whose "wheel" he has turned in business writes:—" From the moment that I set foot upon his threshold, Perthes did me great good, and good only, and in the highest sense proved himself a fatherly friend. May his spirit and his example continue to influence us, and the course of his life encourage the young men amongst us faithfully to devote their means and energies to the higher interests of our calling!"

"**There** is little friendship in the world," says Lord Bacon in one of his Essays, "and least of all between equals. To take advice of some few friends," he adds "is ever honorable." Perthes is not one of those isolated beings who, with a hundred arm's-length friendships, yet move through the word solitary and friendless. "When I reflect," we find him writing, "on the extent of my acquaintance, Goethe's words occur to me, 'The stream rolls wider, and its waves increase;' and I would call out to all to 'hold together with all their strength, alike in the sunshine and in the storm.' To me, at least, it is almost impossible to let any go from me who once stood near; and of all the inward gifts God has given me, I am most thankful for the consciousness of constancy. It has always been exquisitely painful to me to see any one who once **was** closely united to me by head or heart now pass me coldly by."

"**It is** good discretion," Bacon says again, "not to make too much of any man at the first, because one cannot hold out that proportion." Perthes' friendships are lasting, because they have not been hastily or lightly formed. "What you young people call friendship," he writes, now more than ever estimating friendships on their grave and serious side, "**will** certainly **not** last for ever, least of all now-a-days; its warmth and intensity belong not to the immortal element in man, but to the fresh feelings of youth. A few years hence, and feelings, opinions, convictions, will have got developed, which even the most intimate friends will fail to understand. Amongst older men, friendship, except as it belongs to memory, consists in confidence **in** each others' earnest striving after truth ; and this confidence can outlast all changes."

Dwelling more abundantly in the light, he feels, as he hastens on towards the mark, an almost-painfully deepening sense of his unworthiness. " How far," we have him writing, for example, " beneath our wishes and our will are the works and ways even of the old among us! Love without work, and work without love! How cold, too, and weak seems our sorrow for sin! and yet, perhaps," he adds, " God sees more in it than we do, and knows how deep and strong and abiding a sinner's repentance really is."

And on another occasion he writes: " ' Be ye holy, even as I am holy.' These words often pierce me through marrow and bone. Not to shut our eyes, through indolence or despondency, to the sin remaining in us—not to mistake death for life, sorrow for repentance, and imagination for love—not to grow weary in our upward course, or to substitute wishing for willing—this is our ceaseless task here below—a task impossible without faith, but without which faith is impossible too."

His solacing joy at such times is characteristic of the man. " Look," he writes to one similarly exercised, " for comfort to the epistle to the Romans: in it is the whole truth of God, in as far as we need to know it here on earth. ' Fight the good fight to the end'—this is Paul's teaching to us." And again: " I have often, very often, read the epistle to the Romans ; it is the portion of Scripture which has most impressed me, has given me most light, and most stablished my faith."

As he advances in years, a simplicity more and more childlike gathers on him. " My Christianity," says he, " becomes each year more simple. That not to love God is sin, and that to love Him constitutes deliverance from sin—this, as infinite truth, as the solution of every problem, has been transmitted from the Bible to my spiritual life. Scientific inquiries, and absorption of the soul in religious emotion, are of themselves **little** worth. I learn more and more to discern the divine wisdom, which has set limits to revelation : all that we need **for** our happiness is given to **us ;** and were the curtain lifted farther from holy mysteries, men's utter bewilderment would **be** hopeless."

Nature and its scenes of grandeur or of loveliness have not lost their attraction. " You see," he writes, from a rustic retreat to which he has betaken himself for the summer with his family, " I have fled **to** the mountains to drive away the consequences **of** influenza. My hearing is still **much** affected, **and I** have difficulty in making **out** human babble ; **but I** hope to be able to hear the vulture scream and the trout splash. **If** any thing can restore my health, it will be life in the woods. **You know this** place, so I need not speak of its charms. Every thing is in our favor—the sky blue, the woods dark, the meadows green." In that lovely spot he spends his remaining summers—the cottage filled with a succession of

guests—including such men as Tholuck, Olshausen,
and De Wette—who repair to its sunny converse as
to some sweet oasis. A visitor, indeed, without a
sense of natural beauty, rather has his pity than his
sympathy; for such a defect he regards as little better than if his friend had been born without arms
and legs, or deaf and dumb. **But** Friedrichroda and
its aged host are enshrined **in** every memory, as each
new guest departs. To the simple country-people of
the valley, the old man is a perfect mystery. "He
neither burns charcoal," they will say, " nor prepares
tar; why should he persist in threading these long
and toilsome paths of ours, which we must daily
traverse for our day's work?" It is **an** eye and a
heart for Nature which take him there. " O Nature!"
is his holy breathing on such scenes—

> "O Nature! whose elysian scenes disclose
> **His** bright perfections, at whose word they rose!
> > Do thou expand
> Thy genuine charms—
> That **I** may catch a fire but rarely known,
> May feel a heart enriched by what it pays,
> That builds its glory on its Maker's praise."

The neighboring little town enrols **him** among its
freemen—"an honor," says he, "which has given
me greater pleasure **than** any I have ever received."
And, in 1840, another honor is conferred on him,
significant **of** an appreciation more weighty, though,
to himself, less touching. "I could not," he writes,
when, in **1840** the University of Kiel has created

him a Doctor of Philosophy, "have marvelled more
if I had been created Vladica of Montenegro. The
learned company has not for a long time seen such a
bungler as I in their midst; my Latin is as rusty as
that of my Erfurt colleague, Dr. Blucher; and that
is saying much." But the degree is not unmerited.
"The faculty has done well," writes a literary friend;
"he who has practised wisdom throughout a long
career, may well be styled Doctor of Philosophy
even though his Latin be rusty."

5*

CHAPTER IX.

Now consciously nearing **his** heavenly rest, he **grows** week by week more heaven-like. "I have never," says he, one day in 1841, to a friend who has been **advising** him to purchase his country retreat, "**had any** other **landed** property than my travelling **carriage and** my corner in the church-yard ; and, just before the order to march comes, **I do** not want to bind myself down to any earthly spot." And, on another occasion :—"I do not climb **so** high, nor ramble so **far** as of yore ; preferring the familiar paths, where I can live my inner life undisturbed, as becomes a man of seventy, who will not much longer **see** and feel the beauty of this earth." And again, **in the** spring **of** 1842 :—"I yearn for the repose of Friedrichroda ; **perhaps it** is there that the last re**pose of all** will be granted to me—gladly would I rest in that churchyard with its fir-trees. It is not

my physical condition which occasions this yearning,
but I discover in myself an increasing indifference to
all temporal matters; I feel incapable of effort for
anything on this side ; I want nothing more here
below."

Friend after friend is summoned away from **his**
side. Niebuhr goes, and Goethe, and his "loved **and**
honored Nicolovius." And his aged uncle, too, follows. "Thank you, dear Fred," the old man has
written to him, after receiving a visit from him
through snow and storm ; " you love me now just as
you did sixty years **ago,** when you used to ride upon
my knee." **And, a short** time after, Perthes writes :
—"I heard yesterday of the death of my dear uncle.
Schwarzburg is now to me desolate ; the playground
of my childhood is no more. The family is now dispersed. So goes the world ! Who can suppose that
this is our home ?"

Perthes has fought manfully life's great battle.
" How strange it seems to me," we find him writing,
" to look back upon my past life ! Half a century
ago, I was an orphan—cast in extreme poverty into
the world's whirlpool, without information, without
help, without support, a forsaken apprentice in a
cold garret, having to limp about for weeks on frozen
feet because no one attended to me but my poor and
still dear Frederika. All this lies like a dream behind me, now that I am at my journey's end : my
life has not been an easy, nay, often a painful one.
To God be the praise that it ends well !"

He is now entering his closing year. "I believe," he writes to Chevalier Bunsen, "that my end is not very far distant. My soul yearns for more certain nourishment." And to another :—"I know that the prayer, 'God be merciful to me a sinner,' will be accepted of God." In January, a serious illness suddenly reduces his strength ; and though he rallies for a little, his old energy is finally gone. Yet his brave spirit is not weakened. "I found him," writes a friend, who had been visiting him at the end of March, "quite unaltered in mind and heart: he is as bright, friendly, and interesting, in conversation, as formerly. Such a spirit as this is mighty indeed. True, it has lost the absolute mastery over the physical nature ; but still it can assert itself, and force that nature to obey, though reluctantly, and but for a season. I was often surprised to see that when, towards evening, Perthes lay back weary and worn, a little mental stimulus availed to restore life and strength even to the body."

A deeply-tried sufferer, who has gone to his rest, once said :—" Looking back on my past life, my conclusion is, that, want what I might, I could not have wanted the afflictions." The same is the experience of Frederick Perthes. "Pain and sorrow," we find him writing, in these his last days, to his son, "have done more for me than joy and happiness ever did : the prayer for help leads to resignation, and resignation purifies the soul ; but still the fight goes on to the present day. Let us fight to the last, my dear son. If Paul had to complain of inward conflict and discord, no other need despair because he has to do the same."

The Marquis of Argyll, the night preceding his martyrdom, said to those about him, with a calm intrepid voice—" I could die like a Roman, but I prefer to die like a Christian." Not in the stern stoicism of a seared conscience, but in the strong faith and hope of one consciously reconciled, Perthes advances towards the "Celestial City." "God," he is heard whispering **in** hours of extreme pain, **" for** His Son's sake, is **very** gracious to me, a poor **sinner."** And, at intervals of ease, he will write to friends **little notes, expressive of** his calm confidence. **"In hope** and faith," he writes, for example, one day, to Neander, " I am joyfully passing over into the land where truth will be made clear, and love pure." And, another day, to Dörner :—" The consciousness of life being quite over, is to me a very peculiar, and by no means depressing, feeling; rather, on the contrary, exhilarating. I am full of thankfulness to God."

The Bard **of Olney, in one of** his bright moments, wrote :—

" Hope, with uplifted foot, set free from earth,
　　Pants for the place of her ethereal birth ;
　　On steady wings sails through the immense abyss,
　　Plucks amaranthine joys from bowers of bliss,
　　And crowns the soul, while yet a mourner here,
　　With wreaths like those triumphant spirits wear.

> Hope, as an anchor firm and sure, holds fast
> The Christian vessel, and defies the blast."

Frederick Perthes, amidst the rude winds of these last days, is anchored firmly by that holdfast. "Do not mourn for me when I am dead," says the veteran warrior one day, as **he lies** in his room surrounded by his children and grandchildren; "I know that you will often long for me, and I am glad of it. I have, indeed, had my trying days and hours; but God has ever been gracious to me. I die willingly and calmly; and I am prepared to die, having committed myself to my God and Father. Here there is no abiding city; we needs must part: death cannot harm me, it *must* be gain."

"**Oh,** brother!" said John Owen on his death-**bed, to a** friend who had been alluding to his great **work on** "The Glory of Christ," "the long-looked-for day is come at last, in which I shall see that glory in another manner than I have ever yet done, or been capable of doing." The same is the death-bed utterance of Perthes. "The season of faith," says he, one morning, "will soon be over for me; that of sight is near: and yet, how mysterious the **word**! Sight! I shall **see** with faculties which I never have possessed here. Knowing is not seeing. **If** I am to **see, I** must have a new spiritual faculty, conferred by perfect love, in order to make the reception of perfect **truth possible.** Fain would we question how this **will** be brought about; but be it unto thy servant according to thy word."

A friend one day enters his little cabinet, where he is in the habit of reclining in his arm-chair, when able to leave his bed. "His hands were folded," says the visitor, "his eyes were closed, and peace and joy were spread over his countenance. I hoped," he adds, "that God had heard his prayer; but it was not so—he was only asleep, and woke up cheerfully."

In these hours, his one resting-place is the Word. "Hold simply and firmly," he will say, "to that which our Lord has told us: read again and again the fourteenth, fifteenth, sixteenth, and seventeenth chapters of John; he who has these has all he needs, alike for life and death." His two closing months are a kind of heaven begun; and the theme which chiefly animates him is, the divine glory beaming so brightly in these divine chapters.

It is recorded of the Venerable Bede, that he never knew what it was to do nothing. During his last fifty days, he translated into English John's gospel, saying occasionally to his amanuensis, as his breathing was growing shorter—"Make haste, I know not how long I shall hold out; my Maker may take me away very soon." And, one day, towards the close, as a favorite pupil said to him—"Dear Master, one sentence is still wanting," the dying man replied, "Write quickly," and, on the young man exclaiming, a few moments later—"It's finished!" Bede rejoined with a tone of joy—"Thou hast well said, It is finished. Glory be to the Father, and to the Son, and to the Holy Ghost"—and expired. Perthes also has been

an unwearied workman for his God. "A rich life,"
he says, one day, "lies behind me."   And, another
day, a friend who has been with him, writes : "Perthes
belongs to that class of men, with every thought of
whom mental and bodily health is so intimately connected, that one forgets that they, too, are subject to
the universal law of decay. **And** another friend,
Schelling, writes : "It was so comforting, to know of
one in the **world, from** whom, in every case of need,
one **was** sure of sincere sympathy, loving good-will,
and judicious counsel." And still another, the Coun-
cillor Rist, writes : "**I** stretch out my hand to say
farewell—if, indeed, it must be so—to edify myself
by your courage, faith, and joyful trust in the new
birth in Christ. You have been much to us, and
your memory will remain to us most blessed. And
now farewell ; here is my hand : we shall meet again,
dear **Perthes !**"

When Herbert was dying, and a friend was re-
minding **him of his many** acts of well-doing, the holy
man answered : "They be good works, if they **be**
sprinkled with the blood of Christ, and not otherwise."
Perthes is dying in the same meek lowliness of heart.
"Herder on his death-bed," he says, one evening,
"sought only an Idea; Goethe exclaimed—'Light,
light !' It would have been better," adds Perthes,
"**had** they cried out for love and humility." And,
another **day,** after a severe conflict, he says,
"Thanks **be to** God, my faith is firm, and holds in
death as **in life :** for His dear Son's sake, God is

merciful to me **a** sinner. And **as his** spirit is just winging its upward flight, weeping **friends** can **distinguish** only these words—" My Redeemer—Lord—forgiveness."

It **is a** heaven-lit scene, that death-chamber at Gotha. " When he folded his cold hands," writes **his** daughter, who is there, " and prayed from his inmost soul, we, too, were constrained to fold **our** hands and pray ; it was all **so** sublime, so blessed, **we** felt **as** though our Lord Jesus Christ were with us **in the** room. As evening **came** on, and lights were brought **in, a** strange halo **seemed to** encircle his brow, as if already he **were half in** heaven." " **The** last enemy," writes another eye-witness, " loses all his terrors to **us, and** the resurrection appears nearer to **us** than the death. We can think only of his bliss, not **of** our own sorrow. At half-past ten in **the** evening of Thursday, May 18, 1843, he calmly falls asleep. He rests from his labors, and his works do follow him.

> " 'Tis heaven, all heaven descending on the wings
>   Of the glad legions of the King of kings ;
>   'Tis more—'tis God diffused through **every part,**
>   'Tis God himself triumphant in his heart."

6

V.

The Christian Mother:

MRS. MARY WINSLOW.

"To learn much, to love much, and to suffer much, **are the** three requisites for woman."—PROTOPLAST.

"Be not conformed to this world, but be ye transformed by
the renewing of your mind."—*Rom.* xii. 2.

"LOVED *me* and gave Himself for ME!" That is the mainspring of every earnest life. It is the sun rising on the soul's dark night, and ushering in an unending day. The sun may be clouded by the mists of earth;—but it shines there bright and glorious—a sun which shall never set.

Not often, in these days, has the Church witnessed a life more finely sun-lit than the life of MRS. WINSLOW. It is no transcendental pattern, away from our human sympathies; but a calm, steady conflict with life's stern realities, crowned with a fitting triumph.

Woman is specially honored of God. Given by Him as man's complement and help-meet, she executes her mission most worthily by a meek and womanly mien.   The key to her whole being is **her heart.**

> " The world of the affections is thy world,
>   Not that of man's ambition.   In that stillness
>   Which most becomes a woman, calm and holy
>   Thou sittest by the fireside of the heart,
>   Feeding its flame."

And the woman-nature is never so beautiful as when it adorns this its befitting sphere.   The clinging tendril of the vine is not intended to do the office of the sturdy oak: each is perfect after its kind, and is **adapted to its** peculiar function.   **In** like manner **woman is not** intended for the work of the man : they **are each** adapted to their peculiar vocation. Never did **any** woman appreciate more correctly woman's **true** calling, than did **the** subject of **our** present memoir : *she* ran no risk of perverting the graceful and accomplished woman into " a deficient **man."**

CHAPTER I.

Birth—Bermuda—Wesley and the burning thatch at Epworth—The
ship of war—The cask of gunpowder—Antigua—The hurricane—
" Preserved in Christ Jesus"—The ball—" Is this all ?"—Refugees
—" A sinner"—Unhappy—Dawn of hope—Struggles—The meeting-
place—Rest.

I⊤ is in the island of Bermuda, and in the year
1774, that MARY WINSLOW first sees the light. He
who snatched the infant Wesley from the blazing
thatch at Epworth, and the youthful Joseph from
the living grave in Dothan, interposes in her behalf
more than once or twice. The first occasion is, a
sudden **recovery from** illness when about **five years**
of age, after she has been given over by her father **to**
die. But a more striking providence follows. Soon
after, she accompanies her parents, during the French
war, on a visit to England. The vessel in which
they sail is a light barque, carrying a few guns, and
but ill furnished for severe conflict with the enemy.
On entering the Channel, and midway between the

English and French coasts, a ship of war heaves in sight. It is toward night; and, as she appears to bear down upon them, the captain prepares for action. Mother and child are hurried from the **cabin** to what is thought a place of greater safety below. They have not **been** long **there** when the child observes **a** boy come occasionally to the place **of their** imprisonment, and with a large horn **in** his hand take something out of a barrel, having first fixed a lighted candle on its edge and leaving it there. **Observing,** as she sits upon her mother's lap—who is too absorbed in anxiety to notice the circumstance —that the piece of candle is nearly burnt to the edge—little Mary gets down, puts out her hand, and **takes** it away, saying, " Mamma, this will burn the **barrel."** It is **a** cask of gunpowder! " Had I not removed it at that moment," she writes long afterwards, alluding to the occasion, " or, in removing it, **had a spark** fallen **from** the lengthened wick, the vessel and all **on** board **must** instantly **have been** blown to **atoms."** Under cover **of** night, the vessel passes the man of war; and thus another peril is escaped.

And, on her return home across the ocean, during **a** brief call at Antigua a fire bursts out in the house where she is sleeping; and, in a few moments after **the alarm** has been given, the roof falls in with a fearful crash, and she barely escapes with her life. Some years afterwards, the vessel in which she is sailing from New York to Bermuda is overtaken, when within an hour of port, by a terrific hurricane, before which vessel after vessel is seen to go down full sail into the yawning waves; but Mary Winslow is again saved. By these repeated deliverances she is (as she used to express it) "*preserved* in Christ Jesus."

Those who have been so preserved are rarely left without a work to do. Married at the age of eighteen to Captain Winslow, a lineal descendant of one of the pilgrim fathers, she becomes the mother of eight sons, whom **she is** by and bye honored to train, as another Monica, for her Master's service.

That service she has not herself yet entered. One night, returning from a ball, where she has been " at **the** very zenith of earthly happiness," the thought **occurs to** her, as she lies sleepless on her pillow— **" Is** this all ?" Her heart is empty—she has grasped a phantom—and from that hour **she** finds no rest till she finds it at the feet of Jesus.

Various expedients are attempted, to fill the vacant heart. Ashamed to own herself unhappy, " even **to** her dearest friend," she turns from gaiety to " **domestic** enjoyment," seeking peace of mind there. And if a promising family, ample means, and **a** beautiful home could have given it, the treasure would not **have** been sought in vain. But " still," she says, " I **was** unhappy; I was a *sinner*—and this secret conviction beclouded **every** prospect and embittered every cup."

Years pass on, and the void is not filled. Having

retired to a rustic retreat in Essex, she devotes herself, in the intervals of domestic cares, to reading. But she is not happy. The barbed arrow is in her conscience; and the hand has not reached her, which alone can pluck it out. "My mind was restless," she writes: "my soul **wanted** what earth could not supply. And yet I could not describe to any one what I needed or what I **felt.** I was unhappy, at times miserable; my weary soul thirsting for what it had not—and yet I could not answer myself and say what that one thing was."

She next removes to London, her husband fondly fancying that its bustle and excitement may heal the wounded spirit. The change of residence is pleasant to her: she is thrown more among friends; and for **a** while her mind is diverted from its gloom. But **He who** leads His own by a way which they know **not, now** brings her to the place of rest. There has **lately entered** a neighboring pulpit a holy man of God, from whose lips she is to hear, for the first time in her life, **the** message of great joy. Eagerly she listens, drinking **in** every word! After having **in** vain endeavored to save herself, her work always falling short, and leaving her as poor and miserable as ever—she now learns for the first time that she may **be saved** by the work of another—the work of Jesus Christ. **On** one occasion, the preacher picturing her **own very** state at that moment, adds most solemnly: —"If there **is** such an individual present, I will pledge my soul for it that that individual is in the way to Christ." She thinks, if this be true, she may, after all, be saved. Repairing to her Bible, and searching it again and again, she is arrested by the passage—" By grace are ye saved through faith, and that not **of** yourselves, it is the gift of God." But, not long after, she reads in the Epistle of James that we are "justified by **works** ;" and immediately her heart sinks within her, **for she** feels she has no works, and can do none pleasing and acceptable to God. And yet in the Epistles of Paul she reads that we are "justified by faith." There seems a contradiction. Her anxious mind can find no rest : though, animated by that ray of hope which **has** risen upon her benighted soul, she continues to **hear** the precious truth as one hungering and thirsting for divine knowledge.

One night watching alone **by the** side of a sick child, she takes her Bible **and** searches the Scriptures. The question, " How can the sinner be justified ?" presses heavily on her mind. If she can be saved **by** faith in the righteousness of another, **then** there **is hope** for **her ;** but if there be anything **for** her **to do towards** meriting this salvation, **she sees** she must **be for** ever lost. At last the **words** are brought **to** her mind—" Ask, and **ye shall** receive." " Who is it," she asks herself, " **that** says this ? It **is** God. Can God lie ? It is impossible. He *must* **do** what He has said." **She falls** upon her knees. **Her** petition is offered **in the** simple language **of an** untutored child. She knows nothing of **Christian** experience—has heard the Gospel but a few times—and the only thing which has fastened itself upon her mind is the truth that a poor sinner can be saved. Time after time she pleads **that** word, " Ask, and ye shall receive."   **At length,** light breaks in upon her soul.   Jesus seems to stand before her, and to utter those blessed words—" I am thy salvation."   She hails the glad tidings ; her heart and soul respond. Jesus **is** with her—He has Himself spoken—her soul is saved—the grave-clothes, in which she has **been** so long confined, fall off—her spirit is free—she rises from her knees to adore, and praise, and bless His holy name.

This is the finger of God.   " It was no vision of the bodily senses which I saw," she says ; " but I **had** no more doubt that I was a redeemed and **pardoned** sinner—that I had seen Christ, and held communion with him who died that I might live, than **I** had of my own existence."

CHAPTER II.

———

The acorn and the oak—A right start—Trials—" An undivided family in heaven"—New-York—Conversions—Revivals—End of Gospel-ministry—Cecil—The three " ideas"—Activities and awakenings—Unbelief—Return to London—Harrington Evans—Our calling—" Gossiping professors"—A poison.

"MIGHT not the man," asks Vinet, somewhere, " who holds in his hand an acorn, **say,** 'I hold in my hand an oak ?' Is not the whole of a river in its source ?" Just so, the soul which has found a free acceptance through the blood of Christ, may be said to have in it already the whole elements of the Christian life. Mrs. Winslow now finds herself welcomed in her Father's house ; and, **her** person being thus accepted, her **whole** future life of service **and** of suffering is transformed into " a living sacrifice."

" Everything," she once said, many years afterwards, looking back upon this turning-point of her spiritual life, " depends upon a right beginning. One wrong turn in setting out, and all will be wrong the whole of the way. The starting-point for the saint of God is the finished work of Jesus—to know he is pardoned and accepted in the beloved of God the Father. He then can run the race with holy delight; and, though he may necessarily have many enemies **to** contend with, both from within and from without, yet He who has **once** set him **upon** his feet, and bid him go forward, **will** watch over him by day and by **night,** guide him, and **correct him when** needful, and assuredly enable him to hold out to the end." That starting-point Mrs. Winslow has now, after many tossings and anxieties, reached ; and seldom has **a** race been run so patiently and so nobly.

The Hill Difficulty soon rises before her. Suddenly crippled in her resources by certain "disastrous investments," and scarcely less suddenly bereaved of her husband, she finds herself summoned **to a** task such as few women could have mastered. **But** with **a** strong will, and with a heart " at leisure from itself," she sets her face steadfastly **to** the Hill, and bravely ascends.

" An undivided family in heaven" is now her first and her last aim. It is during one of those remarkable revivals with which the land of the pilgrim fathers has been so often visited, that she begins to reap the earliest fruits of this longing. There has been formed in New York a little circle of Christian mothers, who assemble weekly for special prayer on behalf of their families. From these meetings Mrs. Winslow has been seen to return not seldom " with tearful eyes and a glowing countenance," as if He, whose fellowship on the Mount made Moses' face shine, had been with those holy women. In various churches, and in individual families, **a** work of God commences. Three of Mrs. Winslow's sons—all who at the time reside with her—are awakened and brought to Christ. " Not one unconverted soul," we find her writing, **" is** under my roof. All love the Saviour. My house is **a** house of prayer."

These revivals are most instructive facts, and peculiarly humbling. That counterfeits have appeared on the American soil, with only the mechanical imitation of the inward heart-work, is tolerably certain. But what more convincing evidence of the existence of the real thing? " Several **churches," Mrs.** Winslow writes, describing one of those scenes, " have partaken of this heavenly shower. Oh! it is a refreshing season. The Lord is pouring out His Spirit in a way I never before saw or felt. There is nothing like enthusiasm. I am quite inadequate to give you any just **idea** of this most gracious and solemn work of God. It is **to** me something like the day of **Pentecost.** I look back and see with such concern **how I** have loitered **on my way."**

Is not that **the great want of the** present hour? **It** is not philosophy we want in our **pulpits,** nor cold criticism in our pews—it is the tongue of fire— the pricked heart—the awakened conscience. It is real, downright plucking men out of the fire. Cecil was right when, describing the true character of the Gospel-ministry, he wrote: " Hell is before me, and

thousands of souls shut up there in everlasting agonies—Jesus Christ stands forth to save men from
rushing into this bottomless abyss—He sends me to
proclaim His ability and His love : I want no fourth
idea! every fourth idea is contemptible! every fourth
idea is a grand impertinence!"

And when God is working thus in the public assembly, it sends **men** to **their** homes and to their
trades, not to lay aside the Sunday religion with the
Sunday dress, but to carry it about with them as **a**
part of themselves. "Everything under my roof,"
writes Mrs. Winslow, "seems to wear another aspect.
Old things have passed away, and all things have become new. I can say of my children—' Behold, Lord,
they pray.' The things of God open upon them with
deep interest. The ways of wisdom are pleasant, and
everything not connected therewith tasteless. Ask and
expect," she adds, "great things from God. You
cannot ask too much, when you ask in Jesus' name ;
and God cannot give too much, when He gives for
Jesus' sake. **How near** he has **been** to us ! The
angels in heaven rejoice over one sinner that repent-
eth ; and here **are three to** whom Jesus has given repentance and life under my roof. **If** the angels **re-**
joice in heaven, well may I rejoice on earth."

Are we here in England always to be satisfied with
the low standard of godliness which everywhere prevails? **Are** we to go on from week to week, complacently resting in our religious activities, and
content to have scarcely any conversions? What

are we doing? Are we pleading believingly enough
with God for men? and are we pleading earnestly
enough with men for God? " How is it," we find
Mrs. Winslow inquiring, years afterwards, " that we
have no precious revivals here, and that the all-important subject lies with so little weight upon our
hearts? It is because we do not believe the matter-
of-fact, although God has promised, and declared the
truth. When Christ had risen, and some were eye-
witnesses of the fact, yet, when they declared the
blessed truth to the rest, they were as those that
mocked. We testify that these things are so, for we
have seen and felt them ourselves. The **doors have**
been shut about us, and Jesus has been in our midst
within, blessing, reviving, and refreshing us—giving
life to the dead and speaking comforting words to
His saints. It has been the work of an Almighty
God, manifesting His power, and displaying His
love. Oh! the mighty power of prayer! Even the
best of Christians know but little what it really is."

Returning in 1828 to London, and attaching **her-**
self to the church of that venerable man of **God, the**
late Mr. Harrington Evans, she labors for souls **with**
an earnestness **which** not many in a lukewarm age
can comprehend. **"It is** our duty," **she** writes in
her Diary, **"to have our eyes shut, and our** ears
stopped, to everything that is not **a** step in that ladder which reaches from earth to heaven. I cannot
understand some Christians, and they do not understand **me.** I may be wrong; but when I read—

' Come out of the world, and be ye separate; love **not the** world, nor the things which are in the world,' **and** many other such solemn exhortations, with so many exceeding great and precious promises to the overcoming Christian—I am satisfied of the way a believer in **Christ** should walk, and **have** only to regret I **so** often wander from **it** myself. Dear Saviour! keep me near, **very** near, thy blessed self." And on another **occasion:**—" Avoid **trifling,** lukewarm professors. **They are** the bane of the church of Christ. If you can **do** them no good, they **will** do **you** much harm." And again :—" I wish to caution you against a great evil in many churches—I allude to gossiping **professors, who,** when they **meet,** instead of talking of Christ, talk about almost everything else ;—' busy-bodies,' who go from house to house speaking things which **they** ought not. Oh, what a dishonor are **such to the** cause of the dear Redeemer! Rebuke such in gentleness of spirit, and withdraw from them." And still again :—" I am convinced that much intercourse with lukewarm professors does great injury to the believer. Oh, avoid such! Light and trifling conversation acts as a poison to the life of God in the soul."

CHAPTER III.

"Company-keeping with Jesus"—Little cares—The "confidant"—A trial—Evidences—How brightened?—Each day—"Praise him for the present"—Robert Bruce—The voice in the vestry—"Preaching in prayer"—Unkindness—Henry Martyn—The best of all well-doing—The alleys—The cottage—A contrast.

CHRISTIANITY has been described as "a company-keeping with Jesus." Seldom has any Christian more strikingly realized the idea than did **Mrs. Winslow** during the last twenty years of **her life.** "Keep close to JESUS," we find her saying. "**Go to** HIM for all **you need.** Tell HIM all that **is in** your heart. Lay your case before Him as if He did not already know it. This is the **sweet** simplicity of faith which Christ loves. You cannot come too often. Bring to Him your little cares, as well as your great ones. If anything is a trouble to you, however small it may be, you are warranted, nay commanded, to take it to HIM; and thereby you glorify his name. Satan would keep you away from Him; but Christ is as needful for you every step you take to glory, as when you were overwhelmed with sorrow under **a** sense of your awful state as a sinner before God." And elsewhere she writes:— "Be very cautious to whom you open your heart. Make no one your confidant but Jesus. Oh! commune with Him of all that is in your heart. **If** you are wounded, go and tell Christ—if you are **in** need, go and tell Christ—the silver and the gold are His. Live upon Him as little children would live upon a dear, kind, tender father. Oh! how happily will you then pass on your way!"

A personal example of this let us quote. "I awoke in the night," she writes in her Diary, July **13th** (1828); "and a care, something like a trial in **prospect,** presented itself to **my** mind. I could not sleep till **I had** laid it before the Lord. Almost directly afterward I fell asleep. I had unburdened myself to Him who has all hearts in His hands, and my mind was at peace."

Another feature of her Christian life is **to be** noted. "Never," she writes, on one occasion, "never look *within* for comfort. You will find nothing there but what is calculated to humble you. **But look to** JESUS. There is everything in Him to encourage you in your warfare. Oh! live upon Him, out of yourselves." And on another occasion, thus: —"A mistake, common to many Christians, is the habit **of** looking for ever *within* for some evidence of their adoption ; and, finding nothing there, they do not and cannot rejoice. This is a serious defect. It **is** not by looking within ourselves, but, on the contrary, it is by looking quite out of ourselves, and directing the eye alone to Christ—to what Christ is, and where Christ is—that we obtain real consolation ; and in proportion to our faith in Him, we **not** only rejoice, but **our** evidences brighten, and **the** Spirit within, whose office it is to glorify Christ, bears witness with our spirit that **we are** born **of** God."

It **is a** blessed attainment to live for each day, and for each day only. **We** have grace promised to bear *present* evils, but none to bear anticipated ones. Reader ! are you tried with fears **and** anxieties about the future ? Lately, a young person told the writer that such was her fear **for** the future that she had been tempted again and again to take away her life. Few people have been tried more deeply than Mrs. Winslow ; and here is her judgment about the **way of** bearing it :—" I do think, by constantly poring **over** anticipated troubles, we lose the sweet enjo**yment** of present mercies **in the** expectation of **future** evil. I pray to be enabled to praise Him **for the** present, and to trust His love for all that **is to** come. Lord, increase my faith, and let my **joy be** full."

It is told **of the Rev. Robert** Bruce, that on one occasion he delayed so long appearing in the pulpit that a friend went to the vestry, fearing that he had been taken ill.   As he approached the door, he overheard a voice as if of one engaged in earnest colloquy; and, as he listened more attentively, the speaker **was** insisting, that, unless accompanied by Him to whom he spoke, he could not leave that place.   It was the preacher on his knees before the Lord; and when that preacher entered the pulpit, oh, how he prayed and preached!   Often, often does Mrs. Winslow deplore the absence of such praying.   "This evening," we find her writing in her Diary, "attended a prayer-meeting for the outpouring of the Spirit. The fault I generally perceive with most prayer-meetings occurred again to-night.   The prayers were too long, and not to the point.   Everything was touched upon but the one thing we had agreed **to** meet and pray for.   I do wish there were less *preaching* in prayer, and more *beseeching*, as poor needy sinners, for what we want."   And on another occasion, writing to one of **her** sons, she says:— "You know **my** dislike to preaching in prayer. Prayer is the most holy exercise of the soul, and should be the pure breathings of the renewed heart in humble, earnest petition, as in the presence of a holy God.   And when the soul feels in the presence of God, and loses sight of the worms of the dust who are listening, there is no self-seeking or wish to please the **ear of** man, but humbly to get the blessed ear **of God Himself."**

One of our most trying vexations is men's slanderous whisperings.   It is a blessed secret of the hidden life to rise triumphant over this trial. "Dost thou receive," wrote a holy man who lived in Italy two centuries ago, "an injury from any man? There are two things in it—the sin of him that does it, and the punishment thou sufferest; the sin is against the will of God, and displeases Him, though He permit it; the punishment is conform to His will, and He wills **it** for thy good—wherefore thou oughtest **to** receive **it** as from His hand." That man was imprisoned in the Inquisition for eight-and-twenty years; and when he was entering his dungeon he smiled pleasantly and serenely, calling **it his "cabi-net."** Mrs. Winslow is learning the **same** heavenly lesson. "How often," we find her writing on one occasion in her Diary, " has an unkind look or word proved a blessing to my soul! It has made me flee to Christ; and there I have found no unkindness. He has appeared at such times more than to make up for the want of all creature-love and created good." It was Henry Martyn, if we remember rightly, who on one occasion, taking refuge **from** man's unkindness in the secret of the Lord's presence, wrote:—" I shall never **have** to regret that **I loved** Thee too well."

Foster has described the Christian**'s labor** of love for Christ as the best of all the well-doings on this gloomy planet. Mrs. Winslow **still** counts it her **joy to** spend and to **be spent for** Him. "I have just returned," we find her writing, " from visiting the poor and wretched in the lanes and alleys in this great town. I often have thought that the Lord had nothing more for me to do; but He seems to **have** called me to my old work again, and it is one I always had, and still have, great delight in. May He bless it to me, and to the poor to whom I am sent!" And on another occasion describing some work of the same kind down **in the** country, **she** says:—"I have just returned from **a** visit to my poor pilgrim. I walked softly **in,** and found her with her glasses on, attentively reading **a** book she had upon her lap. 'What are you reading?' I inquired. 'The Shepherd, ma'am; the Shepherd who laid down His life for the sheep,' looking up into my face with an expression of sweet peace and content. '**Have** you dined?' I said. 'Yes.' 'What have **you** had?' 'Boiled milk.' This, I found, was her **chief diet ;** and oh, how happy she is! She says she **is** happier than the rich or the mighty in their palaces; **and from my** heart I believe it." And another case she names:—"I went last evening to see an aged pilgrim in **the** village. She abounds in all the comforts of life—has a nice house, comfortable farm, and every thing to make her happy. But she is far from being so; for, although I believe her to be a child of God, she is constantly harassed with the idea that she has grieved away the Spirit, and will be **lost for ever.** I have endeavored to cheer her up by leading **her to** look more to Christ than to herself. I sat with her last night for nearly an hour, and found it refreshing to my soul to speak of Jesus."

CHAPTER IV.

United States—Awakening—"Our great crime"—A convert—"Old-fashioned conversions"—The way of blood—"My confessional"—Assurance—Second Advent—"Watch!"

In 1833, Mrs. **Winslow** is in New York, on **her** final **visit to the** United States. **During** her stay, another remarkable awakening visits the churches. Relating a scene in one of the congregations, she writes:—"The ministers who conduct the meetings seem men of God, and preach as with the great white throne full in view. The grand aim in their preaching and addresses is, to rouse the sinner—to follow him in all his refuges of lies—to knock from beneath him every false prop, and to **show him, that, if** he perishes, the fault **is not God's, but his own.** Next to this, their endeavor is to awaken **the church** itself to activity and earnestness in the cause of God. After the sermon, all who feel themselves lost and undone sinners are invited to come forward and occupy pews in front of the pulpit. The praying part of the assembly then cluster round them, and peti tions are offered on their behalf. This would be a new and strange thing in England; but God sees fit to own it to the salvation of many souls. Last evening, I felt it peculiarly solemn—I felt that *God was there.* Seventeen individuals advanced—many young, some elderly men—deeply concerned. There was no excitement—no noise or enthusiasm. The feeling was deep, silent, solemn as eternity. All knelt and followed in prayer."

And, on the same occasion, she adds:—" While the Church is stirred up to plead earnestly for sinners, the Lord the Spirit causes them to feel their own lack, and brings them to God in humble confession of their coldness and unbelief. Unbelief, unbelief! oh, this is our great crime before God! We will not take Him at His word, fully believing all that He has promised. Did we really believe that sinners will be cast into hell, should we not be more earnest both with them and with God, although we do know that salvation is of God, and that He alone can save a sinner? If the religion of Christ is not *the* business of our whole life, it is nothing, and we are nothing, and shall be found as nothing, or worse than nothing, when He comes to judge the world."

And, the following day, she writes:—" The Lord is doing a great work here; whole families have, in these last two weeks, been translated out of the kingdom of Satan into the kingdom of God's dear Son; and many more are inquiring what they shall do to be saved. I am glad to be where Jesus is passing by. A young lady in the bloom of health and beauty, living in all the gaiety of the world, was brought under the appalling conviction of her awful state before a holy God. For nights she scarcely knew what it was to sleep. A few days after, while she was in prayer, and while prayer was being made for her by the church, the Lord revealed Himself to her soul, and filled it with unspeakable joy. Her eyes were now opened, and every thing appeared changed. She was happy in the Lord, and her countenance was radiant. When her minister entered the parlor and extended his hand, he said, ' I need not ask how it is with you; I see you have been with Jesus.' I must add that this young convert, in all the fervor of her first love, went from house to house amongst her kinsfolk and friends, imploring them to come and hear the gospel."

And once again, a few days later (to Rev. J. H. Evans) :—" I think I never before heard such fervent appeals to the consciences of men, so completely divesting them of all their refuges of lies, as I have this last week. How I do love old-fashioned conversions, where sinners are brought to feel they are sinners, crying out under the conviction, ' What must I do to be saved ?' and are then led by the self-same Spirit to look to Jesus, and are at once enabled to believe and rejoice ! I cannot understand this long process of months' and years' seeking, and seeking, and never finding, until, *perhaps*, at a dying hour. God is the same now that he was in the New Testament times—

Christ is the same—the Spirit is the same—and the sinner is the same. Oh that the Lord might visit you in your part of the vineyard! Endeavor to show sinners their awful condition; scatter their vain excuses; and tell them they must repent and believe the Gospel, or they are lost for ever. They need not be told they have no power to repent and believe: they will soon find they are *powerless*, and begin to cry for mercy to Him who will give repentance, and power to believe **too**. I love poor perishing sinners more than I can express. I have been very narrow-hearted and selfish; and I hate and abhor myself because of it."

The heart rests upon Christ's person—the conscience upon His *atoning blood*. Mrs. Winslow feels, each day she lives, the growing preciousness of such **a Saviour**. "The way to God," we find her writing **now, in** her sixty-second year, " has seemed to me of late **so** delightful—so exactly suited to a poor lost sinner—so suited **to me**. A way sprinkled with atoning blood : justice and mercy as a wall of defence on either side ; and this way leading to such **a** rich treasure-house, filled with all blessing for time and for eternity ! All is in Jesus—the way to God, **the** way of holiness, the way to glory." And a specimen of the way in which she personally applied this truth occurs elsewhere thus :—" You may, perhaps, **wonder** why confession of sin should be the subject upon which I have chiefly written. I had **just** returned, when I took up my pen to address you, from my *confessional*—the throne of grace—so sweetly refreshed and so blessedly pardoned, that **I** could not refrain recommending it to all **I** love and write to, as one of the most hallowed exercises of the Christian. **I** often repair to **it** heavily laden, and return **as** though nestling beneath the wing of the Saviour. If there is a cloud between you and Christ, rest **not** till it withdraws. Go again and again, should there be but a shade, until it is **put** away and you see Him who loves you."

Like not a few Christians of the present day, Mrs. Winslow has not hitherto had her thoughts directed to the Lord's Second Coming. About **the** year 1840, however, she is led into this truth. " I grieve," **she** writes, " that I have so long neglected to search into this glorious subject. As it opens upon me, I feel my soul led out in grateful praise and thanksgiving. Oh, to love Jesus more, and to **have** Him more in our thoughts ! How soon we *may* behold Him in all His glory, coming in the clouds of heaven ! May the Lord keep us watching and waiting, and enable us to say, ' Come, Lord Jesus, come quickly !' "

8*

CHAPTER V.

Instinct of advancing years—A little child—A bereavement—"Clap
his glad wings"—The promise and the precept—A temptation—Foster—Not faint—A pattern—"Only two"—"Love turns the wheel."

IT is an instinct of advancing years to return to
the scenes and associations of youth and of childhood.
In like manner, the instinct of the maturing Christian leads him back with a freshening zest to the
simplicities of his first love. "Who can subdue sin
in us but Jesus?" writes our venerable friend. "I
might as well attempt to remove mountains as to
reason away one corruption of my fallen nature. But
if we, the moment we detect it, carry it to Jesus, He
will do it all for us. This is one of the most difficult
lessons to learn in the school of Christ. I am but
just beginning to learn it; and therefore I am placed
in the youngest class, travelling to Jesus more as
little helpless child, for Him to do all for me and
all in me. My fancied strength is all vanished, my
boasted reason turned into folly; and now, thus living on Christ in childlike simplicity, my peace, joy

and consolation are past expression." And, on another occasion : " Oh, to believe that Jesus is indeed at the right hand of God! on **the** resurrection of Christ depends our eternal all. Upon that single and glorious truth hinges every other. If that **be true,** all that He has said, all that He has promised, **and** all that He has engaged to do, is true."

One **of** her sons is suddenly snatched from her side, and she pours out her heart thus : " Dear **Henry** is gone home, and I am a bereaved mother. He **sleeps** in Jesus. And now thou art beholding **in** all His glory Him whom thou didst long to see coming in that glory in the clouds of heaven." **And she** adds : " He was fully prepared for the **change, and** was more fitted for heaven than **for earth.** The world seemed to **have** no charms for **him.** It had lost its hold for a **long** period. **He was** living in full **expectation** of **Christ's** coming, and now he is with **Him** whom he **so** ardently desired to see. **Day** and night he was looking for Him, as if ' hastening unto the coming of the Lord ; so that Christ was in all his thoughts. When he had to grapple with the ' last enemy,' he feared not death, and, to use his **own words,** ' longed to clap his glad **wings,** and fly to Jesus.' This affliction has wafted me closer to my happy **home.** Oh, to realize it fully, **even** here !"

Grace in the heart always bears the fruit of honest dealing ; and if ever it be accompanied with any crookedness of way, it is because that man has, not too much grace, but too little. " Remember," we have Mrs. Winslow saying on one occasion to her son, **who** is practising at the bar, " that to walk in the *precept* is the way to the full enjoyment of the promise. We must not expect the comfort of the one without the observance of the other. Rather than incur debt, exercise the most rigid self-denial. Go not against **God,** and **God** will be for you. None ever disobey Him but are sure to pay the penalty of disobedience. I speak now of His own children. Never undertake a cause without kneeling down and asking the Lord for wisdom and grace. If Solomon felt it needful to do this, well may you. Christ says, ' Without me ye can do nothing.' Be not fearful you will lose your cause by so doing; but only trust your case in the Lord's hands, and, if a just one, He will prosper you. Walk in His fear, and you need fear nothing **else."**

Reader ! are you ready to faint under the yoke ? Is **Satan** tempting you at this moment to grow " weary in well-doing ?" " Look up to heaven," says Foster, " and **see the** beams of the Divine complacency ! I obtain little of human favor to animate me in my work ; well, but God is pleased. I accomplish too little by all my efforts—but He does not ' despise **small** things.' Do you say, ' I have not resolution and **patience** to go on ?' What ! not to please God ?" And, appealing to the instance of the Master, he adds :—" Think **of** His appointed work, the greatest that ever was to be done on earth. If *He* had been ' wearied,' and left but one thing undone ! If He had shrunk

and failed, what sensation in heaven—hell—earth!
Let His followers advert to that, when tempted to
shrink from service, and to say it is too much. When
this repugnance arises, go and look at Him! Even
imagine that any given Christian service **had been** to
be performed *in His presence*—under His inspiration
—would you then be weary? He is the grand **trans-
cendant** example, to show that a good work must **be**
gone through with : **to** constitute it such, **the conclusion** is indispensable. '**He** that endureth **to** the end
shall be saved.' '**He** that looketh back is not fit for
the kingdom of God.'" And Mrs. Winslow, herself
now far on in **the** "course," summons a fainting fel-
low-pilgrim to new faith, and **new energy, and** new
patience, thus : "**And so** you **are** discouraged? Trials
and difficulties **many ;** faith **tried; and only** three
met. **Did you** expect to undertake **a work for** Christ
and **get on** smoothly, while there **is** every thing within
and without to oppose it? Did you expect faith would
not **be** tried in this matter? In a country-place in
America, a few Christian females engaged to meet **to**
pray for a blessing on their families ; but after **a** while
it declined, **and** continued **to do so until only two** came.
'Shall we **give it up ?' was the** question. **They** thought
of God's faithfulness **to His** promise, **of his** power and
goodness, and **they** resolved to **go on.** They met,
these two only, again **and** again. They pleaded the
promise, and encouraged each **other** by their prayers.
At last *the answer came.* **God** tried their faith ; Je-
sus interceded, and it had not failed. Some who had

left them returned; others followed; and the place of prayer was soon filled. The Lord poured out His Spirit on them, and they prayed in earnest until the blessing was given. The Church felt the holy influence; their children at home began to inquire what they must do to be saved; the mothers directed them to Jesus, and prayed on. God in very deed bowed the heavens, and came down in their midst to bless them. Dear sister, take courage and look up. Expect difficulties—expect opposition, even from your own heart; but you have the Lord on your side. Go forward in the strength of Jehovah Jesus, and God must and will bless you."

And *how* to labor **on** she indicates **in** another letter, thus:—"The Lord has brought me here, I **trust,** for some service He has for me to do. If His servants, we ought to be doing His work; and it is **so sweet** to work when *love* turns the wheel. It is the **love of** God in the heart that sets us all in motion. I am persuaded it is irksome where this is not the case. To work for **God** as **a** hireling is one thing, and to work for Him as a son is another."

CHAPTER VI.

Simeon—" Collar of my coat"—The blacksmith—The " unanswerable
argument" — Baxter—" Taking walks above"—The home—Grand
Salève—Mountain sunshine—Child of the mist—" Worth living for"
—Have God's ear—Sin.

ONE day Charles Simeon stood at the death-bed of a brother. " I am dying," said he, grasping his hand with deep emotion, " and you have never warned me of the state I was in, and of my danger in neglecting the salvation of my soul." " Nay, my brother," answered Simeon, " I have often brought it before you in my letters." " Yes, but that was not enough. You never came to me—closed the door—and took me by the collar of my coat, and told me I **was** unconverted, and that if I died in that state **I** should be lost." That **scene** Mr. Simeon **never** forgot; and oftentimes does Mrs. Winslow appeal to **it** as quickening exceedingly her zeal on behalf of perishing souls. " Oh !" she will be heard saying, as the great tear of **tender** compassion trembles in her eye, " who will warn —**who will** entreat them ?"

And no dreaded "awkwardnesses" hinders the plainest and most downright appeals. It is told **of a** working man, that one cold winter morning he entered the forge of a blacksmith, with whom he **had** held frequent discussions about the Gospel. The blacksmith was an infidel; and only the previous night they had parted, the infidel objections answered, **but** the infidel himself hardened **in** heart as ever. His friend, **on** going home, had, instead **of** going **to** bed, spent **the** greater part of the night in prayer for him. Early in the morning he mounted on one of the horses of the farm, and rode through a drifting snow to the **forge.** Dismounting at the door, **he went** up to his friend, and, taking him by the **hand,** he, with tears in his eyes, said—" I am greatly concerned for your salvation !—I **am** greatly concerned for your salvation !" And, with another **friendly** grasp, he left the forge, remounted his horse, **and hastened** home. " That," said the blacksmith, **describing the** incident, not long afterwards, as the **turning-point of** his life, " that was **the** unanswerable argument—I could not gainsay that !" All who see Mrs. Winslow feel, in her earnest heartmelting appeals, the power of that argument.

Baxter, in his " Saints' Rest," stimulating the soul **to new** attainments in the heavenly life, gives this **counsel :—" Let** thy faith take hold of thy heart, and show **it the** sumptuous buildings **of** thine eternal habitation, and **the** glorious ornaments of thy Father's house, even the mansions Christ is preparing, and the honors of His kingdom; let thy faith lead thy heart into the presence of God, and as near as thou possibly canst, and say to it, 'Behold Him! Here is an object worthy of thy love! here thou shouldst pour out thy soul in love! here it is impossible to love too much.' This is He who hath loaded thee with His benefits, 'spread thy table in the sight of thine enemies, and made thy cup overflow.' This is He whom angels and saints praise, and the 'heavenly hosts for ever magnify.' Open thus his excellences to thy heart, till the holy fire of love begins to kindle in thy breast. And if thou feelest thy love not yet burn, lead thy heart further, and show it Him who was dead and is **alive** for evermore. Draw near, and behold Him. **Dost** thou not hear his voice? He that bade Thomas come near and see the print of the nails, and put his finger into His wounds, He calls to *thee*, saying, ' Come near, and view the Lord thy Saviour, and be not faithless, but believing : Peace be unto thee; fear not, it is I.' Look well upon Him. Dost thou not know Him? Or, if **thou** knowest Him not by the face, the voice, the hands— thou mayest know Him by the heart : **that** soul-pitying heart is His; it can be none **but** His; love and compassion are its certain signatures; this is He who chose thy life before His **own,** who pleads His blood before His Father, and **makes** continual inter-cession for thee. And is **not** here fuel enough for love to feed on? Doth not **thy** throbbing heart stop here to ease itself, and, like Joseph, seek for a place to weep in?" One of Mrs. Winslow's favorite expressions, and not less special joys, is, "taking walks above"—such walks as Richard Baxter found to be his daily strength and rest. "Only think of this," we find her writing (February 10, 1840) to a tried saint: "Jesus is above, and is ready to welcome you home. Let us hourly realize this—realize heaven, with all its glories. What rapture to fall at His feet, and to hear him say, 'Come, ye blessed of my Father!' Oh, that the saints of God would live more in the anticipation of the glory that awaits them! There is much of heaven to be enjoyed even on earth." And, another day, she says:—"My soul seems swallowed up in God. I feel heaven so near, that I am almost in the actual presence. Yes, Jesus is above. Our own Joseph lives."

One autumn morning a traveller left Geneva to ascend the Grand Salève. A thick mist enveloped the valley as he began the steep ascent. Mounting by a zigzag path in the face of the hill, he suddenly emerged into a brilliant sunshine—a sea of mist, as smooth as a chalcedony, still covering all beneath. The chime of the village-bells, the lowing of the oxen, the busy hum of industry, came up from the valley, as if they were things of another sphere; and yet but a brief moment sufficed to carry down this denizen of this mountain-sunshine into the region of mist and of earnest life. Mrs. Winslow's "walks above" resemble that morning's ascent into the Alpine sunshine. Not sentimental journeys into the regions of romance, but occasions of real communion with her living God—they bring her down into these scenes of mist, encircled with a fresh halo of heavenly buoyancy and joy. "Oh, may a view of the blessings awaiting us," she writes on **one of** those occasions, "encourage our hearts to press on to know more and more of the power of Christ's resurrection in our souls, that we may manifest it by a holy walk **and** conversation before a gainsaying world! **Let it be your chief** work, and occupy your best **thoughts. Look** not behind, but press forward. **Heaven is** worth living for, and it is worth **dying** for."

Another of the lessons which **she** learns, in these "walks above," **is—an** ever-freshening confidence toward **the Lord.** "When **I go,**" she writes, "to **the** throne **of grace, I** cannot **be** satisfied unless I feel **I have** the ear of God. I cannot be happy, if I have not communion with Him whom my soul loveth. Go, under all circumstances, and tell Him all. **Oh,** *keep an open heart* with the Saviour of sinners." **And** again:—"Let us live more in holy familia**rity with** Jesus. Nothing is too much beneath **His notice. As** dear old John Newton says, **'If** the **buzzing of** a fly is an annoyance to us, **it is our privilege to** carry it to Jesus.'"

And another **lesson is—an** ever-deepening hatred **of** sin. **"I think** that in general," she says, "we do **but** take too superficial a view of what sin is in the sight **of** God, a holy God, and we do not sufficiently examine our hearts by His holy law. Such **a view** of what sin is would make us cling closer to the cross of Christ; it would send **us** oftener to the atoning blood for cleansing, **and** endear to **us** the **worth** and preciousness of a throne of grace. **It** would also keep us from being mere yea-and-nay Christians, or half-hearted Christians. A slight, imperfect knowledge **of** what sin is, leads to almost **every evil into** which **a** Christian **is** liable to fall."

CHAPTER VII.

The Egyptian statue—Vocal **by sun's** rays—Life-harp—"Hearsay Christians"—An "unknown **God**"—**The** "earthly house" crumbling—Fainting fit—"None like Jesus"—"**Best** time"—Illness—"Not yet"—"Something more to learn"—Port **in view**—"Pin by pin"—Heaven a place—"Deify Christ's humanity"—Snare.

It is **fabled of an** Egyptian statue, that, when the sun **rose upon it, the** strings within became vocal. It **is** no **fable, that** no sooner does the Sun of Righteousness rise on the statue-like religiousness of the poor formalist, than the heart's life-harp is attuned to a heavenly melody of praise. Herself rejoicing in the happy joys of the heavenly life, Mrs. Winslow seems to yearn with a new compassion over **the** lifeless form. "Oh, how few," we have her writing, "really know God! I meet with many *hearsay* Christians, who have heard of Jesus **with** the hearing **of** the ear, but who have no **person**al acquaintance with Him. They have never **come** to Christ as poor, wretched, blind and naked; and, therefore, they know nothing of that peace which the application of the atoning blood alone can impart. They **have never come in** contact with Christ. They only believe what others say of Him, and know nothing of a blessed recognition—a oneness and a holy intercourse between Jesus and the poor sinner, saved by sovereign grace and everlasting love."

And, on another occasion, she adds:—"What communion can a formalist have with God? He regularly says his prayers, but it is to an *unknown* God. There is no response, no interchange of feeling—above all, of love. There is no answer from the Lord, no bending down of His ear, no lifting up of His countenance, no cheering welcome. And the formalist is satisfied;—he does what he thinks his duty; he repeats his lifeless, heartless, meaningless prayers, and thinks he has done well;—and so he lives and dies with a lie in his right hand."

The soul's " dark cottage" is now crumbling down. " I have had one of my alarming fainting fits," she writes, in the autumn of 1851, " and often think I may go off in one of them. God be praised for all His love-tokens. These visitations are nothing more. The oftener the gold is put into a furnace, the more the dross is consumed, and the brighter it shines. In the trial, we cling closer to Jesus; we see more of His loving heart, and imbibe more of His lovely image. We cannot come into close contact with Christ, and not get good. Touch but the hem of His garment, and virtue flows." And, somewhat later:—" I have been feeble; but this I must expect according to the course of things in this changing, fading world. Oh, to live upon Jesus—to live for Him—and, in a measure, even now to live *with* Him!

It is a narrow road the followers of Christ walk ; but it is the footpath He Himself travelled, and it is a great honor put upon a follower of Him to tread in the same. In all my helplessness I lean upon Him. There is none like Jesus, the once despised Nazarene, who trod this earth in loneliness and poverty, despised and rejected of men. The honors of this poor world are not worth a thought. May the Lord keep you more than merely satisfied ; may you always *rejoice* that He has called you to take up a cross for Him who bore so heavy a one for you, that you may hereafter, after a little while, wear a crown ! I am increasingly feeble. Humanly speaking, I think this will be my last summer on earth. Well, be it so ; the Lord knows the best time, and He will take care of His own."

This summer, an illness seizes her, which seems to intimate that ere very long the clay-tabernacle must be "dissolved." But a respite is given. "'Not yet !' said the Saviour," she writes, September 24, 1853 ; "'a little longer trial and conflict in the wilderness.' I have something more to learn of my helplessness and weakness. It is but a little, and we shall pass away ; all our sicknesses, trials, and disappointments are needful to fit us for it. I have, through a long-protracted life, waded through much tribulation ; and now I feel that I have not had one sorrow amiss. The port is almost in view, and how pleasant it looks !"

The " abundant entrance" is not to be much longer delayed. "Shall soon be with Jesus," she says, one day, about a week afterwards, as the port at last heaves actually in view—" shall see Him face to face. Oh, the glorious prospect!" And again : " I am so happy—I cannot tell how happy I am ! Not a ruffle, not a cloud. I wish you to keep my poor wandering mind fixed upon that one blessed truth—Christ's glorious resurrection ; for, if Christ rose again and is alive, I shall certainly rise and live with Him for ever."

Another day, she says : " Oh, how graciously the Lord is taking down the tent, pin by pin ! What an eventful life mine has been ! I have lived much in camp, and have seen the tents struck, and the regiment move off. Such is life. Jesus is all to my soul. Oh, how I realize His presence ! I have a full view of Him at this moment. Heaven is a reality. We mystify heaven ; it is a place. There is a service in heaven for Christ. I wonder if we shall not go over our eventful lives in heaven ? I think we shall."

" I feel," she says, on another occasion, " that one reason why many real Christians do not go on their way rejoicing, is, that they *deify* the humanity of Christ. Jesus is the very same Jesus now that He was when He walked the streets of Jerusalem. Though His body is glorified, He is not altered. His heart is still the same, full of sympathy and love, ready to listen to all we have to say to Him, and to do all we ask Him to do, and in the best possible way." Most weighty words ! Jesus is God—very God ; but He is also man—very man : and to deify His humanity, is to rob Him of His chief glory as the Head of His body the Church.

CHAPTER VIII.

> " I see, by faith, my holy home above,
>> Jerusalem !
> Adorned so richly, by my Saviour's love,
>> With pearl and gem.
>
> I long to enter the eternal gates,
>> And sin no more ;
> My best and sweetest praise **suspended waits**
>> For that **glad hour.**
>
> Then shall my harp possess **no broken string,**
>> My song **to mar ;**
> **And in the everlasting praise I bring,**
>> **No note shall jar.**"

William Carey—A " worm"—The mother—**The** Black River—A struggle—" Our sins"—The Trinity—Sunshine—The glory—" See Him as He is"—" Close intimacies with Jesus"—Not a single cloud—" All real"—" A cloudless death"—" I see Thee"—Conclusion—" First joy in heaven."

When William Carey was dying, he directed **that** on his tomb there should be engraven this epitaph—

WILLIAM CAREY,

Born **1761.**

Died ——

> " A guilty, weak, and helpless worm,
>> On thy **kind arms I** fall.**"**

Not less self-renouncing is Mrs. Winslow. " I shall **enter** heaven," she says, on one of those closing days, a poor sinner saved by grace. I seem to have done nothing for the Lord, who has done so much for me." Reminded of her self-denying labors, especially for her family, and of the blessing which had come upon them, she replies eagerly: "Ah! faithless, faithless have I been to my trust.

> "'Nothing in my hand I bring,
> Simply to thy cross I cling.'

I think many Christians dishonor Christ by refusing to obey Him. Whatever your hands find to do, do it with your might."

Like Christian in the Black River, a conflict intervenes. "Oh, pray for me," she says, at early dawn, one morning, "pray for me! I am under a cloud. Oh, what a night of conflict I have passed—a conflict with death, hell, and the grave! The enemy would conquer me, if he could." "It is one thing," she proceeds, "to talk of death; it is quite another thing, when it becomes a reality, to grapple with it. It is an easy thing to speak of the war in the East— perhaps to plan an attack upon the enemy; but it is quite a different thing to be in the heat of the conflict, the mighty foe contending with you foot by foot. Some go out of the world without a fear; but they know not and feel not the magnitude of sin. To have one's sins all in review before the mind's eye, and eternity in view—*this* is reality, and it needs the TRINITY to comfort and support the sinking soul."

But the sun shines forth once more. "The gloom has all passed," is her joyful exclamation, not long afterwards, "and I have a full view of the glory which awaits me. Oh, the hope of heaven! when shall I be there? To see Jesus, once **a** Man of Sorrows, now enthroned—that very same Jesus who was upon earth, and who **so** often has spoken words of comfort when others could not comfort!"

Disclosing the secret at once of her holy **living** and of her holy dying, she whispers, another day, **to** one who is watching at her side :—"Keep close intimacies with Jesus. We must live upon Christ, **and** we must die upon Christ." **And** again :—"Little faith will bring the soul to heaven; great faith will bring heaven into the soul. I am passing away; but not a single **cloud veils** Christ from my view. I seem as if Christ **were becko**ning me to come, saying, 'Why **do you delay?** Come up hither.'"

The **bar is now** reached, and she is to enter her haven. "Note this," she says, on her closing morning : "there is a buoyancy, a vitality in the principle of the renewed soul, which, in dying, cannot be **de**pressed. The more the body decays and sinks, **the** higher it rises **to** its native heaven." And **again :**— "I am longing **to depart** and to be with **Christ.** All is real. **I long to** end this mortal **struggle.**

> " ' Jesu, lover of my soul,
> Let me to thy bosom **fly.'** "

Too feeble **now almost to** articulate a word, she **looks** one of **her sons** steadily **in** the face, and, lifting her hand, points upwards. Like the martyr Ridley, she has lived so near heaven, that, now that she **is** dying, she has not far to **go**. **Her** voice regaining for a moment its strength, she **exclaims,** calmly and firmly —" a cloudless death ! a **cloudless** death ! a cloudless death !" Then a still interval—and, as life seems ebbing insensibly away, she whispers—" I see Thee ! —I see Thee !—I see Thee !" " What do you see ?" inquires a tremulous voice. **"I** see *Thee !"* once more whispers the expiring **saint ;** " I see THEE !" A few moments longer—and she is with her LORD.

> " When that happy era begins,
>   When, arrayed in thy glories, I shine,
> Nor grieve any more, by my sins,
>   The bosom on which I recline :
> O then shall the veil be removed,
>   And round me thy brightness be poured ;
> I shall meet Him whom absent I loved,
>   I shall see whom unseen I adored."

Such was this honored woman in her life and in her death. " My *first* joy in heaven," said she, on one of those **last days,** " will be to see JESUS." And, on her closing **evening,** she added—" The glory of heaven is Christ." **Reader !** is that **your** heaven ? You can easily judge, **by** this simple test—" **Do** you love the society of Jesus NOW ?" If you do, then **your** heaven is already begun ; but if not—if Christ **be an** unwelcome guest in your heart and **in** your home, the heaven of **the** Bible **is no** heaven for you —you have **a religion for time but** no religion for **eternity. And** shall it be always so ?